I0624987

SAM CRESCENT

EVERNIGHT PUBLISHING ®

www.evernightpublishing.com

EASTON

Copyright© 2021

Sam Crescent

Editor: Karyn White

Cover Artist: Jay Aheer

ISBN: 978-0-3695-0406-7

ALL RIGHTS RESERVED

WARNING: The unauthorized reproduction or distribution of this copyrighted work is illegal. No part of this book may be used or reproduced electronically or in print without written permission, except in the case of brief quotations embodied in reviews.

This is a work of fiction. All names, characters, and places are fictitious. Any resemblance to actual events, locales, organizations, or persons, living or dead, is entirely coincidental.

SAM CRESCENT

Four Kings Empire, 2

Sam Crescent

Copyright © 2019

Chapter One

The bottle of whiskey was almost empty, and Easton Long couldn't stop the constant thoughts and memories from plaguing him. Curled up in his office, he stared at the ceiling. There was a time he'd be passed out by now, but the more he drank, the more tolerant to it he was becoming.

Now, he was onto his second bottle of whiskey, and if he kept on going, he'd probably need his stomach pumped again.

Running a hand down his face, he knew he should drive himself off a cliff, or do something else constructive. It's not like he'd done anything worthwhile sitting around here. Axton, Karson, and Romeo were all better off without him. The Four Kings Empire didn't need him, not anymore, not when they had Paul, and he could go and end it, like he should have done years ago.

The truth was out, and he and his friends weren't

going to pay the price for their parents' bullshit anymore. They were all free.

Easton had hoped it would give him some freedom from this pain, but instead it just made him even more useless.

No one needed him around. His father always said he was a waste of space, and after getting Carla pregnant, it had pretty much cemented his uselessness. His own father, Nial Long, had taken care of the problem. Killed her so he wouldn't be able to run away with her and live his life without the riches.

For years, Nial had told him he'd never be able to hack it broke. Wealth was what defined them all. When Easton had made a bet with his friends, he hadn't expected to fall for her. He just wanted to pop her cherry and move on. Not to fall for her, or to want a future with her.

Carla showed him that being poor didn't mean anything. She had been one of the poorest girls in King's Ridge. Even though he wanted her to fall in love with him, and have sex with her, it didn't mean he intended to get her pregnant. He'd fucked up big time with her, and she had paid the price for his asshole ways.

"You've got to stop thinking about Carla. You can't bring her back," he said.

"And you've got to stop being in this office, drinking yourself to death."

He lifted his hand up to see Axton and Taylor, staring down at him.

"My humiliation is now complete. Thanks for that," he said. "You shouldn't even be here."

"Why? Because you're the only one that owns this place? I had to work late."

"On something I know nothing about, I'm sure."

He glanced down at Taylor's stomach. "You

know what it is yet?"

Taylor put a hand on her growing belly and shook her head. "No, not yet. We're not sure we want to know, you know, extend the surprise maybe."

"That's nice." His and Carla's kid would be just over ten years old by now, if she'd lived long enough.

He would have loved to have been a father. "You're the first one of all of us to have a kid. Congratulations, Axton. You always did get everything first."

"Is he always like this?" Taylor asked.

"No. It's worse on the anniversary."

"Fuck you," Easton said. He sat up, feeling the world spin but not enough to make him sit down. "You think you know me? You think you know what true pain is all about? At least you're getting to see your child born. Me? I didn't get to do anything about it. That pleasure was torn from me because of my father." He got up, and if Axton didn't grab him when he did, he'd be on his ass.

The alcohol must clearly be having an effect.

"So don't try to tell me that you even understand what I'm doing!"

"You're drinking yourself into oblivion because of guilt, Easton. I'm not going to pretend it's anything else, because it's not. You feel guilty over what happened, and you've got other reasons. Reasons you're not even ready to tell any of us."

"Fuck you!" He growled the words as he tried to hit Axton, but it didn't work.

Axton merely let him go, and he collapsed to the floor.

Karson and Romeo finally stepped into his office.

"Why don't you just leave him to pass out?" Romeo asked.

"I'm not going to leave him alone here. He's got an apartment and a life, and he needs to get back to it," Axton said. "We're all in this together."

"Yeah, but one of us right now is a fucking bum. I'm tired of dragging his drunk ass all over the place," Karson said.

Easton rolled onto his back. "I didn't ask any of you here. I was quite happy not dealing with any of you fuckers, so leave me alone." His stomach started to turn.

He didn't roll over fast enough before he began to vomit.

At first, he choked, but then his friends didn't give him a chance to help himself before they were holding him and making him throw up on the carpet.

"This is gross," Taylor said.

"Then get the fuck out. Why don't you do something useful and plot our deaths, or maybe, I don't know, learn how to spread your legs properly and keep your man out of my office?"

He wanted them to hate him, for them all to despise him.

He wasn't good enough to stand by their side.

This was all just a waste of time.

"You know what, I've put up with your bullshit for long enough, but no more. Your ass is going to rehab, and I've already picked out the perfect one."

"I'm not going anywhere. You can't make me."

"With the wealth we've got, we can make you do whatever we want. We're even going to make sure you stay in until you complete a total detox program. Your place will always be here, by us," Axton said.

"You think he needs to do that?" Taylor asked.

"He's going to do that if he likes it or not. He's one of the Four Kings, and we have a reputation to uphold. We've all been really fucking lenient with him, and I'm done."

"Fuck you!" Easton curled up on his side and burst out laughing. He really didn't give a shit what his friends wanted. They had their own lives, and he didn't need to worry about them needing him.

This was his life, and if he wanted to fuck up, he could do that.

"You want me to fuck off?" Axton asked, getting right up into his face.

"Yeah, why don't you take your woman and fuck her properly rather than worry about me?" He saw Axton's hand clench.

"He's wanting you to lose control," Romeo said.

"I know. Easton, you think we don't know you, but we do. We all know what is going on here, and we all know what you're doing."

He glared up at his friends, hating them even more than ever before.

"Get out!" He wanted them gone, but Axton shook his head.

"Not happening."

"I don't know what the hell you're going to—"

He didn't get to finish as Axton hit him, and everything turned black.

****

"What the hell was that?" Taylor asked.

Axton shrugged. "There was only going to be one way of getting him to the clinic. This was it."

"By hitting him?"

"Believe me, he'll thank us for it," Karson said.

"I don't think he's going to thank you for doing this to him."

"He's killing himself, Taylor. I know you wanted to take time and all that shit, but with Easton we don't have time. He's dying inside, and at this rate, he's going to drink himself to death." Axton nodded at the two empty bottles of whiskey.

Easton's drinking had been a problem long before now, but Axton had always found some reason not to complain or be annoyed, or even upset by it. Now he felt so fucking stupid. Karson and Romeo had each come to him with concerns about Easton. Even Paul, their new business associate, had voiced his own worries. Everywhere he turned Easton was fucking up, and they were all carrying him, which wasn't a problem.

He was their best friend and had been by their side for as long as Axton could remember.

There was no way he could turn his back on his best friend; none of them could.

Moving toward Easton's desk, he opened the top drawer, and seeing the small bag of white powder made him even more angry.

Drinking, he could handle.

Even drinking to excess, he could handle.

Lateness was something else he could deal with.

The constant women and the blackmail for extorting money, he didn't even mind. There was no reason to even be alarmed by that. There was nothing Easton had done that made Axton want to kill, but the drugs, that was one step too far.

He didn't know if Easton had already taken any, or if this was just the next step in waiting.

Grabbing a piece of paper, he used it like a glove to pick out the bag for Romeo and Karson to see.

"Now do you think I'm overreacting?" he asked, glaring at Taylor.

"I don't need to be here for this."

He watched as Taylor walked out of the office and closed the door behind them.

"Let's get him to my car," Axton said, dropping

the bag back into the drawer.

"Let me take care of that," Karson said. "We don't need an overzealous cleaner who thinks they're doing us a favor."

"We can pay anyone off."

"Right now, I don't want anyone looking too closely at us," Karson said.

Axton wasn't going to complain. Since the truth had come out about their families' manipulation and blackmail, the police had been making their presence known, which was fine, but none of them wanted to draw too much attention to themselves.

With a baby on the way, Axton didn't want Taylor stressed. He'd already upset her tonight with this thing with Easton. He would make it up to her. For now, she had to wait while he dealt with his friend's guilt.

"You think he's got any idea why he's behaving this way?" Karson asked.

"Nope. It's Easton. He believes he doesn't have to have a reason. This is who he is, and he really does like to play the martyr. Give him a reason to throw himself down on his sword." Axton helped to lift Easton. With the alcohol and the punch, Easton would be out for long enough for them to get him to the rehabilitation clinic.

They had all been warned there was only so much the doctors could do. The true test would be on Easton, if he could survive without the booze or drugs.

He hoped Easton wasn't on drugs. He really didn't want his best friend to be going down that path.

Axton got it, to a point. Over ten years ago, Easton had gotten a girl pregnant, only for that girl to end up murdered by Easton's father. From what he remembered, Easton was willing to sacrifice a life of wealth to be with her. Carla, Taylor's best friend, had been poor. At first Easton was only having a bit of fun, but it had soon changed. Carla had been the girl to change everything for all of them. She'd been the girl Easton truly believed he was in love with, and to anyone who didn't know Easton would have believed it too.

Karson, Romeo, and himself knew the truth.

The guilt eating away at Easton wasn't because he was missing Carla, or that he wanted her back.

No, he was feeling guilty because the truth was, he wasn't in love with her, had never been in love with her. He'd knocked her up and was doing the right thing, and what made it even worse was Easton was thankful he didn't *have* to do the right thing.

****

Easton had a really bad headache. Opening his eyes, he felt the pounding behind his skull, and his mouth was incredibly dry.

He licked his lips and started to sit up, realizing immediately he was in some kind of hospital.

"What the fuck?"

"Water is by you," Axton said.

He looked toward his best friend, who was sitting in a chair, looking way too calm and collected for his liking.

"What is going on?"

"No recollection of the past twenty-four hours?" Axton asked.

He remembered arriving into his office, doing some work, and around lunchtime, he got the bottle of whiskey and began to add little drops to his coffee, until most of his drink was the whiskey.

"Vaguely."

"You remember buying drugs?" Axton asked.

Easton tensed up and waited.

"I will take that as a yes."

Again, he didn't say anything. He had bought the drugs a few weeks ago but hadn't used them. He'd left them in his drawer for when he finally felt ready for that total oblivion the dealer had told him about.

The booze wasn't helping. He'd hoped the drugs would.

It wasn't perfect, but then, his life wasn't perfect either and hadn't been for a long time. He didn't know why he was even trying any more.

"This has got to stop, Easton."

He stared up at the ceiling, wondering if by some miracle it would collapse and he wouldn't have to hear all the bullshit spilling from Axton's mouth. That's what he wanted.

"You're going to be in here for a month."

"A month? A fucking month! How is that even allowed? I can let myself out at any time. I'm not staying here." He sat up.

"You will."

"Why?"

"Because of the Four Kings."

"Oh, please, you guys don't need me, and you've been running things pretty smoothly without me there. Don't give me all that crap."

"If you don't do the month and stick to it, you lose your rights to your position and all of the assets. Not only that, you will be under the police radar as well," Axton said.

Easton glared at his friend. "I had nothing to do with any of that shit. The police granted us full amnesty."

"No, they granted the *Four Kings* full amnesty. You think they're going to take into account wording now that you're gone? I bet your dad told them everything. How you got her pregnant, were going to run away. You know what a piece of work Nial is. You think you can survive poverty, but can you hack it in prison? Pretty princess like you, they'd eat you for dinner." Axton's voice filled him with dread.

The truth was, he didn't even think he could hack it without money. He'd spent so much time relying on being wealthy.

Of having the money as a fallback.

Prison.

He didn't even know if he could hack it for an hour in a jail cell, let alone any stretch of time.

"Why do you care so much? I'm not hurting anyone."

"Your drinking affects all of us, Easton. This isn't you."

This time he laughed. "You're going to pretend that you know who I am and what I'm capable of. Good one."

"I'm not bullshitting here, Easton. I mean it. This isn't you. Whatever you've got going on is going to stop."

"And you, fierce leader, are going to do it."

"It's not your fault that you didn't love her, and even a little part of yourself is relieved she's dead so you didn't have to take responsibility."

Easton stared at his friend. In that moment, he didn't consider him a friend but the enemy.

"Get out. Go and fuck your woman or something."

"You can hate me all you want, Easton. We know you had feelings for Carla, but it didn't extend to love."

"I bet you had a great time telling Taylor that."

"I didn't tell Taylor anything. She doesn't need to hear it. *You* do. We all understand, and we get it. You've got to stop making this harder for yourself. Believe it or not, we all do love you."

This time, Easton laughed.

"We do, otherwise we wouldn't have made this arrangement. Get the help, and when you're out, we can help you stay on track."

Easton didn't want to stay on track. "Get out."

Axton got to his feet. "We do love you."

He didn't say anything.

Axton sighed. "Fine. You can hate me all you want. It's not going to change anything. We've disposed of your problem, and you're going to stay here. I've already informed the doctors you're a flight risk. This is for your own good, Easton, and one day, I hope you can see that."

Silence filled the room.

It felt amazing, wonderful, and at the same time, Easton was sick.

Running a hand down his face, he realized he needed a drink, badly.

Really fucking badly.

This wasn't good for him.

All he did was drink. The drugs were the next step up and he didn't take any of them, bought them with the intention of taking them.

Climbing out of his bed, he opened the second door in the room and found an en-suite bathroom, if anyone could call it that. It was so tiny.

He made it to the toilet, vomiting. He held onto the edge of the toilet as he threw up absolutely everything in his stomach, or what felt like it anyway.

When he was finished, he pulled down the flusher and pressed his face against the edge of the toilet.

Someone had sat their ass on this very toilet seat at one time, and he had his face to it. He was practically kissing another man or woman's ass.

He didn't have the energy to get up and move.

"This is pitiful."

He turned his head to see her.

She wasn't real.

He'd seen her dead body.

Yet, Carla, seventeen-year-old, sweet, smiling Carla, sat on the edge of the bathtub as if she was very much alive.

"What are you doing here?" he asked.

"You tell me. You're the reason I'm here."

"I'm hallucinating. That's what this is."

Carla sighed. "And yet, I'm still here. Clearly, you like thinking of me, sweetheart."

"Axton was right."

She winced. "I didn't imagine you'd say that out loud."

"You're here, like, a ghost, and I'm over a toilet. It's the only thing that makes sense."

"You're concerned by what this all means, rather than wondering why it is you thought of me as someone to talk to in your moment of need. That is crazy talk."

"You're dead."

"I know. I remember."

Now this was all a little too much, and he couldn't handle it.

Getting to his feet, he felt the sickness in his mouth, and quickly washed it out with water.

"Here you go panicking. You need to calm down. You really do."

"I don't want to talk about anything right now." He splashed water on his face. "I've got to get out of here."

"So you're going to run. Isn't that what you always do? When the going gets tough, Easton starts running or in your case, drinking. The drugs were a rebel step, I'll give you that. I didn't see it coming."

"You're in my imagination. It means the only person I'm really seeing is myself."

"I know. You're talking to yourself, and I'm the voice of reason still. What does that tell you?" She stood up, putting hands on her hips and walking toward him.

"I visit your grave."

"Again, we're one and the same, and I know."

"Why are you here?" he asked.

In all the years since her death, he'd not seen her. Not like this. In the moments of drink, he was sure she was close by, but he'd always been so drunk.

"I'm a figment of your imagination, Easton. You tell me why I'm here."

"I don't know."

"I'm guessing I'm here for you to talk to. If you remember when we were younger you were always able to talk to me. You know you could keep all of your secrets with me."

"Secrets that nearly cost me everything. You put everything down in a diary."

"I was a girl. I was falling in love and with a guy I knew I shouldn't trust, and yet, I was doing it. You can hate me all you want. You can even hate Axton, but deep down, you know he's right about this. About you getting well."

"He's fucking your friend, you know. Taylor."

"Good for her."

He shook his head. "I can't believe I'm having a conversation like this." He knew she wasn't there. There was no way for her to be there, and yet, here he was, still talking to her. He was going fucking crazy. There was no other word for it.

"You know you've got to do this, right? The only reason I'm here is because of all of this. Axton's right, and it's killing you to know that your best friend may be

right about anything. He always is."

"I've got this all under control."

"Ding-ding, guess what, you haven't. Someone who has it under control doesn't drink two bottles of whiskey. Someone who has it under control doesn't go out and buy drugs, hoping to score the next high. You're so far from being under control that you can't even see it."

"And this is better for me? Imagining and having full-blown conversations with my dead girlfriend?"

"Ex-girlfriend. I'm dead, and we are so not going out."

Easton gripped the back of his head, rubbing up and down. "Do you ever think about it? What it would have been like?"

"I know you do. I know you think about it at least once every single day. You wonder if you loved me enough to make me happy, for us to be happy. I know more than anything you think about the baby. You want to be a dad more than anything. Axton, he's living a dream for you. I also know you think about her, and the thought is so fleeting, but it's there."

He pressed his hands against his face, trying to calm himself the fuck down, but nothing was happening.

Nothing was … giving him focus.

This was all just too much.

"And because you think about her so much, it makes the pain and guilt you feel just a little harder to bear. She's alive. I'm not."

"Stop it."

"You're the one controlling this, Easton. Not me. I'm simply voicing to you what you're thinking. What you don't want to think about so you drink. So you try to create the oblivion your mind won't let you have." She shrugged. *"You can hate me all you want, but it's the*

truth. You've got to let it go and realize what Axton wants for you is what is right."

"I need a drink."

He didn't leave his room. The last thing he wanted to do was to have imaginary Carla following him around.

"If what you're saying is me, then why do you sound like her? Why does it feel like you're here?" he asked, collapsing to the bed.

"You know all those answers, Easton. You've just got to be willing to listen to them." Carla lay down beside him, and he turned his head.

He would spend hours on her bed like this, staring at her. She always made him smile and feel calm. There was never any judgment in her eyes.

This was how he remembered her.

Happy. Calm. Sweet. Gentle. Everything he missed about her.

The pregnancy had been a big mistake, but he'd promised to take care of her.

"I miss you."

"I know, but we also know it's not enough." She reached out, and as she put her hand against his face, he didn't feel anything.

Because she wasn't there.

This wasn't real.

He was a drunk who had a whole lot of problems and really needed to figure it out for himself.

Chapter Two

"It's not that hard to do. You say, 'Hi, I'm Easton, and I drink way too much,'" Carla said.

Easton's imaginary friend came and went. Whenever he left his room, she magically disappeared, but when he was alone, it was like he thought her into being. She'd either be standing in a corner, or sitting on a counter. He went to the bathroom yesterday, and there she'd been, sat on the counter near the sink. He hadn't told anyone he was imagining his dead ex-girlfriend.

She was some company in this place.

He'd stayed by himself for the most part, taking his meals alone and just trying to get through the program.

The sickness, the shaking, and the withdrawal weren't fun. Not even a little.

Much to his surprise, in order to wean his body off the alcohol, they had to give him just a little, to slowly draw him out of his addiction.

While they were doing that, he was having to train his mind not to drink.

Not to do anything.

Throughout it all, Carla was there.

"Your friends are coming for a visit today," Carla said.

"I know."

"You excited?"

"Yes. The prospect of sitting in a room full of my friends as they know how fucking weak I am is thrilling. Not to mention, I've spent the best part of a week speaking to a girl from my past that we all know died."

"You're not in the best of moods."

He sat down on the edge of the bed. "No, I'm

not."

"It's going to be okay though. They're your friends for a reason."

"We're not friends."

"You don't really mean that."

"I do. We were all forced together, but we're not friends."

Carla sat beside him and tucked her hair behind her ear. He remembered her doing that so many times. Her hair was always too long, and he missed seeing her do that.

"They are your friends. If not, they wouldn't care if you're an addict or not. You're here because even if you don't feel it, they do care in their own way."

"This is the most I've talked to anyone in a really long time."

"How come?"

"I ... I don't know. Talking is not exactly my talent."

She laughed. "It doesn't have to be your talent, Easton. You got to learn to let things go."

There was a knock on his door.

He turned toward it just as a nurse entered.

"Your visitors are here."

"I'm coming."

Trying to discreetly see if Carla was still there, he turned his head, looking over his room. There was no sign of her.

Getting to his feet, he followed the nurse out of the room, and for the first time since arriving at the center, he felt nervous.

There was a separate area for visitors.

Axton had paid for a private room, and as he entered, he saw Axton was sitting with Taylor beside him. Karson and Romeo were also paying a visit.

"Look at you," Karson said.

He was embraced by Karson and then by Romeo, who each slapped him on his back.

"You always did tell me they were the brutes of the club," Carla said.

He looked over Axton's shoulder, and Carla was in the corner, smiling. He wasn't going to freak out.

"Well, how is it going?" Karson asked.

"Good. Good. I'm still alive."

"You've not tried to sign yourself out yet, so that's good," Axton said.

"Now I totally understand why you want to kick his ass. Look at the guy. He has it all. The looks, the wife, and look at Taylor, she is so beautiful. I always knew she would be in high school."

He tried not to think of what Carla was saying. "There's no point in trying something unless I'm going to do it properly." He had no idea what he was saying. Carla started to laugh, but he didn't look over Axton's shoulder.

Taking a seat, he offered Taylor a smile.

"I didn't agree to their methods," she said. "Does it hurt?" She pointed at his face.

"A little, but there was no other way of getting me here right, and I need to."

"You could ask Taylor to look her up. I bet she would love to."

"So, what's new?" he asked.

"You're seriously going to pretend I don't exist right now? You want to go and meet this woman. Why not ask Taylor? She's my best friend; she'd understand."

He tried to drown out Carla.

Axton was talking about a new deal Paul was working on, and he really didn't care.

The truth was, he wanted to know a bit more

about another kind of woman, and he couldn't ask Taylor.

It was a stupid idea even thinking about it, let alone listening to Carla tell him to use Taylor.

"What's going on in here? Have you banged anyone yet?" Romeo asked.

"Ew, why do you have to go there?" Taylor asked.

"Because it must be boring."

Easton looked over Axton's shoulder, and Carla gave him a wink. Taylor caught him looking, and he just forced a smile.

"Are you okay?"

"I'm more than fine."

"Taylor's always been a worrier. I always talked about her, remember? She must hate me for that. You know her better than Axton does by now. You know her little revenge would never have lasted. She was angry, hurt, upset, but above all else, she couldn't hurt anyone else. Well, she could have pissed them off, and it made her very obsessive, but she would have seen the truth."

Carla liked to talk about Taylor a lot. The revelation of her trying to bring them all down didn't fit with the girl he once knew. The girl Carla would talk about all the time. He didn't mind as it meant she wasn't asking him endless questions.

Taylor was a good girl pretending to be a bad one, and what he could respect was her desire for justice. When you lose a loved one, who wouldn't want that?

It didn't work for her, and now she was married to Axton, and pregnant.

"You're following the program?" Axton asked.

"I'm doing it. I'm going to get clean." Easton thought about the drugs in his desk. He ran a hand down his face, to try to stop the shame from rushing over him.

When he purchased those drugs, he had every intention of using them, whereas now, he didn't know what the hell to do anymore. "I didn't use them."

"What?" Karson asked.

"The drugs. I didn't use them. They were there just in case."

"Did you have any intention of using them?" Romeo asked.

"Yes." Part of his program was to tell the truth. He glanced over at Carla, who had a raised brow, before looking at Taylor. He couldn't say anything, not yet.

Even though he knew he should tell someone he was talking to his dead ex-girlfriend, he just couldn't bring himself to … let her go.

What if they made him take something, or wanted him to talk about his feelings? It was hard enough talking about them now with Carla, let alone a complete stranger.

"Are you okay?" Taylor asked.

"Of course he's not okay. Look at him. He's in a rehab center because his life is falling apart and it's all his fault." Carla smiled at him.

The Carla he remembered wouldn't have been such a fucking bitch to him. She'd have cut him some slack.

"The Carla you knew is not the one you see today. We've gone over this already. You and I both know, I'm you. This here is all you. The only way you can deal with the truth is because it's me telling you and not you."

He was going crazy.

This wasn't normal and it wasn't right for him, but for the first time in his life, he didn't feel alone. Even if he was seeing Carla.

"I'm going to stick to the program. I'm not going

to stop. I won't let you down." He looked at each of his friends in turn before looking at Taylor.

The guilt hit him again as she offered him a smile.

"How is the … erm, pregnancy?"

She put a hand to her stomach. "Fine so far. I'm always sick, but I hear that's normal."

"I read about it, and yes, it's quite normal."

"When did you read about it?" she asked, with a laugh.

"Carla," he said. "Before she was killed, I had some time to read on it." He stood up. "I need to get back to my room. I've got lots to do."

"You have a busy schedule here?"

"Yes, and now I really need to get back to it. Lots to do. People to see. Rules to follow." He held his hand out to Axton. "Thank you."

"I bet that one hurt you."

"I appreciate you bringing me down here."

"You're like a brother to me, Easton. No matter what, we've got your back."

He shook Karson and Romeo's hands, and turned to Taylor. "I'm going to head back."

Taylor gave him a hug. "She'd be so proud of you."

He tensed up.

"He doesn't care what I'd think."

"I've got to go." Regardless of how leaving made him look, he rushed from the room, only stopping when he'd closed his own door and collapsed against it.

"Well, I thought that went rather well."

"I shouldn't be seeing you." He turned toward Carla, who was now sitting on his bed. "Anyone else, I'd tell them to get their brains tested."

"True. You're a drunk, a potential addict, a loser

in the making. Yeah, add weirdo to the mix. No one would need a reason to throw you in a cell and toss the key away."

He walked to the bed and collapsed down on it, where Carla was. Seeing as she wasn't there, he settled himself more comfortably on the bed.

"You know, we could talk about her. You rarely allow yourself the chance to think about her," Carla said.

"I'm not talking about anything. I just want to sleep."

"That's up to you, but you know I'm here."

He rolled over, staring up at his ceiling. The color white was so off-putting to him. He didn't like it. Wrinkling his nose, he glanced over to Carla. She was now lying on her back, her hands on her stomach. This was how she would lie when they were younger. When he was younger as she was still the same age.

"I really liked her, which surprised me. I didn't even intend to find anyone else. I just wanted to have a break. You know, take the time to forget about you, and everything that had happened. It was Axton's idea for me to get away, to detach from it all. So I took the chance. It was a camp of some kind. I was only there for three weeks. Not long enough to make an impression of any kind, but long enough that I've not stopped thinking about her. I went back there a year later, but there were no signs of her. It was like she'd vanished without a trace."

"Why didn't you look for her? She gave you her name."

"No, she gave me one name. One name that could have thousands of possible names, and at the time my dad was breathing down my neck. I couldn't go anywhere without him waiting for me to fuck up. So, I gave her up. The three weeks we had, I've cherished."

He rubbed at his temples, feeling the beginning of a headache.

"This is the first time you've spoken about her?"

"Yes. The guys don't know about her. I didn't want to tell them anything of what I experienced those three weeks. They sent me there to get over you, and during that time, it was where I realized, I didn't need to. I didn't want you to die, Carla, but I also knew that I didn't love you. I didn't even know what love was."

"You can't keep living in the past."

He snorted.

"Here I am, talking to you, and you're not even real. I don't know what the hell to do anymore. I'm twenty-nine years old and a fuck-up. How did it get like this?" he asked.

"I'd say you spent too much time moaning about what has happened. This isn't you, and you need to stop feeling guilty for stuff you can't control. Who cares if you hate that Axton is right all the time? Who cares that you're in here? You're in here, and you know what? It means you can have a second chance. There are not that many people who get this chance and you have it. Stop wasting it."

"It's not that simple."

Carla sighed. "It is. You've just got to stop looking for excuses not to believe in yourself. You're not a bad guy, Easton."

He closed his eyes. "I'm not a bad guy you say. You're not even real." He opened his eyes and there was no Carla. "I'm talking to myself in my own room, all alone. Carla died over ten years ago. Right now, I'm the biggest fuck-up in the world."

Staring up at the ceiling, he thought about *her.* The way her blonde hair fluttered out from behind her as he chased her. They would run down to the beach every single day, and he'd pick her up in his arms, spinning her around in the air.

Her smile always captured his heart so that he didn't want to let her go. The reality was, his time with Scarlett was limited.

He'd thought about her many times over the years. Each time wondering if he should reach out, apologize for what he'd said to her on that last day.

Every chance he had at happiness, he'd messed it up in one way or another.

This was his second chance.

No more alcohol.

No more toxicity in his life.

There was a chance he could do this.

Rather than blow this opportunity, he could finally get clean, not rely on the drink or the women. To finally have a clean slate where his own father wouldn't have a chance of ruining him.

The idea seemed a little too good to be true, but he had to do something.

He was dying, and even though he'd tried to take his own life, to finish the endless pain and suffering, he couldn't do it. Did it make him a coward? He didn't know.

Life wasn't supposed to be like this, and it hurt to know he couldn't seem to catch a single break.

This wasn't going to be his end.

He was going to make this work even if it was the last good thing he did.

Chapter Three

One month later

Sitting outside in the garden of the rehabilitation center, Easton felt … different. He'd stayed longer than Axton's one-month request. Only a couple more weeks, and he'd finally discharged himself. His bags were packed, and he was ready to go. The same old life was waiting for him back in the city. His job secured in the Four Kings. The only thing that had changed was he was no longer full of alcohol.

There wasn't even any need for it.

He wasn't yearning for a single drop of whiskey or the body of a willing woman. His life was suddenly his own.

"You did it," Carla said, appearing in front of him.

Even as he gave up all of the booze, he couldn't seem to stop bringing her back. He knew he wasn't crazy. Carla was dead. She wasn't here, but he'd thought her up, and in his mind, he saw her, so clearly.

"I'm getting out. I'm waiting for Axton to pick me up."

"You're ready?"

"There's no reason for me to stay here."

"Good. I'm glad."

"You're not real."

"I'm as real as you make me, Easton. You're me, and I'm you. We're one and the same. I guess I'm the voice that you refuse to listen to. Whatever you need I guess." She winked at him, getting up from her position on the floor. "Are you going to go and see her?"

"No. I didn't know her last name, and I'm not going to hold onto a past that has no chance of a future.

What happened, happened. I'm not going to drag myself down."

She stepped toward him.

He didn't even attempt to reach out to her. There was no point. She wasn't there.

"You should find her. What you did all those years ago was stupid."

"I'm not going to do anything like that."

"You can't keep having these kinds of conversations with yourself. It's not very productive."

"Mr. Long, your friend is here to pick you up," one of the nurses said.

He looked behind him and smiled. "I'll be there in a minute."

The nurse looked at him a few minutes longer, and he didn't break eye contact. Whatever she had seen, he wasn't going to be embarrassed or upset. He'd deny whatever accusation she threw his way.

She nodded and withdrew.

"That was a close one," Carla said.

"When I leave here, you can't come with me." He turned back to look at her.

Over the past couple of weeks, he'd noticed her image was a little fainter, showing him she was nothing but the ghost in his mind. It had been nice to imagine it was her though. The one thing he couldn't deny was how much he loved being around Carla. She'd always been so much fun.

"Easton, you and I both know I'll be wherever you need me. This isn't my choice. This is all up to you." She folded her arms. "What are you going to do?"

He closed his eyes, took several deep breaths, and opened them again.

Carla was gone.

Getting to his feet, he made his way inside. Axton

and Taylor were waiting in his private room.

Axton held his bag. "You ready to go?"

"Yeah, I'm ready to go."

There was no reason for him to stay here. Nothing holding him back.

He'd done the time, and now it was up to him to get out of here.

He followed Axton out of the center, having already signed all the necessary paperwork. Taylor opened the trunk of their car, and he watched as Axton put the bag into it. Then he was standing right in front of him.

Easton jerked back a little.

"I know you hate me, and I wish there was another way for this to have happened. I love you, man."

Axton hugged him.

Easton stared past his friend's shoulder to see Taylor smiling at him, tears in her eyes. Her pregnancy was really showing now, and it wouldn't be long before she gave birth. He'd missed a lot in his friend's life already, and he didn't want to miss anymore.

"You keep hugging me like this and Taylor's going to wonder if you love me or her."

Axton laughed. "Asshole."

"Just saying." He climbed into the back seat and looked back up at the center. No one came out to offer him goodbye. Other than the programs, he didn't get close to anyone. He spent most of his spare time in his room, alone, talking to Carla.

Axton climbed behind the wheel, and then Easton was watching the center fade into the distance.

"Where do you want to go first?" Axton asked.

"My apartment. I need to clean out the trash. Unless you guys did it for me," Easton said.

"No, we didn't do your apartment. Taylor and I

haven't got anything to do today. We'll help you."

"What's Romeo and Karson doing?" he asked.

"They're with Paul. We're working through a brand-new software program, but it's hitting a couple of snags."

"Paul is a perfectionist."

He nodded.

The conversation was all very safe. Easton wasn't sure if that made him comfortable or not. He'd been in a rehabilitation center, and now, he really didn't understand his place. It would be all so easy to conjure up Carla, to listen to her talk.

It wasn't even Carla talking, just him and his thoughts. They were easier to listen to.

Music filled the air, and he was glad for the break.

He'd never been like this, unable to break the silence. The awkwardness. He'd always been the kind of guy to fill it with goofy shit, to make people laugh.

That had all changed now.

He was classified as an alcoholic, or was it a past alcoholic now?

"Hi, my name's Easton Long. I'm one of the Four Kings, I'm an alcoholic, a loser."

This wasn't what he wanted from his life.

Fortunately, the drive to his apartment didn't last overly long. Once Axton parked, Easton grabbed his own bag from the trunk and looked toward his friend.

"You don't have to come up."

"We want to," Taylor said. She pushed her arm through his. "We're all family, right? We're all that's left. We're going to be here for you."

"Great." He hoped he spoke with enthusiasm. He tried, but the truth was, he wanted to do this alone.

He hadn't seen his apartment in over six weeks.

He couldn't even remember the state of the place.

Rather than push them away, he followed them right up to his place. He inserted the key into the lock, and then the wave of old alcohol washed over them.

His apartment was completely trashed, and this was why he'd been wanting to avoid them coming here. On the night before Axton knocked him out, he'd partied hard. There had been a couple of whores he'd hired to entertain him. He had blood work done at the rehabilitation center, and he was all clean, which was a miracle in itself. This was why he'd decided to take this new chance and to hold onto it. He didn't want to let it go, and it would be so easy to do.

"Holy shit, Easton," Axton said.

"Yeah, and I was hoping you guys would have something a little more interesting to do." He closed the door, dropped his bag on the only clean space in his place, and grabbed a black trash bag from the kitchen. He'd never used the kitchen, and there was mess everywhere. Beer bottles, wine bottles, ashtrays, and he didn't even smoke.

He started to pick up all the glass bottles. There was no alcohol in them, but he didn't need to worry about wanting them. Just one look at this place, and he wasn't exactly happy with what he was seeing. This had been his life for so long. He couldn't even remember when it had gone from a couple of beers to three or four. This was fucking crazy.

The party that caused this, he couldn't even remember it. The night was like an old memory, refusing to come to the forefront of his mind.

Taylor grabbed a black bag and began to fill it with metal cans. Axton did the same, but he filled it with trash.

One by one, they walked their way through the

apartment.

Easton opened every single cupboard, and without waiting for his friends' instructions, any alcohol left in the bottles, he tipped out.

It wasn't even a time for second-guessing.

He just opened that bottle, tipped out the contents, and threw the bottle into the black bag.

Time flew, and none of them spoke, which Easton was more than happy with. He didn't need to talk right now.

When all the trash, bottles, and cans were gone, it was time for him to call housekeeping. He needed his space clean, and the only way to do that was to cleanse the entire area.

Taylor and Axton stayed still.

"Are you worried I'm going to fall off the wagon?" He couldn't help but chuckle there. Fall off the wagon, it was so fucking stupid to even think of something like that. He'd never intended to be on the wagon in the first place, and yet here he was, totally on it.

"We're your friends, Easton." Taylor hugged him.

Her stomach pressed against his body, and he … he quickly pulled away. He couldn't handle that kind of pain right now. The stark reminder of why he kept seeing Carla in the first place.

A very seventeen- to eighteen-year-old Carla.

It was that part in his life that was the worst.

The cleaning crew arrived, and rather than stand with his friends, he watched them work. He had a feeling he was going to be taking up another hobby, and it wouldn't have anything to do with drink.

Chapter Four

Over eleven years ago

Easton stared into the campfire. The wood was burning so brightly, he saw all the ambers and golds. The reds of the fire were just exquisite. He loved watching things burn. The way the heat caught everything, and within a matter of seconds, turned it into smoldering ash.

Taylor's scream from a few nights ago echoed in his mind.

The horrible memory of her pulling Carla out of the water. Taylor had looked half possessed. When he realized who it was, his friends held him back. They had to. His relationship with Carla had to be kept a secret. No one in the town could ever know that he fell for her, that he fucked her, that the baby she'd been carrying was his.

Their chance to start a completely new life together was all gone.

He'd not wanted to be a father. When Carla had told him, it had been on the tip of his tongue to demand she got rid of it, or to pay her off.

Him with a kid.

His father was no role model when it came to being a dad. Over the years he'd watched his father fuck any woman he wanted, abuse them for his own sick pleasure.

"You okay?"

He turned to see a blonde girl. She'd already been at the summer camp when he arrived. In the past twenty-four hours, he noticed people gravitated toward her, asking her for help and advice.

"Yeah, I'm fine."

She had pretty green eyes. Her hair was so long and blonde. It fell to her waist, but it didn't look lifeless. The strands looked so soft, as if they had a life of their own. She offered him another smile.

"I'm Scarlett, by the way." She held her hand out.

She didn't look shy or nervous as she waited for him.

He could push her aside, or take a chance.

"Easton." He placed his hand within hers, and shook it.

"You have got one firm handshake there, buddy." She pulled away.

"Look, Scar, look, I did it." A young kid, not older than ten, ran over. He had some kind of bracelet around his wrist.

The camp was for all ages. He didn't even know why he'd come here. In all the summers it had been offered to him, he'd always turned it down. Who wanted to go out into the wilderness, set up camp, sing a bunch of songs around a fire? It all sounded rather corny to him.

"You totally did, champ. Well done. I think Elle is serving hot chocolate."

The kid nodded and left.

"Scar?" Easton asked.

"It's how my name gets shortened down. Scar. I guess I could deal with Lett, but it doesn't ring right."

"How about Lettie?"

She giggled. "That's not my name."

"Nah, but maybe it's what I'll call you."

"I'd like that, Ton." She winked at him.

****

Present day, six months after Easton's release from rehab

Work kept him busy.

Charity work kept him sane.

Carla kept him from going crazy.

Even though he knew deep down she was his imagination, he liked seeing her. Especially when the pain, the guilt, the shame, it all seemed to meld together. Easton had gone to a private investigator in the hope of finding Scarlett. With no last name, and a camp that had burned down, as well as all of the records of who attended it, there was no hope in finding a blonde girl with green eyes. The man he hired would try to find a connection to anyone with that description, but so far, all the leads had been useless. None of the women the PI had found had actually led to anything of any importance. All of the women were wrong. None of them were Scarlett.

He'd spent countless hours thinking of what to say to her when he finally did see her.

"So, hey, loser," Romeo said, coming toward his office door. "There's this new burger place. It's all veggie and shit, but Taylor's craving some veggie so we're all heading down there now."

Taylor had given birth to a little girl. They'd named her Carla. It was rather fitting seeing as Taylor had come into their life once again purely for her need for revenge. She had been sure they had something to do with her friend's death, she just couldn't prove anything. The truth was, there was nothing that needed proving.

His own father had taken care of Carla, and dumped her body in the King's Ridge lake. Thinking about Nial Long always left him feeling bitter. His father was very much in prison, but Easton wouldn't be happy until the old fucker died. No matter how he tried to live his life, his father always seemed to be there, taunting him, doing something that would make him stumble.

No more.

"She's not pregnant anymore. She can stop with all the cravings and bullshit she seems to claim she has," Easton said, grabbing his jacket.

"Yeah, well, she gave birth to a tiny human, and we all have to suffer through the consequences of that."

"Of course we do. It's so fucking lame."

"You're still coming?"

"Of course. I wouldn't miss it for the world." He smiled. "The chance at a veggie burger. Yum."

"Don't scare me. You've already kind of scared me from the fact you love to clean. You even had a new vacuum cleaner arrive at the office, and I saw you using it."

Cleaning had become his crutch. He loved to clean, to watch his space sparkle, and the scent of lavender was a great feeling to be surrounded by.

"You're just jealous. You can't stand me being the clean one now." He pulled his jacket on.

Karson, Axton, and Taylor were already waiting.

Axton carried the baby in his arms. He wore one of those strap things that attached to his chest. It looked so odd to see his friend carrying a baby, but the smile on his face, and there was no doubt, Axton had found everything he was looking for.

In high school, he'd known Axton's obsession with Taylor. It had started at a young age. Even when he tried to hide it, there was no hiding the letters or the roses. Taylor had a love of roses, and he'd put a new one in her locker every time he could, with a brand-new letter.

"You ready?" Taylor asked.

"Yes." Easton followed them onto the elevator, which took them down to the parking lot.

Eric, Axton's driver, was waiting.

Axton and Taylor climbed in first, and strapped the baby in. Easton was the last one to get in, and he took a seat by the window.

"This is nice. All of us going to lunch," Taylor said.

"For veggie burgers?"

"I've got a craving. I can't help it."

Easton laughed. "I got no problem with it." He was hungry and would eat anything right about now.

Conversations filled the car about the new baby, the new software product. When Axton and Taylor were going to have another baby. If they were going to get a nanny. Easton hadn't held the baby yet. There had been opportunities, but he'd always passed them by. He didn't want to hold the baby.

She was cute, no doubt about that, but children were no longer in his future. He'd made a vow to never have kids, to never pass these genes onto anyone else. This was the life choice he'd made for himself, and he wasn't going to change it.

Eric pulled up at the curb of the brand-new vegan place that had opened up. Easton hadn't yet visited, but he'd heard amazing reviews of the food.

He entered in behind his friends.

In the corner, he noticed a child's birthday party.

He ignored the chaos and sounds of kids. Since making his vow to be childless, he'd noticed kids were everywhere. He couldn't get away from them.

They took a table as far away from the party as possible.

"What do you guys want?" he asked.

Easton got their orders, and Romeo decided to come and stand with him as they waited to be served.

The place was really busy, and the scents were spicy and garlicky. It was incredible. His mouth was watering.

The woman in front of him had beautiful blonde hair that reminded him a little of Scarlett. This woman's hair had pink tips at the edges, and it was no longer down to her waist. The dress she wore was blue with multiple flowers on it. There was no denying the full hips and nice, curvy thighs.

Her ass wasn't too bad either. It looked full and round.

Scarlett had been a curvy girl, but she'd been confident in her body. He'd seen her in a bikini as well, and she'd been so fucking hot. Some of the girls had tried to attack her with snide comments about her weight, but to him, she'd been perfect.

The smile as well. He would never forget that smile.

Telling the PI about her smile hadn't exactly helped matters as the PI told him most girls you like have a pretty smile. His PI hadn't been helpful, not even a little bit. His sarcasm was overrated as well.

"Thank you so much."

The blonde turned around, and Easton felt like his entire fucking world had collided in on itself.

No way.

No fucking way!

The woman his private investigator was supposed to be finding, the one who he said was going to be so freaking hard to find, was standing right in front of him.

"Scarlett!"

"Easton!"

"Coming, Mom."

Easton turned his head and watched as a black-haired kid with brown eyes came rushing forward. Glancing up at the banner, he saw it read "Eleventh Birthday."

He turned back to Scarlett, who looked shaken.

"You two know each other?" Romeo asked.

"Mom, you ordered the chickpea patties, awesome." The kid grabbed the tray, and Easton heard Romeo gasp.

"Oh, fuck. Tell me that I didn't just see a little Easton."

Easton looked toward Scarlett, who was staring at him.

"He came when you said Easton."

She pushed her hair off her shoulder and stared right at him. "And?"

"That's my kid," he said.

"And?"

"Why didn't you tell me?" he asked.

"Do you guys really think you need to do this here?" Romeo asked.

"Why didn't I tell you? You really want me to answer that in front of your friend?"

"That's my son."

"That is *not* your son," Scarlett said. "You contributed to his DNA, but other than that, he is all mine." Scarlett stepped right up to him. "Today is his birthday. You better not do anything stupid to spoil this for him."

He didn't get to say anything else as she spun on her heel, heading toward the party of twenty kids, boys and girls.

"Did I ... what ... I'm now officially confused," Romeo said.

"Gentlemen, could you please make your order or allow others to," the man behind the counter asked.

Stepping forward, Easton placed the order, and as he waited to be served his food, he looked back toward the party.

He had a kid.

An eleven-year-old kid.

A son named Easton.

"Come on, Easton," Romeo said, grabbing his arm and helping him. They grabbed their order, but he couldn't look away from the small group.

That was Scarlett. The girl from camp, and she had his son.

"What's going on?" Axton asked.

"Erm, I don't know if it's my place to say anything," Romeo said.

Easton couldn't even think. That little kid. The one standing in the center of all of his friends was his son. Scarlett sat off to the side and clapped her hands. To anyone else, she looked calm and relaxed. He knew differently. She wasn't calm.

Her gaze didn't once drift over to him, but he had to wonder if she was aware of his presence as much as he was of hers.

This couldn't be happening. Not right now. He had a son.

He and Scarlett had only been together a handful of times at camp. He'd been her first, and when the time had come for him to leave, well, he'd made sure she knew the truth about him and about their future together.

"That's my kid," Easton said.

All of his table looked toward the little boy.

"Holy shit, he looks exactly like you when you were a kid," Axton said.

"I bet he's bossy as shit too," Karson said.

"How can that be your kid?" Taylor asked.

Easton looked toward Taylor. "Because Scarlett and I had sex."

"He's eleven. That must mean you didn't wait long after Carla's death to move on." Taylor went pale.

He watched her and didn't avert his gaze. "I didn't."

He wasn't going to lie to her or pretend something didn't happen. Those three weeks were the best of his fucking life. They were the weeks he kept trying to forget along with other emotions but everything else he pushed to one side.

"Oh."

"Taylor," Axton said.

"No, it's fine."

"I was a teenage kid, Taylor. I didn't say to you that I spent a great deal of time mourning."

"You spent no time."

"I'm not going to do this with you. Carla's dead. You can't handle this shit, then go. Leave. I'm not going to pretend I was some good little mourner when I wasn't." He saw Axton glaring at him.

Taylor and Axton were speaking to each other in low tones. She didn't leave. She sat there, and he felt the power of her glare as it singed his face. The burn was very much real.

"I'll stick around. See what you're going to do."

"I'm not going to do anything."

"Aren't you a little pissed you have a son and only now finding out about it?" Karson asked. "If that had been me, I'd be up in his mother's face."

"You don't know what I did to her."

"What did you do?" Taylor asked.

Easton looked her way once again. "I'm not saying what I did or didn't do. It doesn't matter." He picked up his burger, taking a bite. It was pretty good, but to be honest, there was only one thing he was interested in, and she was across the room.

The kids sang to the kid; his kid, Easton. She called him Easton. That had to mean something after all this time. He wasn't going to believe it didn't have any meaning.

They were together for a short time, but she could have named him anything else. The kid looked happy though. He laughed, and Easton sat there with his friends watching as his son opened his presents.

He looked so excited and happy. His own childhood hadn't been so lucky. His father wasn't ever going to win awards for dad of the year. He was in jail now, but his birthdays would come and go with a gift here or there. A car. A woman. Some money. Nothing was ever celebrated with cake.

Scarlett was doing the right thing. His son had a cake. A party. Friends. They were all having a good time.

Had they been in the city this whole time? How long had she been close by without him knowing it? It seemed so surreal to him for this to have happened.

"Are you okay?" Romeo asked.

"Yeah, I'm okay." They finished their meal, and his friends left the restaurant, heading outside. He'd already told them he wanted to try to talk to her again.

The kids were doing some kind of game with one of the waiters, and he walked over to Scarlett.

He watched her tense up as he got close.

"Hey," he said.

"Just leave. Please. Easton has already asked me who you are, and I don't want any complications."

"He's my son."

"I think we both know why you don't know about him. I wasn't going to come looking for you, Easton."

He pulled out his business card. "Please, I want to know everything, but I also get why you don't want me to be part of his life. I wasn't exactly a great role model. I get it. I do. But please, will you consider calling me?"

She stared at his card and sighed, taking it. "Fine.

I'm not promising I'll get in touch or anything."

"He's really mine," he said, looking toward Easton.

"I think you should go. Your friends are waiting for you."

Easton nodded. There was so much more he wanted to say, but instead, he took a step back, giving her the distance she needed. It wasn't easy for him to do, and all he wanted was to ask questions, to get to know his son. To find out everything.

He left the restaurant with one last lingering look. What struck him hard was he saw it. He saw any hope and dreams of a future vanish before his very eyes.

"I know you saw it. The boy is yours, but Scarlett can never be. I saw the ring on her finger, Easton. She belongs to someone else," Carla said.

It shouldn't matter to him about the ring, and yet, he couldn't get it out of his head. Scarlett was married, which meant he couldn't have her. Someone else was playing dad with his kid.

He didn't know what he could do about that.

Chapter Five

Over eleven years ago

"You're all by yourself again," Scarlett said.

Easton sat on a rock overlooking a lake. All camps seemed to be set up near a lake. This one didn't have any known predators in it, but she hated to go swimming. It scared her in case there was something evil lurking beneath the depths.

"I just want to be alone," Easton said.

"Okay." She sat down beside him.

From the moment Easton had joined them, she'd known he was different. His clothes screamed designer and expense, and his attitude told them he was used to getting what he wanted. No one wanted to be around him for fear of pissing him off. She didn't give a fuck if he was happy about it or not. It wasn't her place to tell him what he should or shouldn't be.

"This is a nice place," she said.

"I wanted to be alone. Are you stupid or something?"

"Wow, look at someone who woke up on the wrong side of the bed this morning. Forgive me for wanting to include you." She didn't get up though. She merely sat beside him. Every now and again, he'd turn to look her way and he'd looked pissed off.

She simply smiled at him, offering her best comfort face. It didn't seem to work. He looked more pissed off with her than before.

She had to work on that.

"Look, I'm not here to join in with everything. I don't want to be friends. I'm here to forget about something, and the only way I can do that is to be left alone."

"No, you see, that's where you're wrong. To forget about something, you need to be surrounded by people. When you're with someone they can help you to make new memories. Being alone helps you to dwell on the pain and suffering of everything that is happening around you."

He turned to look at her, and she offered him her best smile. "You're offering to help me forget."

"Why not? I like to help people."

Easton moved in close, and she couldn't help but notice how sexy he was. For an eighteen-year-old, he certainly seemed way more mature than she thought was possible.

When he stroked a finger down her arm, she knew he thought this meant something else. She smiled and took his hand. "I don't mean that, Easton. Sex is not going to make whatever it is going on in your head easier. It'll only make it harder."

"I know what can be harder."

This guy clearly had a lot more pain inside himself than he'd like others to believe.

****

Scarlett Knight walked into her large kitchen. Easton, her son, had already rushed in, probably to find Liam and tell him all about his day. She had agreed to take him to the vegan restaurant for his birthday because he'd been begging. She'd put a generous donation into one of their many charities in order to make it so they would accept their very first birthday party.

Opening the fridge, she pulled out a bottled water, unscrewing the cap and taking a long drink.

She was so thirsty. Her mouth was dry.

She'd gotten her body under control, but only just.

What the fuck was Easton doing there? She knew

who he was and where he worked. She'd followed the story when it was exposed about his father's past dealings. The entire company's parents as well. He was still with his friends, the ones he'd talked about all the time at camp. She wondered which one was Axton and if he still had an issue with that friend and his bossy ways.

She wasn't going to do this.

Her time was better spent not thinking about seeing Easton today or that her son was close to his real father.

"Knock, knock," Liam said, entering the kitchen.

Her husband.

The man she had married.

This man, five years ago, had helped her when no one else would. It had all come with a price, and it had been a price she'd been more than willing to pay to help her son.

"Hey," she said, offering him a smile. "You want one?"

"Nah, I'll take a coffee." Liam stood at the island, tapping his fingers on the counter. His own wedding ring seemed blaringly obvious on his finger.

Had Easton seen her ring? Did he even care? She honestly didn't know what to think of what was happening.

"So, Easton came and told me today that he saw another Easton."

She sighed. "And?"

"And I find that incredibly odd. Don't you? Easton would meet another Easton. It's not a very common name."

"It's a name."

"Yeah, and I also know the meaning behind it. You didn't come to look for me when you came home. Why don't you tell me what is going on?" Liam asked.

"Why do you have to be so …. right all the time?"

"It's a natural gift." Liam jumped up onto the counter as she started the coffee maker.

"Where is Easton?"

"In his room, playing with all the awesome gifts. I wish I could have been there, you know that."

"Of course I do." She leaned against the counter. "It was his father. Easton, the guy he saw. It was him."

"Wow."

"Yeah." She took a sip of her water, not really knowing what to say about that.

"And how did it feel to see him after all this time?" he asked.

"I don't know." She pulled his card out of her pocket and handed it to Liam.

"Easton Long, and you finally saw him."

"I did tell you before he was one of the Four Kings." She didn't know why she'd told Liam everything about her life. Maybe it was so he knew what he was getting into with her. She didn't come without excess, and Easton belonged to another guy that was a lot of baggage. She had told Liam the truth from the word go.

"I know. I guess I always imagined him coming around before now."

"He didn't know I was pregnant. I also told you about that," she said.

Liam still held the card.

She poured him a coffee and handed it to him.

Liam caught her wrist, pulling her close. "I was just surprised he wouldn't come and try to look for you."

"I've told you, what we shared at camp, it wasn't a love match."

"What was it?"

"I don't know. Sex, I guess."

Liam took her hand and kissed her knuckles. He did this often, and she always found it comforting.

"Tell me, is he cute?"

"I think he's cute," she said, giggling. This was one of the many reasons she adored Liam. Their relationship was purely platonic. She would be denying herself though if she wasn't a little sad about that.

Not only was he sexy, but he was one of the kindest, most generous men she'd ever met, and above all else, he took care of the both of them.

He had also been thirty-four years old, and he'd needed her. She'd been hesitant to become his wife after only a couple of weeks of knowing him, but he'd given her an offer she couldn't refuse.

Not only would she have everything she had ever dreamed of, there would be love and security for her son. He'd provide him with everything he needed, a father figure, a friend, a confidant if she needed it. For Scarlett, he'd be the husband to provide so long as she offered her … female services, and not sex.

She and Liam had never had sex in all their five years of marriage.

Liam liked to play the field. He liked men and women, but he had an image to uphold. Their wedding had been sweet, set on a little beach. Liam always told her that privacy was key. With his history, he had to keep his life private. He'd not just come out of the world a thoroughbred businessman. From the age of eighteen, he'd gone into the army, and his career had kicked off, and he'd become one of the best damn soldiers, known for getting the job done. He'd advanced, becoming an agent for the country, to serve, protect, and to make sure people could walk the streets safely. He'd made a lot of enemies, and when he'd retired, he'd built this company, which had been handed to him as a reward, along with a new identity. His past life was one he kept a secret, and she had to play the role of his doting wife, to give his credentials a firm background. She didn't know the full extent of his past, but she didn't need to know. Liam controlled everyone and everything. He was one of the few businessmen in the world that didn't flaunt his success.

Their marriage gave Liam the security he enjoyed. It meant he could come and go as he pleased. All she had to do, if she decided to have a relationship, was to be discreet. Nothing long-term, and no love matches. Liam also demanded he get to know the man or woman she decided to include in her life.

She hadn't fallen for anyone. One relationship when Easton was really young had shaken her to the core. She had heard about violence within the home but had never seen or been part of it.

When her boyfriend had smacked her across the face, she had been shocked. When she wouldn't have sex with him, he'd beaten her up so bad she had to go to the hospital. She had pressed charges, and not long after that, she'd met Liam.

In another life they might have been perfect for each other.

"Are you going to talk to him?" Liam asked.

"I don't know if I should talk to him. We left things so … no, I'm not going to talk to him. I don't owe him anything."

"The man just found out he has a son. You think he's not going to try and see him."

"You can stop that, right?" she asked.

"There are a lot of things I can do. I'm a powerful man, and I can make sure Easton never comes near his son." Liam frowned. "Let's start calling them Senior and Junior. What made you think to call them the same name? This could get complicated."

"After Easton pushed me aside and pretty much told me that it was never going to happen between us, I knew I didn't want to waste time on what wasn't going to happen, so I, erm, I figured naming him Easton would be a reminder to me as well. To always be careful who I gave my heart to."

"It makes a lot of sense, but, sweetheart, I'm going to be real, Easton is not going to back down."

"You said so yourself. You can fight."

"Of course I can, but Easton has something I don't have."

"What?"

"Senior is Junior's father. He has DNA, and I've got nothing."

"But he didn't want him. He didn't want his son."

"Did you ever get to tell him he has a son?" Liam asked.

"No. I still had my pride, and I wasn't going to go hunting for a guy that tore my heart out, stomped on it, set it on fire, and then proceeded to cut it."

"Colorful," Liam said. "He's one-quarter of the Four Kings. He's a powerful man."

"So are you."

"I know, but if he was to pull the company behind him, there's no way for me to stop him. Unless a judge rules different, Easton is going to see his son."

Scarlett glared at the business card.

"You're not going to kill Easton through a single glance at a card. No matter how much you want to set it on fire."

"What do you suggest?" she asked.

"Go and see him. Invite him here so I can get a good look at my competition."

She laughed as Liam wrapped his arms around

her. "Competition?"

"I wasn't meaning Easton. You could be my competition for this guy's affections."

Scarlett didn't want to imagine Liam and Easton together, but it didn't stop her from enjoying the potential view. They were both sexy men. Liam appeared stronger to her, more muscular than Easton.

It would be one sexual fantasy, but no, she wasn't going to allow herself to go down that road. Who hadn't thought of them in a man sandwich before? She could safely say Easton and Liam were the two men in her world that she had fallen in love with without a doubt. It wasn't going to happen though. Not in this lifetime.

"You want me to invite him to dinner?" she asked, running the card across her lip.

"Why not? I don't see a problem in getting involved with Easton. We'll get to know if it's worth calling my lawyers, and we can try and stop any kind of bad press that could come of this."

She wrapped her arms around Liam's neck. "Look at you, always thinking of the future."

She dropped a kiss to his lips, and for a few seconds, Liam caught the back of her head.

"Ew, gross, guys. Come on," Easton said, interrupting them.

She laughed. "Of course." She rolled her eyes.

To their son, they were a married couple. They shared a bed, and kept up the pretense of their relationship.

Scarlett knew it was anything but.

Liam spent a great deal of time in the city, and she could only allow herself to wonder exactly what it was he did.

She grabbed her bottled water. "I better go and figure out a cab, and what to say to him."

"You do that." Liam slapped her on the ass as she walked past.

Rolling her eyes, she kept on walking. She loved being with Liam. It was just missing one thing from their life. Now that Easton had reared back up in her life, she didn't know what to make of it, or what to think.

****

From the moment Liam had met Scarlett, she had been completely honest with him. She'd been a struggling mom, and had even brought her kid to an interview. Of course, she had no idea who he was, and she'd just unloaded her life story. At the time, he had a few different people to interview for his housekeeper, but the sheer desperation in Scarlett's eyes had struck him hard. Scarlett had been honest with him, but he'd not been anywhere near honest with her. Not then, not in the last five years, and certainly not now.

There were parts of his story that was a truth. He was bisexual. He loved men and women, and had had relationships with both.

When he first met Scarlett, she'd been recovering from a beating that a boyfriend had given her. She hadn't gone into details, but he also believed it may have gone a step too far, and the boyfriend may have forced himself upon her even after she said no. Again, she had never said anything, but just the way she was with him, keeping him at arm's length.

He was in love with Scarlett.

There was one of his lies. She wasn't just a convenience for him. He was completely and totally in love with her, and her son. He adored the kid. He was so bright and funny. They gave him a family. The other lie he had told her was he wasn't looking for forever.

He was.

When it came to Scarlett, what wasn't to love?

She was sweet, smart, kind, a beautiful woman, not to mention her curvy, bigger body. Scarlett wasn't embarrassed by her curves, and Liam, well, he loved to feel them against him at night, or at any time. It was night when he got to feel her, and know he wanted her for a lot more than just a quick fuck. She had soft, large hips that were just designed for a man to hold onto as he took her hard, claiming her as his. Her tits were nice and full, and he imagined them in his hands most days of the week. She had a body designed to be loved, to be protected, and he'd made the vow to be that man.

He wanted a long-lasting relationship with a man *and* a woman. Yeah, there was his other lie. He wanted to live an unconventional relationship. Since meeting Scarlett, he'd not been with another woman or man.

He'd tried. There had been the occasional date, but nothing had progressed. He couldn't even bring himself to kiss another woman or man. The nights he spent in the apartment in the city were because he needed a break.

Sharing a bed with Scarlett was pleasure and torture all at the same time. He got to spend hours with her in his arms. Whenever she fell asleep, she was like the dead. He'd watch her sleep, hoping that one day, he could turn his lies around with her.

He loved how comfortable she was with him. The way he could hold her, touch her, love her, and she didn't mind, and she wasn't afraid of him. He couldn't stand for her to ever be afraid of him.

Easton.

The kid's father.

Could it really be possible for him to get what he always wanted? A family. He loved Scarlett and he was willing to give anything a go, but Easton, he needed to meet the man that had once owned a piece of her heart.

He had to see if there was a chance of a future. If there was, he could work with it, help their feelings grow to include him. He wasn't ashamed to be a manipulative bastard. He didn't get where he was today by being the good guy all the time. He'd even warned Scarlett a few times over the years that he wasn't what he seemed.

He just couldn't break her heart or her trust.

Each time he promised himself he'd tell her the truth, she'd enter their bedroom, snuggle down, and he'd hold her, resting a hand on her hip, and he just couldn't bring himself to lose that. He knew it made him an asshole, and so many other words, but he could live with that.

For five years he'd given her time. He'd given her the chance to get over her last relationship, to build her fragile heart and to find herself again.

The woman he met five years ago had been close to shattering underneath the weight of expectation. Of being a mother. Her family had turned their back on her all those years ago, and he'd promised to never do that.

After she finally repaired herself, there was just never a time to explore what could be. Part of it was fear of what she'd think and feel. He wanted everything with her, but not if it came with a price. There were only so many things Liam was willing to gamble, and Scarlett's feelings wasn't one of them.

****

The following day, Easton paced his office. He still didn't get her full fucking name. He'd even called his PI to try to get the details of the woman who booked the birthday party, but again, all those details were private and the people at the restaurant wouldn't budge. Even when money was being offered to bribe them. They wouldn't give any information away.

"You're still pacing," Romeo said.

"That I am still doing. Can't you tell?"

"You have a bad attitude, all because of this woman."

Karson entered the room. "And we didn't even get to know her."

"Yeah, and I think it's time that you spilled the details," Axton said, entering his office.

All of his friends sat in the chairs, waiting.

"I didn't call a meeting, and I don't want to share. This is not a sharing occasion."

"I don't care if it's share-worthy, we still want to know. You're pacing like a crazy person," Romeo said.

"I've not touched a drop of alcohol. I'm still clean," Easton said.

Axton sighed. "None of us said you did or are going to. Why do you think we think the worst of you?"

"That is a tongue twister," Karson said.

"Look, guys, I know I screwed up. I did so big time, but that doesn't mean I'm going to do it again. Of course I'm not. I'm not that big of a screw-up. I'm not that big of anything." He groaned. "I hate this. I really do. Scarlett and I, we have a history."

"An eleven-year-old history," Romeo said. "I'm just pointing that out there. You must have gotten her knocked up not long after Carla's death."

"Taylor's already done the math," Axton said.

"How is she dealing?"

"Okay. She hasn't threatened to leave me. She said it's hard, but at the same time, you can't live in the past. We'll see."

"I don't want to be the cause of you and Taylor falling out."

"You won't be. If things ever end between us, it will all be on Taylor," Axton said.

"You're not going to take any of the blame?"

Romeo asked.

"Nope. I'm in love with my woman. I have been for a long time, and if she can't see that, and she wants what happened years ago to get in the way of that, it's on her, not me. I'm just a man trying to make this all work." Axton shrugged. "I don't want to talk about me. I want to talk about you and what is going on with you."

Easton moved to the edge of his desk. "Her name's Scarlett."

"Do you have a last name?" Karson asked.

"No, I don't know her last name. If she told me, I've forgotten it."

"Classy," Romeo said.

"We met at the camp. The one I was sent on after Carla's death. I tried to stay by myself, to not make any connections, and well, Scarlett was very determined to help me be a distraction. Not for sex." He looked at his friends' smirking faces. "It wasn't like that."

"It had to have been like that at some point for little Easton to come about."

"We did end up having sex, but it wasn't straight away. It was a slow burn."

"A couple of weeks isn't a slow burn," Axton said.

"It was for us. Twenty-four hours a day in each other's company. She was so fucking hot. She's gotten more beautiful, but I can still remember her smile. The way she laughed. I don't know how she did it, but she got me to have fun. She got me to forget all about Carla and the life that was waiting for me back at home."

"It didn't last? You didn't think to bring her home?" Karson asked.

"My father had killed my last girlfriend, and she'd been pregnant with my kid. Scarlett hadn't told me anything of her life. I talked about Carla and you guys, but I didn't tell her anything else. I didn't want it to interfere with my time there. By the end of camp and it was time to go home, I knew I had to end things. We were going to college, and we were going to be taking over the Four Kings. I didn't have room in my life for a woman. Not for Scarlett. She didn't belong in our world. I couldn't be responsible for the loss of her smiles. So I ended it. I did it harshly, so she knew without a doubt not to come look for me. I already had blood on my hands. I couldn't add hers."

"What makes you think you'd have hurt her?" Karson asked.

"Carla."

His friends groaned.

"You're not responsible for what happened to her," Romeo said.

"I'm not? You really think I'm innocent?"

"I didn't say you were innocent."

"If I wasn't so damn stupid in trying to win a fucking bet about popping her cherry and getting her to fall for me, I wouldn't have knocked her up. My dad wouldn't have seen her as a threat, and I wouldn't have been wanting to run away from it all. Carla's death is very much my fault. I didn't kill her, but I signed her death sentence the moment I made the bet." Easton sighed.

"My name's Scarlett Knight."

Easton looked past his friends to see Scarlett standing in the doorway. She knew the truth already about what happened to his ex-girlfriend.

Scarlett wore a pair of jeans and a plain white shirt. She looked amazing, calm, put together. Her blonde hair was bound on top of her head, with strands falling down all around her.

Yesterday she had looked beautiful, today even

more so.

"Scar," he said, getting to his feet.

She had her arms folded across her stomach, and he saw the wedding band on her finger.

"What are you doing here?" he asked.

"You gave the impression you wanted to talk after what you saw."

"You mean my son? How did you find me?"

"You described yourself as one of the Four Kings. This company is called that, so it wasn't hard to guess."

"All this time you knew where I was."

"All this time I was busy raising my son. It had nothing to do with finding you."

"He's mine."

"Do you want to go there, with how you ended everything? I'm not here to pick a fight with you, and especially not in front of your friends."

Easton looked at his friends, who were watching the interaction. They were all fucking nosy bastards. "Axton, Karson, Romeo, this is Scarlett. Scarlett, this is everyone."

"Hi," she said.

There was no smile on her lips. Her gaze went straight back to him.

"You're married." He pointed at the wedding band.

"Yes, for nearly five years now. Liam, my husband, he wanted me to invite you over for dinner."

Easton frowned. "Let me get this straight, your husband wants to have dinner with me? Does he know Easton's mine?"

"Of course he does. We've been together five years, not eleven." She closed her eyes, and he watched her take a deep breath. "We just want you to come over, have dinner, talk. You can maybe meet Easton. I don't know. It's just a chance here to catch up. Talk."

"We're talking right now."

"I'd feel more comfortable with Liam present."

"I'm not going to hurt you."

"I didn't say you would. This is already hard, okay? For me, you have no right to Easton. No right to be in his life."

"I didn't get the chance to have a say in that."

"You did. You're just forgetting everything else that came with that, Easton. I don't want to fight or argue about this. I did what I thought I was right."

"Does your husband always get what he wants?" Easton asked. He didn't even know who the man was, but already, he hated him. The mystery husband got to keep Scarlett, to have her every single night and every single chance he got.

"Do not even go there," she said. "Liam is a good man. A good father. Believe me, this is a gift from him. He doesn't have to comply with anything. Here are our details. Call that number on what you decide." She handed him a card, and within the next second, she was gone.

He glanced down at the name, not seeing it.

This wasn't how he saw today going.

"Fuck!"

Without waiting for any encouragement from his friends, he rushed out of his office and followed Scarlett to the elevator. It hadn't arrived yet.

He stopped beside her. "I'm sorry."

"You don't need to apologize."

"I do. I didn't want this to happen between us. For us to argue when we've not seen each other in a really long time."

She sighed and turned toward him. "I don't want

to argue either. I didn't expect to ever see you again, and I'm really sorry about all of this."

"No, please, don't be sorry. I want to get to know Easton."

"Junior."

"Junior?"

"Liam thinks it will be easier if we call you Senior and my Easton Junior."

"You named him after me?"

"Yes, I don't see why I shouldn't? I didn't want to end things the way they did. It just happened. I'm not ashamed of Easton being yours."

"Does he want to know about me?" Easton asked.

The elevator opened, and he saw her nibbling her lip. "I've got to go."

"I understand."

"Easton doesn't ask a whole lot of questions. I think he's always accepted life as it is. I'm not trying to be mean here."

"It's fine. It's fine. He has Liam."

"Will you come to dinner?" she asked.

"Do you want me to?"

"Don't ask me that. Make your own choices here."

"I'll think about it."

"That's all I ask." She stepped into the elevator.

"How was it having him?" Easton asked, putting his hand on the elevator door to stop her leaving.

"Having a son?"

"Yes."

"It was the scariest, happiest, overwhelming experience of my life."

He let the elevator doors go. He'd missed all of the early years of Easton's life. Junior. He liked that.

Whoever this Liam guy was, he sounded like a

solid guy.

Axton, Karson, and Romeo were still waiting for him when he arrived back in his office.

"We have got a company to run, you know?" Easton asked.

"Of course we do, and I accept that, but come on, you've got to tell us something here," Romeo said.

"Are you going to go?" Axton asked, picking up the card, and then giving a whistle. "I wouldn't be too worried about your boy. He's in really good hands."

"What?"

"Liam Knight. He's a wealthy man. Came out of nowhere with a corporation to rival plenty. He rarely does business with anyone. Rarely seen, and when he is, he always has control of who publishes his image. I even heard a story of him paying over a million dollars to someone so he could have his image back, or something. That could all be rumor though. The guy, for some odd reason, is obsessed with his privacy. This is ... wow, your girl really found a good one." Axton held the card up.

"Scarlett wasn't a gold-digger," Easton said, grabbing the details from Axton.

"She may have been. A kid and in need of opportunities," Axton said.

"You didn't know her, okay? I did. I knew her, and she wasn't like that." He had to defend her so they would understand she wasn't the kind of woman to go chasing after a guy with money.

She didn't come looking for him, and she'd only known Liam five years ... or could it have been longer?

No!

He wasn't going to think about that.

"Are you going to go to dinner?" Romeo asked. "It sounds really good."

"I think I should. I want to meet Liam. Negotiate to see my son? Don't you think I should?"

"I think you should do whatever you feel is necessary," Axton said. "We'll know where you'll be so no worries there."

Easton sat down behind his desk.

"Is this going to be a problem?" Karson asked.

"No. I'm clean and fine. I have no desire to drink. I just want to figure all of this out."

"Duty calls," Romeo said. "Whatever you decide, I'd love to be an uncle again."

"Me too," Axton said.

Karson was the only one to linger in his office.

"If you're going to give me some bullshit that you feel like I'm going to fall off the wagon, save it. I'm clean and clear-headed. I want to know my son."

"So long as you understand this is another life. This boy is going to want to get to know you. Once you do this, you can't pick him up and put him back down again. You've got to stick with it."

"When did you get all wise?" Easton asked.

"A long time ago."

He watched Karson leave his office. Once he made a choice, he'd stick to it. Regardless of his son being eleven years old and not knowing him, it didn't matter. Easton had known his father his entire life and still hated the bastard.

Staring at the card, he knew of Liam. He'd never met the guy personally, but from what he heard, he was a damn beast in the boardroom and was known for getting the job done. No one wanted to get on his bad side, and neither did Easton. If he came after the Four Kings empire, it would be a bloodbath. Liam was known for also having friends in high places. No one really knew what those places were though. Not something Easton wanted to find out, either.

"You really need me to make this decision for you?" Carla sat on the edge of his desk, swinging her legs back and forth.

"I'm starting to think I need my brain examined."

"You probably do, but there's no law to say you can't be seeing things that don't exist. So that was Scarlett. She's pretty."

"She's beautiful."

"That, too. And you have a son. He's just a little younger than the baby you'd have had with me. There is a huge difference though." He turned to Carla, knowing she wasn't there. "You wanted this son with Scarlett. My child with me, you didn't want."

He picked up the phone, and Carla disappeared.

Chapter Six

Over eleven years ago

"Come swim with me," Easton said.

Scarlett raised a brow. He found it cute when she did that. He'd tried to do it a few times, but it was a skill he couldn't master.

"You have got no chance."

"Why not?"

"I'm not jumping in a lake. Do you have any idea what could be in here?"

"Lots of water?"

"No, like sharks or something," she said.

"You promised me you'd keep me company and help me to forget, but you won't come swimming with me."

"You don't need to swim to forget. That is just wrong." She wrinkled her nose. "Come. Lie down. Enjoy the sun." She stretched out, and for a few seconds, he admired her. She wasn't a slender girl and had curves in all the right places. She wore a pair of shorts, and she hadn't gone full bikini this time, which was a shame. She looked hot in a bikini.

He didn't want to go swimming by himself, and seeing no other choice, he picked her up. She wasn't light, and as she thrashed around in his arms, he merely threw them both over the edge and dived into the lake. He held onto her, breaking the surface. She let out a little scream as she came up for air.

"Why the fuck would you do that?" she asked.

"To swim."

"I can't swim."

All humor died from him. "What?"

"I can't swim." She wrapped her arms around

his neck as well as her legs. He saw the fear in her eyes, but he didn't have a problem with her body being flush against his.

"It's okay. I've got you. You don't have a problem with anything being in the water."

"Anything can be in the water, you know. Just think all kinds of horror flicks and you know, we're chomped on." She didn't let him go. "I need to let go of you."

"You don't have to if you don't want to."

"I really, really, really need to."

"Then let go." He only held her ass, but she didn't make a move.

"Please get me to shore."

"I can teach you how to swim."

"I don't want to drown. It ... I ... I'm scared."

He held her a little tighter. "We won't practice here, but one day, we're going to have an indoor pool and then I'll teach you how to swim."

"One day?"

"Yeah, don't you see us being friends for a lifetime?"

"I don't know what I see. Please don't let me fall."

"I won't ever let you fall. I've got you, Scar. I won't ever let go of you."

She held onto him tightly, and he knew he would protect her, always.

****

Present day

"You need to stop panicking," Liam said.

"Easy for you to say. You don't have an ex arriving. I should go through your little black book."

"Little black book?"

"Yes, and that way we could have one of your

exes here to make up the numbers."

"You're wanting to partner Easton up with one of my exes?"

"Why not? It sounds like a plan." Scarlett didn't know what to expect. She'd thought Easton would cancel. Her son was upstairs, playing. They had told him a visitor was coming and that they'd call him down when dinner was ready.

She was so nervous. She had ended up changing three times until Liam had picked out the right outfit for her.

This was just one of the many reasons why she loved him.

"Is Easton bi?"

"No."

"Then I would have invited another guy around to talk to."

She rolled her eyes. "You're just being difficult."

The doorbell rang, and her nerves kicked up a notch. Liam got to his feet. His hands went to her shoulders, and he worked out the kinks.

"Stop panicking. This is all good. You, me, the kid, and his dad. It'll work out."

"I don't know why I'm acting this way."

Liam kissed her cheek. "I'm here."

"How are we going to play this?" she asked.

"Play what?"

"You and me?"

"We're husband and wife. Expect touches and kisses, stuff like that."

She nodded her head. "Right, of course, right. I can do this. There's nothing wrong here."

They walked to the door, and she was really glad Liam was behind her. Without him she would have sunk to the floor.

When she opened the door, there Easton stood. He held a bottle of wine and a gift beneath another arm.

"I didn't know what to bring, and I should warn you, I don't drink at all."

Scarlett took the bottle of wine and realized it was non-alcoholic.

"I also checked that it's vegan as well. Does that count?" Easton asked.

"Scarlett and Easton Junior are the vegans here. I'm vegetarian," Liam said.

She forced a smile to her lips as Liam pressed against her back. They had done this many times. Dinner parties and social gatherings. Playing his wife was never a chore. She adored him, and she was used to being close with him. They shared everything together. He was her best friend and her confidant.

"Come in. Come in," Liam said.

Easton looked a little unsure.

"I will go and pour us all some of this," Scarlett said.

She had to get away from the temptation of seeing both of those men together. She couldn't deny how sexy Liam was. He had never given her the impression he wanted anything more. There were a few mornings he woke with an erection, but she'd always put that down to morning wood.

Entering the kitchen, she breathed in the scent of the tomato garlic sauce. Her son had been the one to ask her if he could go vegan, and it had terrified her. Liam helped, consulting with the best doctors, and they had helped to guide her on what to cook.

He'd made his choices, and at eleven she wanted to respect them. He was a good kid, and she loved him so much.

Grabbing the glasses, she opened the bottle and

couldn't help but wonder why he made a point of saying he didn't drink. Had he encountered problems with drink in the past? She was so confused right now.

Liam wasn't helping matters either. Her body was humming with his touch. She had always been able to ignore the slight yearning he created inside her, but not tonight for some odd reason.

"It's okay, Scar. You can do this."

"Talking to yourself already?" Liam asked.

"I have a feeling I'm going to need something stronger," she said.

Liam took both glasses. "We're going to be fine. You need to stop panicking."

"Who's panicking? Me? I'm relaxed."

He laughed and pressed a kiss to her lips. "Come on. I've got your back. You will always be safe with me."

She believed him.

Following him out to the sitting room, she wondered how Easton Junior was getting on. He'd not come to see who their visitor was, not that she should expect it. He often stayed in his room, reading, playing with his microscope, or working on his vocabulary.

Easton was sitting in the chair near the fire. It wasn't lit as it wasn't cold enough yet to have a fire.

Liam took the other chair, and as they were doing this dance, Scarlett sat on the arm by her husband.

"I wanted to thank you for letting me come here tonight. The invitation was a surprise."

"When Junior said he'd met you, I was curious. You didn't know about him, and now, you can have the option, if that is what you wish?"

Easton looked at her.

"I'd like the chance to get to know him. I know I fucked up with you, and I can't change what we did in the past."

"I know. It's fine. Honestly. I shouldn't have reacted the way I did. It was wrong of me. Stupid. Selfish. I didn't expect to see you there."

"How come you weren't at the party?" Easton asked. "I didn't see you there."

"I had other matters to attend to." Liam smiled.

Scarlett sipped at her drink. This wasn't awkward at all.

Silence fell in the room. Liam looked comfortable like he always did, relaxed, as if nothing could bother him.

She felt sick to her stomach.

"So, how have you been?" she asked. "I heard the Four Kings have merged with another company."

"We have. He's a friend. I can't talk about the specifics."

"I don't need to worry. I know Paul Motts. He's a good guy. His software is outstanding," Liam said.

"How are you okay with this?" Easton asked.

"Okay with that?"

"I have a kid with your wife."

Liam placed his hand on her thigh. Her nipples tightened, and she felt a flood of warmth between her thighs.

She hadn't been in a relationship in a very long time. Not since her last abusive boyfriend.

"I know where Scarlett's heart lies. I don't think that we all have to be monsters to get what we want. I'm an agreeable guy. I like to think of myself as a gentleman. We're civilized, and all we want is the best for Junior, wouldn't you say?"

"Yes," Easton said. "That's all I want. A chance to get to know him, maybe?"

Liam didn't let go of her leg. He started to stroke

behind her knee. She licked her suddenly dry lips as Easton watched her.

This had never happened to her before.

"I better go and call him," she said.

Pulling away from Liam, she rushed out of the room, needing to clear her head again. This was a huge mistake, the biggest one she'd ever made.

"Easton, sweetie, come down, we'd like you to meet someone."

Her son got to the stairs. His sneakers were undone, and his shirt was untucked.

"Have you been climbing that tree again?"

"Yeah."

"You don't need to keep on doing that, baby," she said.

"I want to. I told you. Falling out of it won't stop me."

"You will if I cut off all the branches." She wrapped her arms around him and started to tickle him.

"Mom, Mom, I'm, like, eleven now. I've got to be cool."

"No, you don't have to be cool," she said. "You'll always be my baby."

"I need a brother or sister so I can be cool."

Easton said that as they entered the library. Two sets of smoldering eyes looked her way, one sharpest blue and the other deepest brown. Both of them hit her hard, and she wanted to sink to her knees and worship both of them.

Tonight, in the shower, she was going to have to fix her overactive imagination. There's no way she'd be able to sleep with Liam tonight without her doing something stupid, like dry humping him, or begging for more. This wasn't like her, not even a little bit. Sex had been enjoyable in the past, but it hadn't been something that made her act like this.

"Hello," Junior said. "You're the guy at my party."

Easton sat forward. "Hey, Easton," he said.

"Your name is Easton as well," her son said.

"Yeah, it is." He looked toward her.

"Sweetie, there's something I need to tell you. It's, erm, this man here, he's your father."

Her son's eyes went wide. "My dad? He's my father?"

"Yes."

Junior glanced behind Liam, who had sat forward.

"Are you okay?" Liam asked.

"Where have you been?" Junior asked, looking at Easton.

"He didn't know about you. I never told him," Scarlett said. She wasn't going to let Easton take the fall for this. No matter how much she hurt, *she'd* been the one to make this decision. She didn't know what Easton would have actually done, but there was no going back. She'd made this decision all on her own. What was shared between the two of them, happened eleven years ago, and it wasn't her son's fault. This was between her and Easton.

"You know about me now?" Junior asked.

"Of course. It's why I'm here. I'd like to get to know you." He pulled the present in front of him. "I got this for you. I don't know what you're into, but at your age, I loved cars."

Junior took the gift, and Scarlett sat on the arm of the chair, watching.

This scared her.

What if her son wanted to be with Easton more than with her? Was she ever going to be able to share her son with Easton?

Easton moved to the floor as Junior unwrapped the car.

"You okay?" Liam asked, whispering the words.

"Yeah, no. I don't know. I think I'm going to go and get dinner ready."

She got up and ruffled Junior's hair, needing that connection more than anything. He didn't push her away but called her name in that annoyed voice he did.

If he could still do that, she was happy. This could work.

Entering the kitchen, she pulled the sauce from the oven and gave it a stir. She tasted it and quickly went about chopping some extra parsley.

Just as she'd put another pan onto boil with all the pasta, Liam entered the kitchen.

"You really don't seem yourself," he said.

"I'm fine. Really. I think it just hit me what I did. I didn't even try to go looking for him. I've told you how it all ended."

"You feel guilty?"

"Yeah, I do. It's insane. For a long time now, I just wanted to move on. Forget about Easton and the past. Now, he seems to be very much part of my future."

Liam walked to her side, and his arms went around her. The moment he held her, she felt completely protected and safe. This was how it had always been with Liam.

"It's going to be okay." His lips were close to her ear, and she wanted him to kiss her so badly, to put his lips on her neck, to suck hard.

She was losing her mind. Why did she want this?

He gripped her hips and spun her to face him.

"What's going on?" he asked.

"Nothing." She didn't look at his lips, but she

wanted to. "Let's just get through dinner and then we can deal with whatever else we have to face."

She pulled away, but Liam caught her, his lips pressing hard against hers. She wanted to wrap her arms around his neck so bad, and for him to never stop.

Instead, she pulled away and acted like what they were doing was the most natural thing in the world.

It wasn't.

They were not in a relationship.

Liam was her husband in all the ways that counted, but not this one.

"I better get this finished. Will you show them to the table," she said.

"Of course."

He touched the base of her back one last time, and she watched him go, wanting him so badly.

****

Liam wasn't a fool. He knew what was going on with Scarlett.

From the moment he touched her thigh, he saw the reaction in her body. The way her nipples beaded at his touch and how she turned a little closer to him. He'd been noticing these subtle changes for the past couple of months, but he'd not broken the status quo between them.

With Scarlett, when he finally took that chance with her, he wanted her to know he was ready. She scared easily, and her fear of rejection constantly guided her to make bad choices. The truth was, all she wanted, was to be safe, and he offered her that.

When he entered the sitting room, Easton and Junior were sitting on the floor, playing with the car he'd brought.

Easton was everything he imagined he would be. Strong, hard, broken. He needed someone in his life to offer him the same comfort that Liam gave to Scarlett.

"Dinner is nearly ready," he said.

"What is it?" Junior asked.

"It looks like your mother's favorite pasta."

"Awesome. Dad, you're going to love it."

Liam looked at Easton to see the shock on the other man's face.

"Go and see if your mother needs any help."

Junior left them alone as Easton got to his feet.

"I didn't expect that."

"No, I don't imagine you did."

Easton laughed. "This is kind of awkward."

"Why?"

"You're married to a girl I've got a kid with."

"With all due respect, Easton, I've known her longer than you."

"Where did you two meet?" Easton asked.

"At work." It wasn't a lie. She'd come in for a job interview, and he extended the invitation to something more. They'd been living perfectly content for five years now. For all intents and purposes, Scarlett was his most successful relationship to date. "She made a lasting impression."

"Were things hard for her with *him?*"

"With Junior?"

"Yes."

"You're going to have to talk to Scarlett about all the other details. I'm not going to share secrets here. She'll tell you what you want her to know. I want you to know that I'm more than happy with you being part of Easton's life. You can consider yourself one of us, part of our family."

"I'd like that."

"That doesn't mean I intend to ever do business with the Four Kings."

"I won't take that as an insult."

"I don't want to bring business out of work."

"Are you guys ready?" Scarlett asked. "Dinner's on the table."

They both followed her. The table was a small one. He did have a separate dining room with a much longer table when they had guests. Also, Scarlett never cooked for their guests. She had done it once, and the evening ended in a disaster. The one thing he hated was bad manners. Some of the women had made catty and uncalled-for remarks. Scarlett wasn't some award-winning chef. She made good food, and he loved to watch her cook. She made his home feel like one, rather than just a showplace for people.

Scarlett sat beside him, with Junior on the other side.

"You can sit here, Dad," Junior said.

Easton offered a smile, and took the seat next to his son.

Scarlett looked at Liam in fear, but he simply smiled at her. All was good for him. He wasn't going to take another man's child away from him.

"Mom, this is so good."

"I knew you'd love it, sweetheart."

"Dad, Mom is totally learning how to go vegan. I saw this thing online and it was so scary, and I don't want to ever hurt an animal again."

"Vegan?" Easton looked up.

"Also, at school, we're learning about the effects on the environment," Junior said.

"Easton really cares about nature, and he came home and begged me to go vegan. Of course, I was nervous. This is a whole new step for me," Scarlett said.

"You're doing good though, kid. He's been vegan for six months now," Liam said.

"Liam refuses to give up his cheese and chocolate," Junior said.

He chuckled. This was what their family could be like.

He just wished Scarlett wouldn't be so nervous.

They got through dinner, and then Junior took Easton upstairs to show him the bedroom.

Liam grabbed the dishes, taking them into the kitchen.

"You really think this is a good idea?"

"It's his dad."

"I've not seen Easton in a long time. I don't know. I feel you're being too trusting."

Liam wrapped his arms around her waist, pulling her against him. She didn't fight him, and he used the advantage to kiss her again. This was one bonus of having company, he could make any excuse in the world to kiss and hold her.

"I wish I had your enthusiasm."

"It takes a couple of extra years to get used to it."

She placed her hands on his chest. Her fingers stroked over his heart.

"I don't know what to do anymore," she said.

He tilted her head back with his finger beneath her chin. "You don't have to do anything. Easton's not going to try and take him away. I won't let him, and we're going to make this work. All three of us, will make this work in some way or another."

She took a deep breath. "You're right. Of course, you're right."

He kissed her again. "Let's get these dishes done."

"Yes, let's." She pulled out of his arms, and he watched her for a few seconds work the kitchen. This was her domain, and she did love to cook. Junior had given her a couple of new challenges with demanding to go vegan, not that it was an actual instruction.

Scarlett would do anything for the boy.

There was still a spark between Easton and Scarlett, even as she tried to deny it. The chemistry was still there, the fire sizzling between them.

He wasn't going to lose Scarlett, but he might be able to find a way of bringing Easton closer to them.

Liam was used to getting his way. He didn't falter or stop; he simply pursued his target until he got what he wanted. He stayed one step ahead of the game.

This was no different with Scarlett and Easton. He could make this work for all three of them. Grabbing the dish towel, be began to plot as Scarlett cleaned the dishes.

There would be some way of working this out. He was sure of it.

****

Easton didn't want to leave. Seeing his son, chatting with him, playing with him—he'd missed so much, and now was the time to go.

Scarlett came out, following him to his car.

"This house is amazing," he said.

"Liam's owned it for years. He wants to make it a family home."

"How come you and Liam haven't had any kids of your own?" Easton asked.

She laughed. "Wow, you're just coming right out and asking that?"

"Why not? You're both incredible together. You know what you want. Why can't I assume that one day you'd have more kids? You're a great mother."

"You've seen me for one night and you can make that assessment?"

"No, I make that assessment based on the three

weeks we knew each other," he said. Tonight had been a revelation for him. Meeting his son, playing with him, experiencing an overwhelming feeling of love and protection. He'd also realized the love between Scarlett and Liam was very much real. What he did notice was the way Liam kept watching him, assessing him. He didn't know if it was because of his connection to Junior, or for some other reason.

"That was a long time ago, Easton. You shouldn't live in the past. I'm not the same person as I was then. A lot of things have changed."

"A lot of things change, but not the way you are. That will never change."

"You always did have this belief I was some kind of saint."

He chuckled. "Nah, I didn't think you were a saint. Just kind, gentle."

"I'm not a fairy tale character, Easton."

"I know."

"I want to ask you a question," she said.

"This should be good."

"Why the non-alcoholic wine? I don't get it."

Easton rubbed the back of his head. "I did a stint in rehab recently. My drinking had gotten out of control. I'm an alcoholic, recovering." The first sign of recovery was admitting you had a problem. "I've not touched a drop since I got out a few months ago."

"Congratulations. I had no idea."

"I won't ever drink again. Not in front of our son. I promise you."

"I know. I remember the guy you once were and you never drank. At least, not at camp."

"I've changed a lot over the years."

"I saw the exposé on the news about your father, about the Four Kings family. I'm sorry."

"Don't be."

"He's the one that killed the girl you told me about, right?" she asked.

Another of Easton's many mistakes when it came to this woman. "Yes."

"I'm really sorry."

"What happened to Carla was a long time ago."

"You haven't moved on though," she said. "You must have really loved her."

He didn't say anything. In his head, he was screaming he didn't love Carla. To his shame, he never had. She'd been a distraction. Real love came after, but the guilt with Carla would always be there.

"Do you love Liam?" he asked.

"Yes."

She didn't even hesitate. The smile on her face confirmed her feelings as well. It was pointless that he even tried to dwell on the relationship.

"He seems like a good guy."

"He's amazing. If you take the chance to get to know him, he's everything."

"How old is he?" he asked.

"He's thirty-nine years old, Easton. Why?"

"Don't you think he's a little old for you?"

"Ten years older is not that old. He's good for me, and he's wonderful with Junior. See, we're even calling Easton Junior because of him."

She was in love with Liam, and he had no chance, not with her.

"Thank you for coming by, Easton. It means a lot to me."

"I'd like to get to know him more, and you, and Liam." He didn't want tonight to end. It was the most fun he'd had in a very long time, and it was all because of her.

"You can see Junior anytime, Liam as well. He's a great friend. You can't get to know me. I'm not part of the equation. I better go."

"I didn't mean it like that." He totally did, but lying was something he had yet to give up. "You're the mother of my child. I want us to be friends." He wanted a lot more, but he'd settle for just friends. If her relationship was solid with Liam, there was no reason to fight it. But if, for whatever reason it wasn't, he may have a chance at winning her back.

"We can always be friends. Good night, Easton. Have a safe journey home."

She turned her back and walked back into the house. He watched her go, turning to the left to see Liam watching them.

He held his hand up, feeling jealous of this man. Liam did the same, closing the window as Scarlett entered.

He'd fucked up with Scarlett all those years ago, and there was no taking it back. His son would know him though, but anything else he wanted with Scarlett would have to wait.

Chapter Seven

Over eleven years ago

"That's it, you've got it. Trust me. I'm not going to let you go," Easton said.

"I can't believe you were able to find a pool in a camp. How did you do it?"

"I'm good at finding things I want. If you're at camp, you're going to need to learn how to swim. All the kids look to you, and if they were drowning, you couldn't even save them."

"That's not nice." She dropped her legs beneath the water and stood up. "There's you. You can save someone."

Easton thought about Taylor pulling Carla's lifeless body out of the water. He couldn't save anyone.

"There's only so much one person can do."

"And you're willing to let all of that lie with me?"

"Yes."

"I'm a woman."

"I'm not a sexist kind of guy. I believe in equality for all," he said. "Besides, you know I'd help you. I will cheer for you. I'll get a costume and learn all kinds of dance moves."

She chuckled.

"Focus. I don't know how long we've got before someone comes looking for us."

"Do you think you can teach me everything we need to know in two and a half weeks?"

The camp didn't last longer than that. He already had the guys texting him, asking him how it was going. Romeo wanted to know if he was having sex with anyone. He hadn't told any of them about Scarlett. She was his little secret.

The annoying girl that wouldn't leave him alone and made sure he participated. They didn't need to know about her.

Once he left, she would be nothing more than a memory. For over an hour, he got her to paddle across the pool, just the width, not the length. He gained her confidence until at the final minute, he let her go, and instructed her to swim the width of the pool. The moment she did it, she stood up, and threw her arms over him.

"Do you have any idea how scary I've found that for years?" she asked.

"I'm guessing a whole lot."

"Yes, yes, yes, thank you. Thank you so much." She pressed her lips to his, and Easton was so taken aback, he didn't respond.

Before he got a chance to respond, she pulled away.

It wasn't one of those kisses; it was a polite, sweet, tender kiss. One between friends.

"You're the best."

Easton had to get himself under control. Feeling Scarlett's curvy body pressed against him had gotten him all kinds of excited, and they were just friends. This wasn't about him taking a girl. This was about him getting over another. Only, one look at Scarlett and he wanted so much more.

****

Scarlett had put Junior to bed and excused herself to take a shower. Liam had been drinking a brandy in his office when she left him. He'd been watching her and Easton's interaction, and she felt a little guilty.

She did love Liam, and she'd never leave him. With Easton, there was pain, a great deal of it she hadn't spoken of, and also a yearning. Only, the yearning was not just with Easton.

Liam had done something to her tonight, and now, her body no longer felt like her own. It felt foreign to her.

Her nipples were puckered, and her pussy was slick. She was so aroused, and she'd not experienced this in a really long time.

Removing her clothes, she stepped into the warm shower. Water cascaded all around her. She tilted her head back to have it wash away all of her worries. She put her hands on her stomach, turning away from the water to soak her hair.

Slowly, she ran her hands up to her breasts, cupping them, feeling the nipples tighten. With one hand on her breasts, the other, she moved between her thighs, touching her clit. She was so aroused as she gasped out.

Liam's touch had flicked a switch, and now she wanted his hands on her, touching her, caressing her, showing her exactly what he could do to her.

She wanted his brand of touch all over her body.

Pressing two fingers inside her, the heat flooded her body, but it wasn't enough. Her touch wasn't giving her the kind of pleasure she craved.

"You're doing it all wrong," Liam said, startling her.

She'd been so lost in her thoughts, she'd not heard Liam enter the bathroom, let alone open the shower stall.

"Liam, what are you doing here?"

"I'm coming to bed, but seeing as you're doing this." He removed his shirt, showing his impressive, muscular chest. He had a few splashes of ink across his chest and arms, but it was always hidden from sight whenever he left the house.

Next, he pushed down his pants and boxer briefs.

Within a few seconds, he stood in the shower stall.

He reached out and stroked some hair back from her face. His hands fell to her shoulders, and he spun her around so that her back was now to his chest.

Liam didn't make a move to touch her, and she didn't stop him.

This was so far beyond a fantasy. This wasn't a fantasy. This was real life.

Liam, her husband, was standing in the shower with her.

"Is this because of Easton?" Liam asked. His lips were so close to her ear, it made it impossible for her to pretend not to hear.

"No."

"Then what is it? I've never seen you like this."

"I don't want to say."

"Tell me, Scarlett. You can tell me anything."

She sank against him, feeling his warmth once again surround her. "It's you. It's all you."

They were words she didn't want to speak, and yet, saying them for him to hear, felt right. This was what she wanted with him. They slept in the same bed, kissed, hugged, and were a couple in most things. This had never happened though. Whenever she was aroused, she'd always taken care of it herself.

This was different. This arousal came from something else.

Liam.

He'd made her wet and hot, and desperate.

He kissed her neck. He'd done it many times in the past. Only this time, it was so much more. His lips grazed her earlobe, and his teeth scored the flesh of her neck, making her gasp.

This was more than she could have imagined. So much more. His hands didn't move from her shoulders.

He held her tightly against him.

"Please, Liam."

"All in good time. Pleasure is not to be rushed. It's to be explored, to be given time to really develop before you explode."

He pulled her hair down one shoulder, and the tips of his fingers grazed down her body, stroking over the buds of her nipples.

She gasped.

"I love that I did this to you." He cupped her tits, pressing them together. She pressed her thighs together. He bit down harder on her neck, and she cried out, the intense pleasure shocking her with the force of it.

Liam let go of her tits, and his hand ran down her stomach.

"Do I make you nervous?" he asked.

"No. I've never felt anything like this."

"No desire?"

"No."

"Then I'm glad it's me that's done this." He pressed against her ass. The hard ridge of his cock was evidence of his excitement to be in this situation with her. Would this ruin everything between them, or would it only enhance what they had?

"I don't want to ruin us."

"We're better than what we want, Scarlett. I love you. It's never going to change. It doesn't mean we can't enjoy each other, and I don't want to see you suffer. You have a right to pleasure like everyone else."

He cupped her pussy, one finger sliding between her slit, stroking over her clit, before gliding down to thrust inside her, and she cried out his name. It was just a single digit, and yet, it was everything and so much more. She'd not had physical sex in so long.

The last person had been her abusive ex.

She had never told Liam how far it went, and she didn't want to. Those were bad memories.

Liam was not that guy. She wasn't afraid of him, and her body was on fire.

He added a second finger, thrusting them in and out, before drawing his fingers up to her clit, to tease across her nub. His other arm held her up, keeping her stable as he worked her pussy. Her legs felt like jelly as he touched and played with her. His lips never stopping as he kissed at her neck.

"You're so beautiful, you know that? I've always imagined what it would be like for us to have this. For us to be together."

"Why?"

"You're a woman I want, Scarlett. You're a great person, the best mother, and I love spending time with you."

"You've never said anything."

"I will never spoil what we have. It means more to me than sex."

He added a third finger. At the same time, he pressed her up against the wall, and she put her hands to steady her, the cold tile making her gasp as her flesh hit it. Liam tilted her hips. He didn't stop playing with her pussy, but he began to play with her body, cupping and squeezing her tits, stroking down her back. His hard cock rested against her ass.

She wasn't afraid. She wanted him to plunge inside her, to take the next step and make her his.

The ring seemed to taunt her. She was Liam's in all things but this. They had never done anything like this.

With his fingers inside her, he used his thumb to tease across her clit, and she just couldn't take it anymore.

She came hard, crying out his name. The sound echoed around the bathroom, flooding her senses with need.

Liam's lips were on her back, traveling up her neck.

"I love the sound of your orgasm, but now, I want to hear you scream louder." He picked her up and carried her into their bedroom.

He dropped her on the bed, spreading her legs open, and before she had time to come down from the first arousal, his lips were on her again, drawing a second orgasm from her. She didn't think they could ever come back from this.

She knew what her relationship had been missing with Liam, and now, she also knew she'd never be enough for him.

With Easton suddenly back, her feelings were all messed up. Even as he'd caused her so much pain in the past, she knew she still had feelings for him. Glancing over at Liam, she had to wonder, would he ever be enough for her?

****

After a night of giving his wife scream-worthy orgasms, he knew it would be too much for her to see him, so he'd left their bed early.

Junior was already up and ready for school. Rather than have a driver take him, he grabbed one of his cars, and drove him to school, promising to be by to pick him up. Before leaving, he'd left Scarlett a note saying to call him when she woke.

They would need to talk, but for now, he had other plans.

With Junior safe in school, there was only one place he wanted to go. Putting his foot to the gas, he drove toward the city. He didn't live too far from the city, an hour's drive tops. He wanted to be available for his own company but still be a recluse. His home was set back into the country, and he loved it. The privacy it offered was incredible. There was no reason to ever leave his property.

For the most part, Liam's life was modest. He stayed grounded, and never in all of his years, had he ever felt … the need to believe he was special or that he was worth more. Of course, he'd encountered this kind of attitude but rarely indulged in it. He never did business with this kind of personality either.

To him, who had known true danger and the hardest work, there was no such thing as a sense of entitlement. Far from it in fact.

Arriving at the Four Kings Empire, he parked his car in the opposite parking lot. Entering the Four Kings Empire, he was impressed. He knew how the company was founded, and how there were once five main people, only for one of them to be cast out. He had no idea the reasoning for it, just that it had happened.

The building was alive with activity. It was an incredible atmosphere to be part of.

He went straight to the reception desk and offered the sweet redhead a smile. She had this forced smile on her lips as if she'd rather be anywhere else but working.

"How may I help you?" she asked.

"I'm here to speak with Easton Long."

"Do you have an appointment?"

"No. He'll want to see me."

"I'm sure he would, sir, but I'm afraid unless you have an appointment. No one sees one of the Kings unless they have authorized it."

"Penny, do you have any idea who you're talking to?"

Liam turned to see a man with dark hair and blue

eyes. Karson Cross. When Scarlett had told him who Junior's father was, and who he was associated with, he'd made it his business to find out everything.

This man was the main soldier of the group. He was more than happy to do the dirty work. The man had ink on his neck, that was hinted at just beneath the collar, and he had an air of danger around him.

"This is none other than Liam Knight. He's the stepfather to Easton's son. Believe me, Easton will want to see him."

Liam kept his smile in place. "What he said, darlin'."

"I'm so sorry. I had no idea." Penny's face had gone a shade of red.

"We offer a value of services here. I've heard one too many complaints. With how you've just treated this man, I'm not impressed. Consider this your final warning. One more complaint, or rude behavior and you're done," Karson said. "Would you like to follow me?"

Liam met Karson's strides with his own, walking toward the elevator. No one dared to get on while Karson was inside.

"You're the bully."

"I'm not the bully. I'm the guy that has to do what he has to do. No bullying involved. I apologize for her rude behavior."

"It is a continued problem?" Liam asked.

"None of your concern, I'll handle it."

"My expertise is anyone who is rude in the workplace, is not working in the best environment. There are other factors, of course, and it could just mean the woman is not a very nice person overall."

"Penny's a fucking bitch and a slut. She's been trying to fuck her way to the top, and hoped to get one of us to put a ring on her finger. None of us are biting. She specifically wanted Axton, but we don't fuck our employees," Karson said.

"Apart from Taylor, as I recall. Axton has married her and has a kid. Congratulations."

"Your assessments and observations are not needed or required."

"You're like a little robot, aren't you?" Liam asked.

Karson glared at him. "Are you here to hurt Easton?"

"No. I want to have a little chat with him. Man to man."

"Easton's been through a lot. If you intend to take his child away from him…"

Liam found it incredibly cute when Karson stood tall, trying to intimidate him. To anyone else, they would be cowering in a corner. Karson was not a nice guy. Not even by a little bit.

Liam was powerful for a reason. He could handle himself.

Liam stood up and stared at Karson. He stopped smiling and dropped his carefree act.

"I will do what I see as fit for my son. Easton has only just found out about Junior. Do not think to threaten or intimidate me. Believe me, I don't get scared easily. My advice, if you've got a woman intent on being with one of you, it's a sexual harassment suit waiting to happen. Make sure others are aware of her intention or it could end badly for all of you."

The elevator opened, and Liam stepped off.

All it took him was a few seconds to see where Easton's office was.

Leaving Karson behind, he made his way straight to Easton's office. He was alone, bent over his desk, reading something.

He knocked on the door, and Easton looked up. He had really sexy, brown eyes.

"Can I come in?" he asked.

"Liam, what are you doing here?"

"I thought it was time we had a chat."

"I didn't do anything wrong last night, did I?"

He chuckled. "No. I nearly didn't come here. One of your receptionists stated how important you all are."

Easton sighed. "Penny."

"Yes. Karson put her in her place."

"I'm sure he did. She's been a problem. I bet you're looking around the place thinking about what you'd change." Easton stood up, walking around the desk. "Please, sit. Do you want some coffee?"

"Please, and a bagel if you have it. No meat, obviously," Liam said.

Easton instructed his PA before entering the office again. "So, what would you change?"

"I don't make it my business to assess companies for change. This is not my area of expertise, and I have no desire to change it. I'm not interested in the Four Kings Empire. Never have been."

"You're confident."

"I've not gotten where I am by being anything less."

"Did you know I was the father?" Easton asked, perched on the edge of his desk.

"Yes, I did. Scarlett and I have no secrets."

"Why didn't you come after me?"

Liam chuckled. "You think I'd come after you by the past you had with my wife?"

"Did she tell you all of it?"

"How you ended it? Yes. She did. I've got no vendetta with you, Easton. Scarlett and Junior are my priority. I saw you talking with her last night. I even saw the way you looked at her throughout the night."

Easton tensed up.

Liam wasn't going to back down. Scarlett's reaction to him gave him hope. It was the first time she had ever shown any raw sexual desire, and one taste of her, would never be enough.

Last night he'd given Scarlett three orgasms before she passed out. For most of the night, he'd held her, thinking about how he was going to approach this little hurdle.

Having Easton come around more often would be the key—only, he'd want him around when Junior wasn't always there.

"Scarlett is my wife, and I love her very much. Junior, as far as I'm concerned, is my son. I'm only his stepfather. Scarlett told me about your stint in rehab."

"She told you?"

"We share everything. Be aware of that. There's no media record of you going to rehab."

"It was kept under wraps. I don't feel comfortable explaining this to you."

"Nothing to explain. You're recovering?"

"Yes. Not touched a drop in a long time now. It's no longer an issue."

"And finding out about Junior?" Liam asked.

"I consider it a blessing. You can stop with the personal questions now. I don't have to justify myself to you."

"I'm getting an overall perspective. I made a vow to Scarlett to love and protect her always. It means I have to ask the uncomfortable questions, if you know what I mean."

"I get it. I won't do anything to harm either of them, I promise."

"I know. I would like to extend an invitation out to you for the weekends."

"An invitation for the weekends?" Easton asked.

"Yes. I know Junior would love having you around, and it will give you time to get to know your son. Weekends he's not at school, and it won't confuse him. Scarlett can also get used to having you around. You'll have a room at my place. You won't need to convalesce between drives. You arrive Friday after work, leave Sunday, or Monday to start your day. How does that sound?"

Easton stared at him for several seconds without speaking.

Liam waited.

"Let me get this straight, you came down here to not only invite me to see my son more but to also stay at your house, with my son, and your wife. My ex-girlfriend?"

"Scarlett was never your girlfriend. She described the event as a camp fling that resulted in her being pregnant."

Easton's face went bright red. "I still had sex with your wife."

"Over ten years ago. Your point being?"

"Don't you see me as any kind of threat?" Easton asked.

"No. I don't. I'm offering you a chance here, Easton. A chance to know your son and to become friends with my wife. This will be amicable." And it would also start what he wanted as well.

He didn't know what Easton's feelings would be, but something told him to keep trying. If it didn't work, he'd still continue to allow father and son visits.

What he'd started with Scarlett couldn't be undone, and he had no intention of doing so.

"You have my contact details. Let me know what you decide. I've already kept you enough, and now I need to go home. Lovely to see you."

"Your coffee and bagel," Easton said.

"Maybe another time. You enjoy them. You look like you need to eat something. You've got to stay healthy now, Easton. It's important you do so."

With that, Liam left.

It would appear he had another person to take care of. Easton wasn't doing a good enough job of it, but Liam had no problem taking over.

****

The bagel and coffee arrived, and Easton sat on the edge of his desk, not moving. Did he really just have a conversation with Liam Knight?

"Do I need to go and fetch the lawyers?" Axton asked, entering his office.

Karson and Romeo came in behind him.

"I ... no. It's not about that. It's about Junior, my son. He's offering me the chance to get to know him."

"Take it," Romeo said. "What have you got to lose?"

"Do you really think a guy like Liam Knight would offer this without something in return?" Karson asked.

"You don't know him, Karson."

"What if he didn't know the whole truth?" Karson asked.

"He did. Scar and Liam share everything together."

"How sweet," Romeo said. "There has to be some lies going on. All relationships work on lies."

"Not all of them," Axton said.

"True, but white lies are the key to any relationship surviving."

"I didn't lie to Scar when I was with her. I couldn't."

"How did it end between the two of you?" Axton asked. "You never mentioned her."

"You did look like death when you came off the camp. I always figured it was because of Carla," Romeo said.

"He didn't love Carla. We all know that," Karson said.

Easton glared at his friend. "I did."

"No. You didn't. It's why you went off the deep end. With Taylor around, I bet horrible guilty feelings have been manifesting in all kinds of badness of late. We need to fire Penny. I don't care that she was rude to Liam. Bastard probably deserved it, but she's bad for business."

"Then handle it," Axton said. "What are you going to do about this thing with Liam? If you have any feelings for Scarlett at all, you're going to have to nip them in the bud."

"I, I want to know my son. I do know that. When it comes to Scar, I don't know. I don't have a clue what to do. She's the mother of my son, and I've ... missed her."

"You've missed her in what way?" Romeo asked.

"I've thought about her many times over the years. What I did. How I ended it. It was bad. I don't know what to do, guys. I'm sorry." He ran a hand over his face, feeling like the worst kind of man in the world. "Everything is happening so fast."

When Liam had been in the office, he had truly felt like he could handle anything. He took a bite of the bagel, and the spinning in his stomach stopped. He sipped at the coffee. It was sweet and hot, and went well with the bagel.

"I can't walk away from this. I have a son, and I want the chance to know him. For him to know me. I played with him last night. With the toy car I bought him. He's eleven but at least I got the chance of that."

"You ever thought about petitioning for custody of him?" Karson asked. "She had him for the first eleven years. You got nothing. Now you can have him completely. It's a win-win for you."

"No, I'm not going to do that." Liam wouldn't allow it. "He's offering me a chance at weekends."

"You're going to be a weekend dad?" Romeo asked.

"For now. I just want to get to know my son." He paused. "My son."

"Yeah, it has a nice ring to it," Axton said.

"Wow, I'm a dad."

"You're only just realizing this?" Karson asked.

"No, I mean, I knew that I was a dad, but now that I'm faced with it, and it's all so new, you know. I'm a father. I've got a son." He ran a hand down his face in an attempt to clear the fog. It didn't work. "What if I turn into my father?"

He looked at each of his friends.

"Not possible," Romeo said.

"My father was a monster."

"Exactly. It's why you'll never be him. Already you want to do right by your son. Do you think Liam's an okay guy?" Axton asked.

"I don't know. I don't really know him. Junior was happy around him, and Scarlett, well, she's more than okay."

He'd seen the arousal on her last night. It wasn't exactly hard to see. The dress she wore showed just how happy she was to have Liam's hands all over her. He wasn't jealous. Scarlett wasn't his.

He'd given up that right to her.

"I'm going to do it. Weekends I'll spend with Junior. If you need me for anything, call me or email me. I want to get to know my son." He also wanted to get to know the girl he'd left behind.

Chapter Eight

Over eleven years ago

"You're a hard one to pin down," Scarlett said, taking a seat beside Easton. He sat on one of the logs, staring into the burning flames.

"Am I that obvious?"

"Did I do something wrong? Is that why you're ignoring me?" She tucked some hair behind her ear. She'd been considering a haircut for a couple of months. It had taken her years to grow her hair this long, but at moments like this, it always seemed to get in the way.

"You couldn't do anything wrong." He smiled. "At least I can tell everyone I know I've taught you how to swim."

"You did, and you were super patient with me."

"Why didn't you learn before?" he asked. "You clearly come to camp often. The kids know you."

She shrugged. "I never had the time. I find water a little intimidating. You never know what's lurking beneath. I help out at camp and have been here since I was fourteen. It's how I know everyone. Doesn't mean I like to join in with everything. Thank you for teaching me though. I don't be taking any dips in the lake or anything."

"You're not going to go streaking?" Easton asked.

"Hell, no. Running through the water naked is so not my thing."

He laughed.

As fast as he started to laugh, it died. Like a switch went off in his brain that told him to not be happy.

"What is it?"

"It's nothing important. I've got to head back

home soon."

"And you don't like home?" she asked. They didn't talk about their life away from camp. She was happy about that. It wasn't like she had much fun waiting for her at home. Her parents had a lot of expectation from her. It was nothing but exhausting work and planning. Everything she hated.

"I don't like any part of being home. It sucks. There's no point talking about it."

"I know it can suck to be around your parents."

He snorted. "Believe me, I know."

She reached out, taking his hand. "While you're here, you don't have to think about any of that. You're here with me, and they don't matter. Cut off your feeling of home, and just embrace what you have now."

****

Present day

With her second cup of coffee resting on her knee, Scarlett stared at the front door waiting for when Liam arrived.

She woke up to an empty house with a single note from Liam letting her know he had a few errands to run and he'd taken Junior to school.

Last night couldn't be avoided.

He'd made her come multiple times, and to thank him, she'd passed out.

What did this all mean?

Their relationship wasn't supposed to be about sex, or anything. This was … ugh, she didn't know what it was.

She sipped at her steaming cup of coffee, and her nerves were completely and totally shot. In all the years she'd been married to Liam, not once had she ever been nervous about talking to him.

She heard his car pull up onto the drive, and her

hands began to shake.

Gripping the cup tightly, she waited, and the door opened. He wore a crisp white shirt and a pair of black pants. His hair was a mess, but for some reason on Liam, it always looked great.

"You're awake, and from the look in your eyes, you're not happy, which is shocking."

"Did you not want to talk to me this morning? Is that why you didn't wake me up?"

"Whoa, okay, I didn't exactly anticipate this being a smooth conversation, but I'm not avoiding you."

"It feels like it. I didn't even get to say goodbye to Junior," she said. "You know I love to wish him a good day. It's part of our routine."

"Routines are designed to be broken. Is there more coffee?" he asked.

"Yes."

He walked away, but she wasn't done. Following him into the kitchen, she put her cup down on the counter.

"Did you not enjoy last night?" he asked.

"You know I did. You know I enjoyed it multiple times. This is not the point. We don't have a sexual relationship."

"And we can change that." He turned toward her. "There's nothing in the rule book to say we can't make changes or decide to do something different."

"We have rules in place to protect each other," she said.

"From what?"

"From heartbreak and … everything. I can't think of it all right now. I'm confused, okay? I thought you wanted a man in your life."

"I do. I've never lied to you. I find both men and women attractive. It shouldn't come as any surprise that I want you."

Scarlett stared at him, shocked. "You're only seeing this now? After five years of marriage? We've shared a bed."

"Do you even remember how we started to share a bed?" he asked.

"When we had guests and for Easton so he wasn't confused."

"Wrong. Sharing a bed didn't start for those reasons. You came to live with me after we were married as per our agreement."

"I remember."

"You screamed during your sleep. You'd have these horrible nightmares about your ex and what he'd done to you." She tensed up. "I couldn't take it, so I started to sleep with you. You'd wake me up screaming. I'd come to your room, settle you down, and fall asleep. We did this for nearly three months, before I just started to sleep in the same bed. Whenever I wasn't there, you'd have bad dreams. It's one of the reasons I either took you and Junior with me on business trips, or I made sure all business could come here. We started sharing a bed."

She'd completely forgotten about the nightmares. The attack of her ex had scared her, but little by little, Liam had given her back herself.

"Thank you," she said.

"You don't need to thank me, Scarlett. I love you. You know that."

"You want a future with a man and a woman."

"I've got the woman I want. I just, at the time of making this agreement with you, I didn't realize it."

"I'm confused."

"So am I," he said. "Believe me. My feelings for you have been growing." He put the cup on the counter and moved toward her. "They didn't happen overnight, and I know, deep down, you've got feelings for me too." He cupped her hip, pulling her in close. "You can pretend all you want."

"I'm not going to do that. I can't give you what you want." She couldn't resist looking at his lips. They'd been on her body last night, and he'd felt so good. "I don't have a penis."

He laughed.

"I don't know if I want to share you," she said. Tears suddenly filled her eyes and she tried to take a step back, but Liam wouldn't let her.

"Nothing between us has changed. You're still my wife. We're still the best of friends. None of it has changed. I won't let you run from this, from us." He wrapped his arms around her. His lips went to her neck, grazing over the pulse.

"I don't think I can do this," she said.

"Let me worry about everything else. I've never steered you wrong. I will never cheat on you. Never."

She pulled away, and he wiped away her tears with the back of his fingers. "You won't be with someone else?"

"No."

"Promise."

"I've never lied to you." He dropped a kiss to her lips. "Ever."

"Where did you go this morning? You were gone a long time."

"I went to see Easton."

She tensed up. "Why?"

"I'm waiting for him to make a decision on joining us on the weekends. It's only fair he gets to share in Junior. What do you think?" he asked.

"You've already asked him without consulting me."

"Because I know you think it'll be a good idea. You always told me you felt a little guilty for not telling Easton at any point during your pregnancy."

That was true.

When she held her baby in her arms after giving birth, she knew Easton should have been there. As the dad, he had a right to witness the birth of his child, but she still didn't reach out. This was on her, and she didn't want to tear father and son apart. She'd made a mistake, and she had to deal with that.

"What about you?" she asked.

"I'm not going to be replaced by anyone." He dropped another kiss to her lips. He pressed her up against the counter. The jeans she wore were in the way of feeling him. The hard press of his cock was almost too good to be true.

Liam lifted her up, placing her on the counter. "Do you realize, Mrs. Knight, we've been married five years and of those five years, we've never once consummated our marriage?"

"Yes."

His fingers went to the button of her shirt.

One by one, he slid them open.

She didn't say a word, feeling her whole body want his touch, want his hands on her.

He pushed the shirt down her arms, but rather than let it all the way off, Liam tied the shirt up, keeping her arms locked behind her back.

"What are you doing?" she asked.

"I'm going to have some fun, and I want you completely at my mercy. Do you trust me?"

"You know I do."

"Then know I'm going to be making up for five years of lost time. Five years of not touching this body because you've not truly been mine. You're mine now, aren't you?"

She thought about Easton. He'd taken a part of her many years ago, only to stamp on it. She'd never given another man a real chance with her. Even the boyfriend who hurt her, he'd known from the start he was second best.

"Yes, I'm yours, Liam. I'm all yours." She spoke the words with conviction. There wasn't anywhere else she wanted to be.

Easton was a distant memory. She had no intention of being with him for a lifetime or for any length of time.

Liam grabbed a knife from the drawer.

She held her breath as he slid the sharp blade beneath the fabric and cut.

The bra fell away from her body, and she heard him groan.

"Do you have any idea how much torture it was to see you getting naked? To know you were going to be all mine one day. You'd strip down, and I'd see how curvy and sexy you were, and I've spent many times in the shower, imagining all the things I want to do to you and these sexy tits."

She gasped as his tongue stroked across one hard bud. She watched him as he flicked back and forth before sucking the bud into his mouth, and moaning.

The pleasure was instant, and she closed her eyes. There was nothing for her to hold onto. She was completely at his mercy.

He pressed her tits together, and she moaned as he licked and sucked at each of her nipples.

"Tell me, Scarlett, have you ever thought about me fucking you?" He helped her off the counter, but didn't allow her to break free from the bindings.

"Yes."

"I better warn you right here, right now, I can do the hearts and flowers stuff. I can be the sweetest boyfriend in your life." He popped open the button on her jeans. He went to his knees before her and heat flooded her body. "But, when it comes to the bedroom, I don't like a little virgin." He helped her out of her flipflops, and then the jeans.

He took her panties down as well.

While Liam was fully dressed, she stood before him, naked.

He stood up, the tips of his fingers dancing across her skin as he stared down at her. He held her waist.

"You like it dirty?"

Liam lifted her back up onto the counter and spread her legs wide. "I like to see how I make my woman wet. I want her pussy to be dripping, she's so aroused." He held her thighs and kept her open. "Just like you are now." He slid his fingers across the fine hairs of her pussy. "I'm going to shave this all off. I don't want anything in my way." He stretched her lips, and she watched him.

Two fingers filled her pussy.

"How long has it been with a man?" he asked, working his finger in and out of her cunt.

"A really long time."

"Five years? Before we were married?"

"Yes." Tears filled her eyes.

"You don't have to be afraid anymore. I'll never hurt you, Scarlett. You want to stop this, you can. I only want your consent and to love what I do to your body. Nothing else. He's not here to hurt you anymore. Remember, I took care of it. I take care of everything when it comes to you."

She smiled up at him. "I only want you." She cut off all other thoughts and feelings. There really was only him. She didn't care for anyone else.

He worked another finger inside her, and she gasped.

"You're so tight."

His thumb, like last night, stroked across her clit.

"I want to feel you inside me, Liam."

"When I'm done making you come."

He licked her pussy, and she watched him, his fingers thrusting deep into her pussy as his tongue stroked over her clit.

The pleasure was intense, and she felt the beginnings of her orgasm. The moment she came, Scarlett felt embarrassed by how quickly she'd found her release.

Liam lifted her up in his arms, removing her shirt, and she held onto him.

"I've never done that before," she said.

"You're going to get used to it. I'm a man that knows what he's doing." He held her a little tighter. "Hold onto me. We're going to the bedroom."

She wrapped her legs around him. "I can walk."

"I don't want you to. This is where I get to take care of you."

Liam walked all the way to their bedroom. He placed her down on the bed, and she watched, amazed and in love with who he was. He was everything to her.

Again, the niggle of Easton kept coming back, but she pushed it aside.

Liam removed his clothes, dropping them on the floor before returning to her, his lips on hers as he moved her back against the bed.

She gasped as he spread her open. He wasn't a small man, and his cock rested between the lips of her pussy, the tip bumping against her clit.

Liam pulled away from the kiss, grasping his

cock and teasing it to her entrance.

She stared into his blue eyes as inch by inch, he sank into her. Her cunt stretched to accommodate him. She cried out as he slammed in hard, going as deep as he could.

He took hold of her hands, pressing them either side of her head. "I'm never going to let you go. Not ever. You're mine, Scarlett."

"And you are mine," she said.

"Forever."

Liam pulled out of her, only to slide back in.

He was the perfect fit. It only took a couple of thrusts for her to get used to the feel of him within her.

The pleasure was instant, consuming, everything she ever wanted, and more. This was Liam, her husband and soul mate.

There would never be a guy like him, and she wasn't going to do anything to ruin the happiness they had with each other.

****

"I don't think you should shave me," Scarlett said.

"I think you need to relax and trust me."

"I do trust you, completely. No doubt at all from me, but you're talking about shaving my personals."

Liam laughed.

They were in the shower, and he'd brought in a stool for her to sit on so he could remove all of her pubic hair, but she now seemed nervous.

"How about I remove yours, you remove mine?" he asked.

"You'd trust me next to your…"

"Cock?" he asked. "It's so cute that big, grown-up words get you all flustered."

"Stop it," she said.

"This is going to be fun. I told you that."

"So, you shave mine and I shave yours?"

"That's the deal I'm giving you. What do you say? You want to go give it a try?" he asked.

He waited while she thought it over.

"Okay, but I get to do it today. Straight after you."

"Agreed."

"Hold on, show me both of your hands. I know the kinds of games you play. I don't want to see anything crossed here."

"I'm all yours for the taking," he said.

"Deal," she said, inspecting his body to make sure he hadn't crossed anything.

"You're cute when you're nervous."

"You think I'm cute all the time."

"I do, don't I?" he said. "Spread those pretty thighs open. Let me get to work." He'd already washed her thoroughly. The sight of his cum leaking from her pussy had turned him on, but now, he got to play with her pussy and make her perfect.

"What does a man give you that I can't?" she asked.

Liam paused, looking up at her. "You really want to know?"

"Besides the obvious, unless you don't have sex."

"I do have sex. I enjoy it."

"Do you enjoy sex with me?" she asked.

"You're asking a lot of questions."

"I'm sorry. I'm just trying to understand. I'm not wanting to pry."

He smiled. "Baby, you can pry all you want. It's why I told you total honesty from the start."

"Have you ever been in love with a man?" She slapped a hand across her mouth. "I will stop."

"First question, besides the sex, I enjoy it. I enjoy exploring men. Our bodies are different. I'm just attracted to both. I love cock and pussy. Yes, I love sex with you. I don't compare the two. No, I've never been in love with a man. I have been in lust."

"How does sharing a man and woman work?" she asked.

He looked at her. Now this he hadn't been expecting. He wondered if she was thinking about Easton or if this was a genuine curiosity question.

"You can make it work how you want. For instance, for me, I love to see both my man and woman getting pleasure."

"So the man would also be there with your woman?" she asked.

"Yes. I wouldn't keep them a secret. I'm not the jealous type. I always saw it as a big happy family. Only no one has a claim to the other, and you both belong to me."

"You'd be the one in control?"

"I'd be the one who was able to help and to make sure no one was feeling left out. I don't know if you've noticed, but I have a knack for helping people. I enjoy doing it. Taking care of them, protecting them, making them safe." He slid the blade across the lip of her pussy. She tensed up, but he didn't stop. Rinsing out the blade, he kept working, taking his time. Scarlett had a really pretty pussy to play with.

"I love it when you take care of me. Even when I was puking my guts up, you were always there for me."

"I don't have an on-off switch. I like to take care regardless. In sickness and in health."

"Would you want to share me?" she asked.

He stopped shaving and looked at her, removing the blade from her skin. "Would you like to be shared?"

"I don't know. I'm … trying to imagine you with someone else, and I can't help but get jealous."

"Stop imagining me with another woman."

She laughed. "Good point."

"See yourself with another man," he said, going back to her pussy. "How about Easton?"

"You want me to imagine you and Easton, together?"

"You saw him last night. It's not hard to picture him."

"But he's the father of my child, and you only met him last night."

"And this morning. I'm still waiting for the call."

She shook her head. "It's weird."

"Is it weird because you still have feelings for him. Or you're jealous? Or, you don't like him anymore or find him attractive?" he asked.

"I honestly don't know," she said.

"Do you hate him?"

"A little bit. He broke my heart, Liam, but at the same time, seeing him again, it's like the past doesn't matter. I think it should, but I can't hate him. He's not the guy who hurt me."

She sounded so sad. His grip on the razor tightened. Hearing that slight catch in her voice was too much. He couldn't allow anyone to hurt her.

"He seems like a nice guy. You know him better than I do. I only know the facts that I've got on him."

She laughed. "I don't want him to be hurt or put in any kind of danger. What happened between us was in the past, and I'm not going to keep bringing it up. Talking about him being shared is off limits. I don't think I can handle that."

"Scarlett, you're a strong woman. You can handle anything and everything."

He finished shaving her pussy. Running his fingers over her, it felt so smooth. "Your turn." He handed her the razor. She left the stool, and he took a seat, letting her do with his cock whatever she wanted to. "I'm now at your mercy."

"I can't believe you're trusting me with this." She stood, and he watched her pressing her thighs together.

"Does it feel weird?" he asked.

"Yes. You know it would, didn't you?"

"Yes. You'll get used to it."

"I don't think that's possible. This is strange." She shook her head and sank down to the floor.

"Now, this is a pretty position for you." He stroked her head.

"Are you sure you're not into Dominant stuff? BDSM, and you know, the other stuff?"

"I'm not, but I can appreciate certain positions for fun. Like this one, I like it a lot."

She rolled her eyes.

"If I was a Dom, that would have earned you a spanking."

She giggled. "Would you like to spank my ass, Sir?"

"I'd love to do more than spank your ass." He pulled her onto his lap, sinking his fingers in her hair, and grabbing her ass. "One day, I'm going to fuck it."

"You really do know how to talk dirty."

"You've not seen anything yet of what I'm capable of." He kissed her hard, nipping at her lips.

"Will I be able to handle all of you?"

Liam stroked her ass cheek. "I think you'll be surprised at just how well you can handle me."

****

Easton knocked on the door and Liam was there, opening the door.

"You know for a successful businessman, where's your butler?"

"I like my privacy, and when you've got money, people like to sell you out. I don't trust anyone. Besides, it's rare I have to open the door. It makes me feel human." He stepped away from the door, and Easton walked over the threshold.

"Where's Scarlett and Junior?" he asked.

"In the dining room, working on his homework. Do you want to go on the tour now, or later?"

Homework.

"I'll take the tour now." It would give him time to settle his nerves. This was really happening.

Liam took the bag from him.

"I can handle that."

"Don't worry about it. I can deal with it. Let's go." Liam went straight for the stairs.

"You don't have anywhere else to show me downstairs?" Easton asked.

"Yeah, but we can put your bag away and do the tour upstairs, then down, and you don't have to worry about where you're sleeping."

They walked up two flights of stairs to get to the second floor.

"At the far end of the hall is Junior's room. I'll let you have a look. He's always liked his own space, and he likes to invent things." Liam opened the door.

Junior's room, his son's space was separated into two parts. One half was a bed and a normal, neat-looking bedroom. The other looked like a laboratory or science geek's headquarters.

"I don't suppose he's good at computers?" Easton asked.

"He is, and it's how he watched some of the rather unflattering videos which turned him vegan. It scared Scarlett, but I've put more security in, and well, I warned Junior if he tried to get past my firewalls and passwords. He's a great kid. Scarlett is a great mom."

"You didn't know her at all when she gave birth?"

"No."

"What about her family?"

Liam hesitated, and Easton waited.

"Look, I don't know how much she wants you to know, but she had it rough. Her parents threw her out for being pregnant. A lot of vile words were thrown her way; slut, trash, bastard. She left with nothing, and she survived. She waited tables while she was pregnant. I paid her medical bills. They were ruining her when I met her, but she had also been beat up pretty bad."

"What?" Easton asked.

"There is a lot you don't know about her. She's a fighter, but she needed help. It's hard for her to accept it."

"Do you love her?" Easton asked.

"More than anything."

"You're older than her." He didn't know why he was even bothering to bring it up. A little over ten years wasn't old at all.

Liam laughed, folding his arms. "Are you jealous of me, Easton? You think you can come in my house and take my woman?"

Easton didn't cower or back down. "I want to make sure Scar is happy."

"She is. Remember you're here because of me, not her. If I think for a second you're crossing the line, I will end you. I take looking after my family seriously. I'm inviting you to be part of it, not destroy it."

Easton held his hands up in surrender. The truth was, he wanted to punch Liam in his smug bastard face.

This man had everything Easton ever wanted, without all the fucked-up shit in his life. For the past couple of days, he'd been trying to figure out what Liam's deal was. What did he want from him?

All of his life, people had an agenda, something from him. What was Liam's?

"I just want to make this work," Easton said. He would pick his fight with Liam when the time was right. He wasn't strong enough.

Junior knew Liam. His own kid didn't have a clue who he was.

"Good. Come on, don't touch anything. Junior's very particular about who touches his stuff. He protects it like it's an actual life."

He left the room, and his kid was a stranger to him. He wouldn't allow that to last, no matter what.

"This is my and Scarlett's room, and we made this one up for you." It was the room between his son's and Scarlett's. Would he have to hear them fucking?

He was starting to think this wasn't a good idea.

His feelings for Scarlett confused the fuck out of him. He was angry with her for not telling him she was pregnant. Then he'd think about how she looked on the last day when he threw her feelings for him, back in her face.

Liam opened the door. The room was huge.

"Wow," he said. "Is it wrong you feel like a sugar daddy right now?"

Liam laughed, and Easton liked the sound. It was good to be around someone who didn't get off on pain and destruction. He'd not been in a house like this since living in King's Ridge.

He'd handed his father's home over to the police to complete the investigation. Once that had been completed, he intended to sell it off, or demolish it and sell it as a building site. He wanted nothing else to do with it.

The past already haunted him enough as it was.

Liam put the suitcase on the bed.

"When you're here, I want you to be comfortable. I only allow the best."

"I can see that." And he could. Liam truly loved his luxury, and Easton liked it. Even though the home was large, it was lived in. It was nice.

His son clearly thrived here, at least from what he'd seen.

"I'll let you get settled in. This home is now yours. Please, join us when you're ready. Easton, I'd like for us to be friends and for things not to be weird for us." Liam held out his hand.

Easton looked at it. "I'd like that. I don't want there to be any complications with this. Just for things to go smoothly."

"Excellent. It's good to know we're on the same page." Liam shook his hand, and he had a firm grip. "See you downstairs."

He watched Liam go and closed the door behind him. He honestly didn't have a clue what he was fucking doing.

Chapter Nine

Over eleven years ago

Easton didn't want to be alone. Whenever he was, his thoughts always went to Carla. The girl he'd been in love with. The girl he'd lost.

Running fingers through his hair, he tried to think of anything but the dead body Taylor pulled out of the water. Guilt crushed him.

He'd not told any of the guys he'd intended to end it with Carla. His father had found out about the relationship and had threatened to hurt Carla. Then she had to go and tell him she was pregnant. Running away with her seemed the only solution to keep her safe. Now he wasn't so sure. Everything just ended up all fucked up, and he hated the uncertainty in his life. How messed up it had all become.

"You're hiding again," Scar said, coming to sit beside him.

He was on a rock overlooking the lake. "I'm surprised you're not scared in case I throw you in."

"You don't look in a playful mood."

"I'm not."

"Do you want to tell me your thoughts?"

"No."

"Then I can sit here and just listen to the world going by without anyone affecting me."

"I'm not the best company right now."

"Me neither. I don't mind."

He didn't believe for a second she could last any amount of time without talking or saying something.

Staring out across the lake, he waited, but Scar didn't say or do anything. She sat. There wasn't even a sigh that crossed her lips.

When he glanced toward her, she had her knees pressed against her chest and her head resting on them.

"You okay?"

"I'm fine, Easton. Just family stuff. You know, the usual crap."

"I get it."

Scar reached out for him, taking his hand, and he stared down at it, liking that she reached out to him. He could handle whatever was thrown his way, just so long as he had Scar.

****

Present day

"You're so cool," Easton said, looking through the microscope at a clipping from a plant.

"It's not that cool yet. It's just science, but I don't want to harm anyone or the environment. I want to save it."

"That's awesome, buddy." Easton sat back on one of the chairs and smiled over at his son. "You amaze me."

"Dad, why didn't you come and find my mom?" Junior asked.

Easton sighed. "I didn't know she was pregnant with you."

"If you'd known, would you have come and found us?"

"I'd have done everything in my power to come and find you. Protect you." He opened his arms, and his son walked into them.

He was growing up so fast, and the fact he still hugged him meant a lot to Easton.

"I'm never going away again. You've got me for life, sweetheart. All the time. I won't ever let you go. Not ever." He pulled back and held his son's arms, giving them a squeeze. "Are you bulking up?"

Junior laughed before stifling a yawn.

"You need to go to bed."

When he'd arrived downstairs a few hours ago, Junior was still doing his homework. Easton had sat and watched as Scar and Junior worked through each item. He'd been shocked by how much was set, only Junior liked to work, and he saw the passion for answers.

There was a time he'd been just as passionate to find answers only to have them squashed by his father.

He stopped trying to find an answer for everything and simply enjoyed his life without questioning what was happening. This had been his error and one he didn't intend to make again.

Easton made his way toward the bed, pulled back the sheets, and Junior climbed in.

"I'm glad you're here."

"I am, too. I'm glad you're giving me a chance to get to know you."

"Mom said you're part of the Four Kings. Does that mean I'm a prince?"

Easton chuckled. "I wish. No, my life is not that glamorous." He sat on the edge of the bed, explaining to his son the Four Kings Empire, and where it came from.

"But what if you made more friends? Will you change it?"

"For a long time, it has only been the four of us."

"What about me?" Junior asked. "I can be your friend, and so can my other dad. He's so cool and smart, and funny. He's also super clever."

Easton smiled. "It looks like I'll have to talk to my guys about improving the name."

"I'd like that. Will I get to meet them? Your friends? I bet they're cool."

"Way cool and bossy. Believe me. They are all super bossy. I'm the coolest."

Junior laughed. "Night, Dad."

"Night, son." He leaned down kissing his son's head. "I know, I know, I won't be able to do that for some time, but give me a few things to enjoy."

"Okay."

He got up and walked toward the door. He switched off the light, and Junior turned on the nightlight.

He took one last lingering look before closing the bedroom door. Being a dad was everything to Easton. He'd missed so much.

Easton didn't go to his room but headed downstairs. He found Liam in his office, on a call.

"I've got to take this. Scarlett's gone for a swim," Liam said.

He nodded and made his way into the kitchen. Grabbing a bottle of water from the fridge, he decided to go and check out the pool. Last time he'd been with Scar, she'd not been able to swim all that well.

Liam had given him the full tour downstairs as Scar and Junior did the dishes.

Entering the swimming pool room, he paused, watching Scar as she swam from one end of the pool to the other. She stopped at the opposite side of the pool, dipped under the water, and pushed her hair off her face.

"Hey," he said. "I see you've gotten stronger."

She turned toward him. "Easton. Where's Liam?" she asked.

"Making a call. He said you were here. I figure I could see if you'd gotten stronger."

"As you can see, I have."

He kicked off his shoes, rolled up his pants, and sat on the edge of the pool, pushing his feet into the water.

It wasn't exactly paddling or an ocean, but the

water felt good on his feet. "Junior's in bed."

"He's probably not," she said.

"He yawned, and I put him to bed."

"I'm not saying you put him to bed wrong. He's probably reading one of his comic books or something on the science world. He'll read for a short time and pass out. I go in before bed, and close whatever he's sneaked into his room."

"Wow, and here I was thinking I'd done a good job."

"You have. You just got to know Junior to know he's a sneaky little rascal. All in good fun though. I love him so much."

"You've done a good job with him."

"Thank you."

"Was it always easy?" he asked.

"Why do you ask?"

"I've only just met you again after all this time, and I'm curious. There's so much about you and Junior, and even Liam, I don't know."

She swam to the middle of the pool, and he was able to see her clearly.

"No, it wasn't easy. After I got pregnant, my family, when I told them but refused to name the father, they kicked me out. I was called a slut and whore and disowned within an hour. I became homeless. I had a small amount of money from working, so I was able to rent a place, far, far away from them."

Easton wanted their names. He wanted to fucking pummel them and hurt them. How dare they push her away. Family was supposed to take care of each other, not punish.

"Anyway, I waited tables in the city. I took as many jobs as I could while also expecting. It wasn't easy, but I saved money, and then of course, I had the baby.

The expense went through the roof, and earning money while raising a child wasn't easy. I was able to do it though. I took Junior with me everywhere I went. Along the way, I met a guy. We hit it off, and I thought I'd finally found the one, you know. That ended badly, and as I was recovering, I met Liam. We got married, and here we are."

He noticed she brushed aside the other guy.

"Liam's incredible," Easton said.

"He is."

"I don't know if he's a magician or something. Whenever he touches me, I swear, I feel more calm and relaxed."

"He has that effect on me. For a long time, I'd have nightmares, and whenever he wrapped his arms around me, the whole world didn't matter. All I cared about was him."

Jealousy struck him hard.

"Are you all talking about me? I get the sense you are," Liam said. He was carrying a walkie-talkie.

"Is he still awake?" Scar asked.

"Yes, and reading." Liam put the walkie-talkie down. "We have one to keep an eye on him. He's a great kid regardless."

"Why don't you hire a nanny?" Easton asked. "It shouldn't be too difficult to find one."

"I love raising my son myself. I don't need a nanny."

"And I don't like the invasion of privacy it often creates. The key to a successful marriage and having your life not smeared across the tabloids, is to be careful who you have in your circle of friends."

"And I'm in the circle of friends?" he asked.

"I'm sure you'll understand why privacy is so important. After having your name over the press, it must be a relief to get away from it?" Liam asked.

Easton watched as the other man pulled off his shirt.

For the first time, he was admiring another man's body, which he'd never done in all of his life. He'd never been attracted to men before.

Averting his gaze, he found Scar watching Liam as well. Her teeth were sunk into her lip, and he saw the arousal in her face.

Liam pushed down his pants and dived into the pool.

Easton watched as he swam to Scar, wrapping his arms around her and taking possession of her lips.

"Why don't you come in and enjoy the water?" Liam asked.

Scar looked at him even as Liam trailed his lips down her neck.

He wasn't ready to leave the room, especially if it was going to lead to them having sex. He wasn't that stupid, or maybe he was.

Being around Scar, she was awakening old feelings within him, and he didn't even know if he had a shot.

You know you don't have a shot. You're in their home, sharing their son, even though he's yours.

Getting to his feet, he pulled his shirt over his head and dispensed with his pants.

After coming out of rehab, he'd lost a considerable amount of weight, and he'd started to go to the gym in order to bulk up.

He was rather impressed. Liam, out of the two of them, was by far more muscular, but Easton didn't think he was too shabby.

He dived into the pool and broke the surface.

Scar had already moved away from Liam and was

doing some gentle strokes.

"I taught her how to swim," he said, the words blurting out of his mouth.

"She told me," Liam said.

"She did?"

"No secrets, remember?" Liam shrugged. "You did a great job."

Just once he wanted to be or do something that didn't include Liam. It seemed pointless to him.

"I know about your time at camp," Liam said.

"So you know I was her first."

"Easton!" Scar glared at him. She swam toward them and stood up. "I don't know what you're trying to do, but stop it. Liam invited you here to be part of our family. Not to start waving your cock around as if it's some kind of contest." She shook her head.

"It's okay, Scarlett. I know what he's doing." Liam smiled. "I'm guessing you still have feelings for her, as otherwise you wouldn't be reacting this way."

"Liam, don't," Scar said.

Easton didn't say a word.

"I've got no problem with you having a crush on my wife. I get it, believe me, I do, but if you're planning on using Junior to get to her, then you're mistaken."

"I'm not going to use my son to get anyone or anything." Easton gritted his teeth. His hand clenching into a fist. "I apologize. I shouldn't act this way. I'm sorry."

"Accepted," Liam said.

He watched as Liam began to swim leaving him and Scar standing, watching him.

She whirled around toward him. "Don't do this, I mean it. I don't know what you're trying to prove or what you hope to gain, but stop it."

"Come on, Scar, I didn't mean anything bad

about it. I was just stating a fact."

"Ugh, please, enough. Liam's not the kind of guy that needs to get his man parts out and measure them, okay? You're not going to win me back. I'm staying with Liam."

Easton couldn't resist taking a step closer. "There was a time you told me you loved me. That you'd fallen hard and fast, and you just wanted to spend the rest of your life with me."

He saw the tears in her eyes and knew he'd pushed too far.

"Yeah, I know. I remember. You know what else I remember? You pushing me away, throwing my feelings for you right back in my face. Thanks for the reminder." She moved to the edge of the pool and climbed out.

He watched her go, wanting to take it all back.

"Scar."

She didn't stop but kept on moving.

He wanted to call her back, to stop her from leaving, but he'd been a dick and now he had to suffer for it.

****

For the past three weeks, Easton had been coming to her and Liam's house. After the disaster of the first week, she'd ignored him every single time he came around. She knew she was being a bitch and it wasn't fair to him at all, but it didn't change the fact he'd deliberately reminded her of a time in her life she wanted to forget, needed to forget, and would do anything in her power to forget.

It was already a problem because she knew deep down she should have done more in order to find him, at least to let him know she was pregnant. She'd been an idiot and stubborn, and now seeing him with their son made what she did that much harder to bear. She'd made a huge mistake, and she was going to have to live with that for the rest of her life. Easton wouldn't ever get back any of the time spent with Junior.

This wasn't how she wanted to live her life though. Junior talked about Easton constantly, and it was hard for her not to love hearing how animated he was when he did talk. There was a frostiness with him toward her, though, one she couldn't control, not that she wanted to. She just wished she hadn't been such a huge disappointment to him. She knew she'd made a mistake in keeping them apart. It was her biggest regret. Junior had even told her he wished she hadn't kept him apart from Easton because of how awesome he was, and that he should have known.

She would deal with Junior's disappointment, and hope in time, he would forgive her.

At least her relationship with Liam had only gotten better. Their sex life was amazing. Every single night, he teased her body, showing her things she didn't even know she was capable of feeling, and she was addicted to his touch, craved it, yearned for it, and welcomed it at every single turn.

"I've got to take Junior out for an hour. He wanted to go to the store for something," Liam said, coming into the kitchen.

"Can't you order it online? Have it delivered tomorrow?"

"It's okay. I'll be an hour at most. I'll call you when we're on the way back."

"Wait, what about Easton?"

"Invite him in. You know the drill, Scarlett." Liam cupped her hip, kissing her cheek.

"What if I told him to stop coming?"

Liam sighed. He pulled away and rested his ass

against the counter. "You want him to stop coming?"

"I'm thinking about it."

"Scarlett, I love you so much, but I think you need to have a think about why it hurt you so much when he told you those things that he did."

"You heard him?"

"Kind of hard not to hear him. You still have feelings for him."

"No, I don't. That's just stupid and insane."

"And yet here you are, upset, emotional, and all because of him." Liam pulled her into his arms. "I won't mind if you want him."

She tried to jerk back in his arms, but Liam wouldn't let her go. "I'm not going to judge your choices." He kissed her cheek. "I think this will be good for the two of you to finally get this out."

"Are you ready?" Junior asked. "Mom, I am going to make Dad go crazy with what I've got planned."

"Just so long as it doesn't blow up the house. I'll be fine."

Junior laughed, and she saw them both out of the door.

Alone.

She wrapped her arms around herself going straight to the kitchen. Her security blanket. This wasn't supposed to be so hard. Not with Easton, not with anyone.

Why did he have to say those things?

She knew her son was happy to be with Easton, and even Liam enjoyed having him around.

Scarlett paused.

Liam enjoyed Easton's company.

Now, she frowned. What if Liam had a … crush on Easton? Did he like him that way? Liam had been honest about what he wanted in a relationship, but she'd never asked him to delve any deeper than necessary. Was that a mistake on her part?

Rubbing at her temples, she tried to think of Liam and Easton together. It aroused her to think of them having sex, but that was only a fantasy.

The doorbell rang, and she walked slowly to the door.

Easton was there, waiting.

When she opened the door, Easton smiled, which slowly died when he looked at her.

"Liam's had to take Junior out to the store. They'll be back in a little bit," Scarlett said.

She rushed back to the kitchen without shutting the door. She heard it close and Easton's footsteps as he followed her.

"We're alone?"

"Yes. You can go and do whatever it is you want to do." She had absolutely nothing to do, and now she wished she had something to keep her hands busy, to do anything but look lost.

"We need to talk."

She lifted her gaze to his. "We don't."

"I didn't mean to bring up the past."

"And you did. Our past isn't exactly a good one."

"It's not the devil either, Scar."

"What is it you want from me? We have a son, I get that, but you don't need to throw reminders of how little my feelings meant to you."

"I lied," Easton said.

"What?"

"Your feelings, eleven years ago, they didn't mean nothing to me. They meant fucking everything. You think it was easy after those three weeks to do what I did?"

Her heart was pounding, her mouth open.

"I fell in love with you. I wanted to be with you."

"You're lying."

"I'm not. I'm not lying. Not to you. Not anymore. Before I came to that camp, I met a girl. I told you about her."

"Yes, she died."

"Yes. My father killed her. He made sure I knew that under no circumstances was I to marry 'below my pay grade.' I was nothing more than a pawn for him to use, to play. Carla was carrying my child. I intended to run away with her, to keep them both safe, but before I got the chance to, they were ripped away from me." Tears filled her eyes at the pain she saw within his. "Do you know the worst part?"

"What?"

"I didn't love her. I didn't feel the way you made me feel all those years ago."

The tears fell down.

"I wanted to be with you, but I had no idea who you were. When you told me you loved me and how much, I was ecstatic, for a couple of seconds at least. I was allowed to be happy that you could love someone like me."

"Someone like you?"

"I'm not a good person. One girl had already died, and I didn't love her like I thought I did. But you, the girl that was so fucking annoying she wouldn't leave me alone. A girl who … couldn't swim. Who would sit with me in long silences and they wouldn't be awkward. A girl who called my name as I made love to her. Yeah, I fell in love with you, Scar. I've never forgotten you, and it kills me to see you with someone else. Do you know the even crazier part?"

"What?" She really didn't know what to say or do.

"For all the jealousy I feel, I love watching you with Liam. Call me confused. I love and hate it at the same time."

She sniffled and looked away.

"I know you've been ignoring me, and I deserve that. I'm new to all of this. It scares me. It fucking terrifies me more than anything else in the world. I don't want to lose you or Junior, or even Liam. Each Monday when I have to leave, I feel a part of myself is being torn from my body, and I won't ever get it back. Friday is my favorite day of the week."

"You don't deserve me ignoring you. And I think it's everyone's favorite day, Easton." She offered a smile.

He took a step toward her, and she took one back.

"No, you don't understand. I get to see you, Junior, and Liam—for me, that is one hell of a day. These weekends are the best part of my life." He cupped the back of her neck. She put her hands on his chest but didn't push him away.

"Easton, it's only been three weeks."

"I've been miserable for eleven years, and this is the only happiness I've felt. I don't want to lose that."

"Then you've got to stop."

He slammed his lips down on hers, and for a few seconds, Scarlett let him. She didn't kiss him back, but the young woman inside her wanted to. She wanted to forget the past eleven years and be at camp again, laughing and joking with the broody guy who didn't have the ability to smile.

She wanted it, and yet it scared her.

Pulling away from him, she shook her head. "I'm a married woman, and I love Liam." She put some distance between them. "You're going to have to go and put your bag away."

"Scar?"

"I don't cheat. I took my vows seriously. Please, go and put your bag away."

Guilt washed over her, and she hated that she had wanted to kiss him back. With shaking hands, she started to prepare dinner. She didn't see Easton, and when Liam came home, she heard Junior shouting to his father. She didn't know what happened next, but Liam came into the kitchen.

One look at him, she just couldn't handle it.

"What's wrong?" Liam asked.

"Easton kissed me." She felt the tears once again. "He kissed me, and I didn't hate it."

Liam wrapped his arms around her, like he always did, and she wanted to sink into him.

"You should hate me," she said.

"It's not possible for me to hate you or to feel anything like that."

She lifted her head, staring into his eyes, confused. "Why?"

He cupped her face, and his lips covered hers. She kissed him back, feeing the need rising up. Her attraction to Liam wasn't dying down; it was getting stronger.

Liam broke from the kiss. His lips trailed to her ear. "Now he has kissed both of us."

She jerked back, confused. "He's kissed you as well?"

"No, I took the kiss from your lips. Now we have both been kissed."

"Liam?" She frowned. "Are you wanting him to be your male? Your boyfriend?"

"We need to talk about this in private."

She had to talk about it now. Grabbing Liam's hand, she marched him up to their bedroom.

Easton was outside Junior's door.

"We're going to talk for a few minutes. Good to see you, Easton," Liam said.

She closed the door, resting her back against it and staring at her husband, who took a seat on their large bed.

"You want him to be your man in this relationship?" she asked.

"I've been thinking it would work for all of us, yes."

"Easton's not interested in a sexual relationship."

"I don't know. There's a lot you don't know about a man."

"I think you're wrong."

"And if I was right and I invited Easton into our bedroom and into our life permanently, would you accept it?"

She opened her mouth and closed it. She didn't have a clue what to say. Could she accept him?

"He hurt me," she said, but she was starting to sound like a broken record and she knew that.

"How did it feel kissing him? Did you like it?"

She nodded her head. It felt too much like a betrayal to say the words aloud.

"Then how about we approach him?"

"You can't trust him."

"Scarlett, we can."

"You don't know him."

"I know he wants you more than anything else. I've seen the way he looks at you. How his gaze lingers and there's a yearning in his eyes, and it's all for you. Every single part of it is for you. He will do whatever it takes to have you, at least once."

"No. You're wrong."

"Do you trust me?" he asked.

"You know I do."

"Then how about you show a little faith in me?" Liam stood up and walked toward her. "This is where our relationship is heading, Scarlett. I won't lie to you. I won't manipulate the facts. I will always give you the cold, hard truth."

"Even when I don't want to know the answer?" she asked.

"Even then. Now, let's go out there and have a nice dinner. I know you want to." He kissed her cheek. "Leave everything else to me."

****

Later that night, after Junior had gone to bed and Scarlett had gone to have a relaxing bath, Liam invited Easton into his library to have a late-night drink. He knew of Easton's addictions, so the drink of choice was hot chocolate.

He'd made the drink himself. It was a damn good hot chocolate. Not as good as Scarlett's but a second best.

"I kissed her," Easton said, taking a seat.

"Everyone seems content to tell me about a kiss I didn't see."

"Scarlett told you?" Eaton asked.

"No secrets."

"Yes, of course. I should have known. No secrets between the two of you."

"Did you enjoy the kiss?" Liam asked.

"Look, man, I don't feel comfortable sharing those details with you. Scar and I, we've got a past, and I can't deny that I blurred the lines today."

"You did." Liam smiled as Easton looked uncomfortable.

"Are you going to take my son away from me?"

"Last time I checked I wasn't a monster, Easton. I

believe Junior has a right to know his father, and regardless of what that means for me, I will never keep you from your son. Unless you hurt him or Scarlett in any way. I'm also not stupid. I know you and Scarlett have a past. A history I can't rewrite and neither of you can change."

"I won't cross the line again."

"Wherever temptation is, you will cross the line. It's natural for you to. You still have feelings for her after all this time."

"My feelings for Scar never changed. I couldn't have her, and I didn't have a choice in letting her go."

Liam sighed. "I get it. Believe me, I do. She's an amazing woman. From the moment I saw her, I knew she was a fighter. The kind of woman I wanted by my side."

"Look, whatever you're going to do to punish me, get on with it. I'm not good with waiting for something to hit me in the face."

Liam laughed. "You think I want to take you outside and beat you up?"

"Why not? It's what I'd do if Scar was my woman."

"But you see, she's not your woman, and I'm not the kind of man who'll take people out into the street and beat them up. I happen to have a higher regard and respect than that."

Easton looked around the room, and Liam watched him. He was so broken inside. Did anyone see that? How nervous he was all the time. The guilt was like a marker on his skin, dragging him down, and completely consuming him until there was nothing left. Liam saw it, and he recognized it. This guy, he needed someone to love and to care for him. He just didn't know how to go about asking anyone for that kind of help. Liam knew he and Scarlett could give this man the kind of love he was looking for.

He hadn't ever seen such pain and suffering. Even Scarlett when she came into his life wasn't like this. She could still smile, barely.

"I was thinking we could make a deal of some kind," Liam said.

"A deal? Seriously? You want me to grab my friends and have a business decision at a time like this."

"I didn't say a business arrangement. Let's refer to it as a more personal one. Something between you, me, and Scarlett." Liam took a sip of his hot chocolate and saw he had intrigued Easton with his offer.

"A personal arrangement?" Easton asked.

"Yes. One where you don't need a lawyer, just common sense."

Easton stood up. "Wait a minute. Are you seriously considering sharing Scar with me?"

"I'm thinking of us each sharing each other. You won't be allowed to disclose of our private information with anyone. I demand utmost privacy and discretion. Scarlett and Junior are my priority."

"Wait a fucking minute, are you for real right now? Does Scarlett even know what you're proposing, or does it not matter to you?"

Liam smirked. "How about you take some time to think about it and you leave Scarlett to me? I'm not promising this will be an overnight success, but she has feelings for you."

"She hates me."

"No, she wants to hate you, but she has many other feelings besides hate, of that, I can assure you."

He released a breath, not really sure what to think in that moment. "I can take some time. You mean share her completely. She'd belong to both of us?"

Liam nodded. "Yes."

"I'm going to need some time."
"Take all the time you need."

Chapter Ten

Monday morning

Easton sat behind his desk, not really seeing any of the work in front of him. All he could think about was Scarlett and Liam's offer. He'd kissed her, and she hadn't pulled away. Liam knew the truth, and yet, he didn't kill him.

He didn't know what the hell was going on inside his own freaking head right now.

"You're missing me," Carla said, *suddenly appearing.*

"I don't have time for you."

"Of course you do. It hasn't slipped your mind that the weekends you spend with your new precious family, you forget all about me. What Liam offered you, you want, only you're too chicken shit to take it." Carla sat across his desk.

He rubbed at his eyes, feeling the beginnings of a headache.

"I need to tell a doctor I've been seeing things."

"Why? It's not like I'm real. You know I'm not real, and we both know I'm just your subconscious helping you make decisions. Especially the ones you find a little too scary. Like watching a certain guy get naked to go for a swim."

"He was wearing boxers," Easton said.

"Pretty much naked and you can't deny how aroused you get looking at Scarlett with Liam. There is something going on there, and your denying it is only going to make everything worse, just saying."

"I didn't ask you for advice."

"Who are you asking for advice?" Romeo asked, entering his office.

Carla disappeared.

"Nothing. It's nothing. Just got a lot on my mind."

"How are things going over the weekend? Do you still love being a dad?"

"Yes."

"Seriously? You've been doing this for nearly a month now and all I'm going to get from you is a yes?"

"What else do you want from me?"

"I don't know. Maybe a little excitement. Like, oh yay, I get to be all happy and thrilled and shit. You've got a son, and I don't know, I expected more."

Easton dropped his pen on the desk and rubbed his hand across his face. "I love being a father, okay? Love it. I wish I'd been there for everything. I don't like not knowing all the little parts of my son."

"But?"

"But, I—" He stopped. Liam didn't want any of their personal or private life mentioned. How far did that go? He knew he could trust his boys, but did it really extend to something like this?

"But what?"

"I'm in love with Scarlett," he said. He wasn't going to tell anyone about Liam's idea or plans. They weren't going to work. There was no way Scarlett would let him share her with Liam. He'd seen the two of them together; it wouldn't happen.

"Whoa, and this is a bad thing because?"

"She's married to Liam."

"You don't want to win her back?"

"How can I win her back?" Easton asked. "When I ended it, I was brutal. I was mean. I was everything Karson was and is. That's how bad I was."

Romeo held his hands up. "And you can't make amends?"

"I don't know how."

"You want this girl to like you? To love you?"

"Yes."

"Then you need to start learning how to say you're sorry. I'd love to meet this woman again. I don't feel I got a good enough vibe from her at the restaurant. But you also need to realize she was in the wrong as well."

"No, she wasn't."

"Easton, no matter what, she kept your son away from you. That has to hurt, and don't you think it was wrong of her to do that?"

"I know why."

"Doesn't make it sting any less or make it right. This woman, you like her, love her, but you need to understand, she's no saint either. So, when do I get to meet her again?"

"I want to enjoy this for myself. I'm not in the sharing mood."

"Totally get it, but we're your best friends. You know that, right? We'll be here for you no matter what."

"I get it." He gripped the back of his neck, feeling the tension building within him. "I've got to get my shit together."

"I can't wait to meet the little guy."

"He's not so little. He's eleven."

"Wow, it still seems only yesterday we were eleven years old."

"That was a lifetime ago."

"Not so long ago. I'll be seeing you."

Romeo left his office, and Easton sat back in his chair.

He felt … drained.

All he wanted to do was to go and see Liam, to talk more, and he also wanted to talk to Scar.

Picking up his cell phone, he dialed her number. Liam had given him her number on the first weekend he spent with them. He didn't know if Scar was even aware he had her number.

"Hello," she said.

"Scar, it's me."

"Easton? What's up?"

"I was wondering how you felt about meeting me?" he asked.

He cringed at the desperation in his voice.

"For lunch?"

He glanced at the clock. "Sure. I can do lunch. Erm, we can meet back at the vegan place if it makes you more comfortable."

"Okay. I'll be there in an hour."

"Don't bring Liam."

"Easton?"

"I'm not going to try anything or make you uncomfortable. I'd like to have a conversation away from your home, and between the two of us."

"I'll come alone. Bye."

She hung up the phone, and he put it back in the cradle.

Taking a deep breath, he stood up, only to pause as he saw Taylor in the doorway. She held her daughter in her arms.

"Hey," she said. "I feel like we've not gotten a chance to talk since you came back home."

"I've been really busy."

"I can see. Do you mind if I come in?"

He didn't have a reason for her to not come in, so he pointed at the chair in front of his desk.

She sat down, and the baby sounded so cute. Little Carla.

His gut twisted.

"Did you hear the conversation?"

"With your kid's mother? Yes, I heard."

Easton felt perspiration dot his brow. "I'm heading out to lunch soon."

"I won't keep you. I promise. I know we've had a lot of history, you and I. With Carla. I know you said you once missed her."

"I never wanted her to die."

"I know."

"Erm, I don't think you should hold yourself back anymore," Taylor said.

"Hold myself back?"

"Carla's in the past, and you need to start living in the present. You've got to find a woman to settle down with and get your happy ending."

He sat back in his chair frowning. "You do surprise me. I figured with your whole revenge plot you'd hope I'd die and save you a whole lot of problems."

"I made many mistakes in my life, Easton." She smiled down at her daughter. "She isn't one of them. There was a time before Axton and falling in love I'd have gladly seen you miserable. I'm changing, and I want you to be happy, just as much as my husband."

"Thank you."

"I also don't want you to feel the need to keep it from me. I hope we can be friends, and I can prove to you, I'm one of the best."

"I like that."

"I better go. Axton wanted me to stop by, but I came to you first." Taylor stood up. "Would you like to hold her?"

"No, I'm fine for the time being. I'm not ready to hold a baby." He also didn't wish to have the reminder of all he'd lost with Junior.

"Another time."

He never planned to hold the baby.

Taylor left him alone, and he was able to deal with a few important contracts. He was heading out of the office when mail arrived. He placed the large bundle on his desk, only to pause when he caught sight of one letter, stating the prison where his father was being held.

He took the envelope, flipping it over, and glancing at it.

Nial Long was the only person who would bother to write to him. Rather than open the letter, he shoved it in his pocket and made his way to his car in the underground parking lot. Sitting in his car, the letter burned a hole in his pocket, but he ignored it and pulled out of the building. The fresh air didn't feel good to him.

Why would his father get in touch with him now?

He'd not heard from him since the arrest. Nial had asked for him to post bail, and he'd refused. There was no way he was going to allow a monster on the streets.

He arrived at the vegan restaurant just as Scar did. She parked right beside him and offered him a smile as she climbed out of the car.

"This will rarely happen," she said, laughing. "I'm usually late or way too early. Never on time."

"Me neither. This is nice." He offered her his arm. He noticed he hesitated for a second before taking his arm.

He didn't speak about it as they entered the restaurant. The place was busy with the lunchtime rush. They stood in the line, ordered their food, and then took a seat in one of the only available two seat tables.

"I'm thinking we should have gone back to my office. We'd have more food and time."

She chuckled. "This is more than fine."

"Does my office scare you?"

"No."

"Being alone with me?"

"Easton, you don't scare me. I told Liam about the kiss, and he didn't mind."

"About that, I'm pleased you brought it up." He leaned forward, wanting to be close to her. "How well do you know your husband?"

"Really well. I know him better than I know anyone else. Why?"

"He offered me something the other day, with you, with him." He saw her cheeks start to turn red. "I don't think you know him as well as you think you do."

Scarlett took a deep breath.

He waited as she composed herself. "You're right. We should have done this in your office. I'm aware of what Liam has offered. He talked to me the night he offered what he did to you."

Now it was Easton's turn to be taken aback.

"And you're still with him?" Easton asked. "He offered to share you." He kept his voice down.

"I know. He believes you and I have … unfinished business. I don't know if he's right or not, but Liam, he knows me. He knows my limits, and even though I find his approach somewhat clinical and direct, I know he will only have my best interest at heart. Is this why you wanted to have lunch? To try and turn me against Liam?"

"I hoped you had all the facts before I made a decision."

"Liam's not a monster, Easton. He cares a great deal. There's a lot you don't know about him, and if you're willing to give this a shot, then so am I. There, I've said it. You broke my heart, crushed it, and it took me a lot to get back up and pick up the pieces, but I did.

I'm willing to take a chance and to either end this thing once and for all, or for us to find some way to get past it. I know what I did was wrong. I shouldn't have ever kept you away from your son, and I apologize for that, I really do. There's no way I can make up for all that I took from you. But what I don't need is you trying to tell on my husband. I love Liam, and I will defend him at every single turn. I need to go."

"Your food," he said, trying to stop her from leaving.

"I'm not hungry."

He watched her go, wishing he'd kept his fucking mouth shut. Sitting back, he saw no reason to rush back to the office. His best friends would only want to know what was going on, and he didn't want to tell them how he'd fucked up with the only woman he loved, for the second time.

After ten minutes of eating, his cell phone went off.

Of course it was Liam.

"You want to tell me the deal is off?" Easton asked.

"No. I'm wondering when you're going to realize we don't have secrets. I don't believe in prolonging what I want. You're going to need to realize this if you decide to be part of us. I can make all of your wishes and desires come true, Easton, but only if you're honest with yourself and truthful with me."

Liam hung up.

Dropping his cell phone onto the table, Easton dropped his head back, wanting nothing more than the world to open up and swallow him.

At every turn and corner, he was fucking up.

He grabbed the letter out of his pocket and slid it open, tearing into it.

It was a single piece of paper.

Easton,

I'm sick and tired of all this shit. If you were any good at anything, you'd be seeing your friends are not really your friends. They only want the company. Your share of it. They will try to take you down, steal your stuff, and spit you back out. I need out of here, and you need to grow some balls.

I didn't raise a quitter, or did I? Do I need to remind you of what punishment will await if you don't do as I ask? Get a lawyer and get down here. I've got plenty of stories to tell, or I'm going to make sure Axton says goodbye to his wife and kid.

There was no signature. The threats were all the same. He had no doubt his father had some influence on the outside. He'd need to show this to the cops and to Axton.

Everything had gotten so fucked up, and he didn't know why.

****

Scarlett threw her bag to the floor and growled as she did. She kicked off her shoes, removed her jacket, and slammed the palm of her hand against the wall.

"What did the wall ever do to you?"

"It got in the way," she said, turning to find her husband without a shirt. "You're working out again?"

"I've got to keep in shape for my young lover." He winked at her.

"Yeah, right. I don't see your little plan working at all. Easton wanted me to know the facts of my husband."

She tried to walk past him, but Liam picked her up and carried her back toward his gym.

"Liam, put me down."

He slapped her ass, and she sighed. Heat flooded

her pussy, and as he put her on the press up bench, she stared at him. He trapped her between his hard body and the bench. His lips felt like a brand against hers.

She banded her hands around his neck, moaning as he slid his hands down her body, cupping her hips.

"Do you have any idea what you do to me?" he asked.

He moved his hips between her thighs, and the hard press of his dick against her core had her moaning.

"Why did we wait five years?" she asked.

"You weren't ready. Time, Junior, life, it all got in the way, but it meant that you got the chance to fall in love with me instead." He lifted up her shirt, tossing it across the room, before he pushed her skirt up. It was one of the wraparound skirts, and he unbuttoned it, the skirt sliding open. Next, he tore at her panties, and when he got to her bra, she helped him remove it.

She was now naked for him, spread out.

"You're the prettiest feature in my gym."

He sat down and rested her legs over his. Liam stroked his fingers down her sides, his thumbs rubbing across her full hips.

"You're sexy as fuck," he said. "I wish I didn't have to wait, but for five years, I've made you mine. I showed you how to trust me."

"And I fell in love with you. I never lied when I told you my feelings. They're all true."

"You own my heart," he said.

"It's not enough though. You want more."

"I always want more." He stroked his fingers through her wet flesh. "And you deserve it as well. If Easton was here right now, he'd be able to lick and suck at your tits. Your mouth would be full of his cock, and I've got a feeling he's got a nice big one. I bet you'd choke on it as well trying to swallow as much of him down as you could."

He thrust three fingers inside her, and she moaned, arching up, wanting more.

"Please, fuck me, Liam." She would gladly beg for more of him. When he'd told her about his discussion, she had thought Liam was insane to even suggest it. Only now, she saw the potential there.

The kiss she'd shared with Easton, no matter how brief, had meant something. She'd liked the hard touch of his lips against hers, the rush of pleasure being in his arms once again.

The crush she had on him when they were younger had never gone away, and it had only gotten stronger.

What Liam offered was the chance to explore this with Easton but to do it in a way that wouldn't cost her her heart.

She couldn't handle any more heartbreak and had told Liam the same.

"I will, all in good time. The trick to having a nice good fuck, darlin', is to not rush it. You rush it, and you're going to miss all the pleasure points." He turned his fingers within her and played her body, rubbing against her G-spot, heightening her pleasure without even stroking her clit. "It's about getting you used to my touch and preparing you for what I'm about to do to you. Think about Easton. Yeah, that's it, think about him watching as I play with you. I've seen the way he looks at you when he thinks no one is looking, and he'll want this with you, Scarlett. To finally get you after all this time."

His thumb teased her clit, and she cried his name.

"Keep your hands on the bench. Don't move a muscle. You're at my mercy, and I get to see those perfect tits shake as I play with you. You were designed to be fucked, Scarlett."

"Then stop teasing me and fuck me."

"All in good time."

"We're supposed to be making up for what we lost."

"And we will. I'm not in any kind of rush. I feel how tight your pussy is getting. You're soaked through. Is it me or Easton you want?"

"Both."

"That's okay. You're going to get us both." He pulled his hands from her pussy, and Scarlett could do no more than follow the movements as he put her into another position. This time, she straddled the bench and his hands held her in place. The angle was a little uncomfortable until he worked his cock inside her.

She didn't know how he managed to work so fast to be inside her.

He banded her hair around his fist, tugging on the length, and he gave her ass a slap. They both cried out.

"You like a little pain, don't you, sweetheart?"

He couldn't fuck her hard like this, but his long, slow strokes nearly brought her to the peak. He gave her ass another thwack, and she cried out, the burn doing wonders to her pleasure.

"Yes."

"Good. I'm more than happy to give you what you need so long as you're willing to take it."

He let go of her hair, and she pushed it off her face to look at him. At the same time, he spread open her ass, his thumb stroking over her anus.

"What are you doing?" she asked.

"There is so much pleasure you don't even know about, but that's okay. We're going to explore it together." He spat down on her ass, and she gasped as he pushed his thumb inside her.

At first it burned, as if she was a little too tight for him. He didn't pull away or stop, working her anus until the burn turned to ecstasy and she wanted more.

His lips brushed across her ear before he bit down on the lobe. "You feel that burn, the ache, the need."

"Please, Liam."

"I know what you want, and don't worry, I will fuck your ass very soon. I'll consider it a pleasure, but for now, I'm going to get you used to the feel of me inside you."

She didn't know if she was going to be able to last.

All too soon, he pulled away and lifted her up so she was on her knees. Liam stood, and as he grabbed her hips and began to fuck her, she was blown away by the pleasure. He held her hair, and she pushed back as he thrust forward, begging him to not stop. This fire between them, it was indescribable. She couldn't believe this man had been in her bed for all this time and only now she was finally getting to know what it would be like with him.

The trust, the love, everything combined together, and as she came, Liam let out a growl, his cum flooding her pussy.

Afterward, he picked her up in his arms and carried her out of the gym.

He took her upstairs to their en-suite bathroom.

"We're going to have to pick up Junior soon," she said. "You don't need to keep carrying me everywhere. I don't want you to hurt yourself."

"It's no trouble," He put her in the shower, stepping in behind her.

"You promise me this isn't going to cost us anything?" she asked.

"It's not going to cost us a damn thing. I've got it

covered, and Easton won't tell anyone," he said.

"How can you be so sure?" She had no reason to doubt Liam, but he didn't know Easton like she did. Eleven years was a long time, but he'd been through a lot, and she didn't want to put any kind of pressure on him. She already felt guilty for not telling him about her son. At any point in the last eleven years she could have told him.

"Because he's still very much in love with you and as any man in love, you do crazy things. Even if it means sharing the one you love most with another man." He cupped her face, tilting her head back and kissing her hard.

She moaned against his mouth, never wanting him to stop.

Liam was the one to break the kiss first. He trailed his lips down her body, picking up the soap.

"How long has it been since you were with someone else?" she asked.

"A very long time. The moment I realized my feelings for you, I stopped. I didn't want to have to make a choice," he said. "When we first married, there was someone. He didn't want to make a commitment, and it was fun. You'd said you didn't want a relationship of that kind. Also, I've never been with a woman in all the time we've been together."

"It didn't last with the other man?"

"No. I didn't love him, and I ended it before things turned ugly." Liam pressed her up against the wall. "You're all I want."

"And Easton. You want him. You can't deny that."

"I'm not going to."

"What if he doesn't want you?"

"He will."

"Are you going to manipulate him?"

"No. I'm going to make him happy. It's all I want." He kissed her harder, and Scarlett forgot about everything else.

****

On one of the rarest of occasions, Liam was in the city. He stood outside the Four Kings Empire again, waiting for Easton to come out and join him. He'd already called ahead to make sure he was available for lunch.

Scarlett had gone to the school for Junior, and they'd be back late. He had errands to run in the city and didn't see a reason why he couldn't take Easton out to lunch.

Easton appeared in the doorway. He was alone, and Liam admired the sheer strength of the man. He wasn't well-kept. The suit he wore didn't fit him well enough. It was too tight around the arms and chest, and looked over large when it came to fitting him around the waist.

He'd have to take the man shopping. Easton looked up, and Liam held his hand up.

Several women had tried to approach him. Even though he wore his wedding ring, it didn't exactly work as a deterrent for the women. With him being married, they saw it as a challenge, which he didn't get. For the most part, he was an old-fashioned kind of guy with family values.

"I'm surprised you called," he said, approaching.

"Why not?"

"I told Scar about us."

Liam chuckled. "I told you. No secrets."

"You think it's the success to a happy marriage."

"It's one of them. The other is making sure your woman is happy as well. Are you ready to go to lunch?"

"Yeah, I know a good sandwich place if you're okay with that?" Easton asked.

"Lead the way."

"How can you walk around without any guards?" Easton asked after a few seconds of silence.

"I don't need guards. I keep my life private, and it has served me really well so far. I don't have to worry about everyone trying to hurt me. I don't make public appearances. Any donations or charities I support are all behind the scenes. I like my life. No one would have any reason to recognize me."

"Is that why you're wearing the glasses?" Easton asked.

"No, it's just bright out, and I don't want to be blinded by the sun." Liam chuckled. "Not everything has to have excess meaning." He noticed how people stopped and stared at Easton.

None of them really saw the broken man, but they certainly admired him.

Easton, along with the other Four Kings, had been in plenty of magazines and newspapers. Their exploits at one point had been legendary. There was also a kiss and tell exposé on them done a few months ago.

Liam had read about three of the four men who liked to share a woman. She'd gone into graphic detail, which only served him well. If Easton liked to share, it would make this new venture even more fruitful.

He *would* have to share though. Liam wouldn't be pushed aside.

Liam's love for Scarlett was pure, and he would die for her, it was that strong. With Easton, it was the same. All he needed was a little time to help Easton shine as well. For him to know that he wasn't alone anymore. Yes, he had his friends, but now he also had Liam and Scarlett, and they weren't going to let anything happen to him.

"I don't know why I bother trying to be honest. The press will get their story regardless."

"You haven't used the right methods in protecting yourself. Being wealthy makes you a target for greedy people. You've got to learn to spot them. It's how I knew Scarlett was the real deal," he said. "She came to me for a job as my housekeeper. She had so many bruises on her face. She looked a mess. I saw the kindness in her eyes." He smiled. "It was cute watching her stumble over her words. It was refreshing."

"When we were in camp, she didn't know who I was or my wealth. I kept so much from her, only telling her what she needed to know. She deserved so much more from me."

"You are aware Scarlett was once wealthy in her own right?" Liam asked.

Easton stopped walking. "What?"

"Her family, her name wasn't always Knight. Her name was Tallia. You should recognize the name. They're not rich on your scale, but they are well-known."

"No fucking shit. You're kidding me?"

"Nope. Scarlett Tallia, heiress to a small fortune. She was set to marry some bachelor. I forget his name. The family lost all of their wealth in the housing crash. Her family is struggling to stay afloat." Liam smiled.

"Let me guess, you're the one making sure they have a hard time?" Easton asked.

Liam had made it his mission to hurt all of those who had hurt Scarlett. With Easton, he always held back because he knew Scarlett loved him. There no denying his woman's attraction to this man, even after what she'd told him he'd done. She never wanted to admit it, but she did love Easton, and no matter what teenage assholery had happened between them, the love hadn't died, and Liam had no intention of pushing Easton away, especially as he saw the other man loved her. With Easton becoming part of them, he wanted to do *something* to show Easton that he was loved and wanted by the both of them.

"I have a way of prolonging my torture," Liam said. "Her parents disowned her without a backward glance. I take exception to their treatment of her. Since learning the truth of who she is, I've made sure to make their life uncomfortable. Victory is not in a quick death. It's in learning your opponents' weaknesses, drawing them close, and taking their fortune right from under them."

"Wow."

"Scarlett could have died because of them. She had no choice but to survive on her own." Liam looked at Easton. "You got a problem with how I handle those who hurt the people I care about?"

"So long as it doesn't break the law."

This time Liam threw his head back and couldn't control his laughter. "You're funny."

"I'm being serious. She would hate it," Easton said.

Liam shrugged. The Tallia fortune was crippled, and he loved to watch them search for an investor. No one would touch them, and it's exactly how Liam wanted them. He had a meeting set up for three weeks, where he would reveal the cause of all of their problems. By that time, they would be broke, and Scarlett would be free.

"Easton, I'm not a crook or a criminal. I will never do anything wrong, I promise. I have spent my life making sure I protect this country. I won't let anything jeopardize that, and I know how to protect the ones I love." He would simply do whatever it took to take care of those he loved, regardless of what others said.

Chapter Eleven

Over eleven years ago

"Tell me one of your hopes and dreams," Scar said.

Easton glanced across the picnic table, not really sure what her question was about.

"My hopes and dreams?"

"Things you hope to achieve for the future. That kind of thing."

"You tell me one of yours."

"That's cheating. I asked you first."

He chuckled. "Tell me something and then I'll know what you mean."

"It's not a hard question."

"To you, maybe not, but to me, it's pretty fucking hard." He didn't believe in hopes or dreams. He was nothing more than his father's puppet who liked to play with him from time to time.

"Fine, fine. One day I hope to settle down, fall in love, and be in an actual loving relationship."

"Seriously? That's a hope and dream."

"If you knew my family, you'd totally understand why I have that kind of dream." She pushed some hair off her face. "Come on, it's your turn."

"This is a lame game."

"It's not. Come on. We clearly don't have great lives back at home. Tell me what it is you'd love to do if your family or friends had absolutely no control over anything you did."

Easton looked at Scar across the picnic table. She twirled her spaghetti around her fork, and she looked in control, calm, as if these questions were not hard. They were. He didn't have a chance of ever fulfilling his dreams.

"If I didn't have to worry about what happened at home, I'd find someone who only loved me for me. What do you think?"

"You're wanting someone to love you?"

"Pretty much. Lame huh?"

"No, not at all. I rather like it." She grabbed her soda, lifting it up. "To falling in love. Hopefully, there will be someone within our future who'll love us no matter what."

He picked up his own soda and tapped it against the metal of hers. "Here's hoping."

****

Present day

Rather than wait for the appropriate time at five o'clock to leave work, Easton left at lunchtime. They had a little time before Junior needed to be picked up. He'd never felt this nervous before.

This decision he was about to make scared the crap out of him. It was such a huge move, and he'd not discussed it with any of his friends. He imagined they would think him crazy to share a woman who gave birth to his kid, and deep down, he really did think it was a little whacky for him to be sharing anyone.

Taking a deep breath, he was about to knock at the door, but Liam opened it.

"You're early."

"I've made my final decision."

"And you're here."

"I think we should all talk about this. I'm getting mixed messages inside my head, and I need to clarify them"

Liam moved out of the way, and Easton crossed over the threshold.

Scar stood behind her husband. Her cheeks were

flushed and her hair bound up on her head. She wore a white dress, and she looked stunning.

"Easton," she said.

"Scar."

"Why don't we take this in the dining room? You two, sit, relax, have some fun, and I'll go and make us all a hot drink." Liam didn't give them a chance to argue.

Scar sat down, and Easton took the seat he usually did at dinner.

Silence fell between them. She stared at the table, and he couldn't take his gaze away from her. In the past eleven years, if it was even possible, she'd gotten more beautiful.

To him, Scar had always been a stunner, but there was something more to her now, a womanliness that had been missing years ago.

"It's a nice week we're having," he said.

Silences of late always seemed to annoy him.

"It is." She had a smile to her lips. "You've made a decision?"

"Yes. I'll wait for Liam to be present. He seems to know what he's doing more than us. It must be his age."

"He's a man used to getting what he wants." She rested her elbows on the table, arms crossed. "How are you coping with everything? I imagine it has been a really huge adjustment for you. Finding out about Easton, I mean Junior, you mentioned going to rehab. We've not really talked about it."

"I'm handling everything great. I have no desire to drink. Finding out about Junior, he was the best thing to ever happen to me. I only wish I could have been there when you gave birth. Was it a hard birth?"

"Not so much. All births are difficult and come with complications. Compared to most I had a good birth, you know. I did whatever I could to take care of our son. Please know that. I would never allow any harm to come to him."

He reached across the table, which required him to stand up so he could touch her hand. "I know you'd never harm Junior, or allow anything to happen to him. I've seen you with him, and I stand by my earlier judgment. You're an amazing mom."

Her cheeks went a darker shade of red. "You're just trying to charm me now."

"No. I believe it. Besides, if I was trying to charm you, I'd mention how pretty your hair is. I miss the length I remember, but I can't do anything about the length, now can I?"

She teased a strand around her finger. "Do you remember brushing it for me? You'd spend hours, and I think in a strange way, it always calmed you while you brushed my hair."

"Is it weird, it did?"

"No, not at all." She chuckled. "This is nice. We're talking about it, and I've missed this. I've missed you."

"I've missed you too. So much. I wanted to find you," he said. Liam had told him the only way a relationship of any kind worked was by telling the truth. He didn't want there to be any secrets between them.

"You did."

"I did. I didn't know your last name, and my PI had a hard time tracking you down."

Scar smiled. "Liam takes care of all kinds of things like that. He knows if someone is tracking me. I've got family who didn't care how I got pregnant or my love of my unborn child. They wanted me to get rid of it."

"You've not spoken to your family?" he asked.

"Not since the day they kicked me out." She shrugged. "I was pregnant, scared, alone, and it was the most terrifying moment of my life. I survived though."

Easton squeezed her hand a little harder. "I'd have been there."

"You broke my heart, Easton."

"It was all lies. Every single word of it. I couldn't take you home with me. Hearing you say you loved me and you saw your hopes and dreams with me, it meant the world to me."

"Not enough to stop you from leaving though. We could have been together," she said.

"I didn't want to leave you. I told you why I had to."

"Let's not talk about what you did or didn't do," Liam said. "This is the chance for both of you to have a fresh start, and the only way to do that is to be open and honest with each other." Liam put down three cups of steaming coffee in front of each of them.

Easton let her hand go and took a seat. The coffee smelled wonderful, and he took his, sipping at the steaming liquid without a care for any burns or scalds.

"Have you made a decision?" Liam asked.

"I have, but first I want to know what Scar knows." He looked directly at her, wanting the truth from her. "I'm not going to go forward if she's being pushed into this."

Scar smiled. "I know everything. Liam wants to share me with you, and you with me." She looked toward her husband. "There is a lot you don't know about us, but I want this, if you do. I don't believe in force." Easton noticed as she held Liam's hand just a little tighter, almost as if she was afraid to speak. "And I think if we're discreet and lay some ground rules, this could work."

"You know this is about me fucking you, with

your husband, without him. All of it?"

"I know he's trying to make a family with us, yes. It doesn't surprise me. Does it surprise you, Easton?"

"Everything right now surprises me."

"What's your decision?" Liam asked. "Once we know what you want, we can move on and make a chance of this."

He sighed. Locking his fingers together, he looked at each of them, in turn. "I want this chance more than anything. It's a yes. What I don't want is to hurt Scar again." He looked at her. "I know I hurt you once, and I'd do anything to change the pain I've given you."

"Excellent," Liam said.

"You need to tell him the truth," Scar said, looking toward Liam. "If he's involved in this, he has a right to know."

"A right to know what?"

Liam and Scar stared at each other, and he watched the man nod his head.

"I'm bisexual," Liam said. "It has been a dream of mine to find a man and a woman to share my life with. Scar knew of this, and before our marriage I was involved with another man, but it ended badly. I wasn't willing to give up my woman. Of course, she didn't know I was going to develop feelings for her."

"Our marriage was originally a contract," Scar said. "You cannot under any circumstances speak of this to anyone. If you do, you void all contact with your son." Scar gave Liam's hand a squeeze.

"This is an NDA with special requirements. At any time, you speak to the press or violate our privacy, you forfeit your right to your son, and any children we may have."

Easton stared down at the document. "Excuse me?"

"I take my privacy seriously. Anyone who comes into this kind of arrangement must be willing to take risks here. For your silence on our family, you will get full access to your son, even if this doesn't work out. Talk, and I will end you."

Easton looked toward Scar. "You accept this?"

"The happiest of my entire life has been with Liam. At first, I thought it was a little … full, but I know he does it out of love. This is his life and our life. I signed my own years ago. What you're doing is not only protecting Liam and yourself, but Junior and me. Any kind of kiss and tell could be dangerous, and I won't have that."

"Neither will I." Liam held out two other forms. Easton hadn't realized he'd brought with him a file from the kitchen. "Here are two NDAs signed by Scarlett and myself. You're protected just as much as we are."

"How?"

"In the event of your reputation being damaged, you can contest for full custody, or shared custody. You will also be compensated. I told you, I protect all the people I care about."

Easton stared down at the two forms, and they had signatures. "Wow."

"You will be part of the protection I offer, Easton. I know it must take a great deal agreeing to this."

He looked up at Liam. "Hold on, does this mean you find me attractive?"

"I will not give any further detail unless you wish to continue and sign the form."

Easton stared at the form. It wasn't a terrifying concept. After having his entire life smeared across the tabloids and his father in prison, there really were worse ways about keeping your life private.

With the flick of his wrist, he signed the NDA.

He wouldn't ever have to give up his son because he valued privacy and respected Liam for doing everything he could to protect the family he held dear to him.

"Excellent. Yes, I find you attractive. I want to see you and Scarlett together as well. Do you have any other questions?"

"I'm still absorbing the fact you find me attractive."

"What's not to love? Your eyes are so dark and smoky, and even though you have the worst fashion sense in the world, you're hot."

"Is this odd for you?" Easton asked, turning to Scar.

"I don't know. At first, I thought it would be, but now, I think it's kind of hot."

"Have you told any of your friends?" Liam asked.

"No."

"You cannot tell them what we have. Not until you are sure of their loyalty."

"The Four Kings are loyal."

"Your entire company is built on a hierarchy of lies and blackmail. Do you even know what a best friend is?" Liam asked.

"Let's not delve into the business here. Easton's been part of the Four Kings for a long time. Since birth if I remember. We don't want to start an argument about loyalty. He knows his friends, and you're not going to control every single element of his life, even if you want to." Scar patted Liam's hand.

"So, how does this work?" Easton asked.

"You've shared women before."

"They were women I didn't care about, and it was only for sex. She'd come to the office or one of the clubs, fuck each of us, and we'd play with her. This is not the same. This is different, and you know it."

Liam leaned back in his chair. "Tell me what you want to do?"

Easton started to get nervous. "Me?"

"Yes." Liam glanced down at his watch. "We've got a couple of hours before I need to pick up Junior. What would you like?"

"I'd like to kiss Scar," Easton said. "To pick up where we left off."

"Scarlett, baby, what would you like?"

"I'd like the kiss."

He saw her nerves as well.

She looked toward Liam. "I'm scared."

"Don't be." The playful husband was gone, and Easton watched as Liam helped Scarlett to her feet. "I love you. More than anything. I want to see him with you. This will not change our relationship one bit. I will love you for a long time, and this won't change that. Remember, I'm a bit different. You knew it when you married me."

She laughed, resting her head against his. "You're right."

"Easton, come and kiss our woman," Liam said. He stood behind her, his hands on her shoulders.

Getting to his feet, Easton moved closer and stood in front of Scar. "You want this?"

"Yes. I do."

He stepped closer and pressed his lips to hers.

The past, all of it faded, and he saw his future and it was with this woman. He didn't know if he'd ever be comfortable with Liam, but he wasn't willing to ruin this with Scar.

****

At first Scarlett didn't know what to do with her hands. Liam didn't let go of her shoulders, and for his presence, she was thankful, more so than ever before.

She didn't want him to ever leave or for him to think she would push him aside for this man.

There was a time she loved Easton and there was still part of her that did, but he'd broken her heart once. She wouldn't trade Liam for Easton, but she also wouldn't trade Easton for Liam. Her life had gotten so confusing.

What Liam offered, was a chance of something more. Each time he spoke of them together, not just the sex but being a family for Junior and for each other, it felt so right. She didn't know how it was possible to be right.

Easton cupped her cheeks, tilting her head back, and deepened the kiss. She opened up, and his tongue slid inside, making her gasp.

Sinking her fingers into his hair, she released a moan and behind her Liam ran his hands down to cup her ass. Both men were igniting a fire within her, and she didn't want either of them to put it out.

Easton broke from the kiss, but his lips were not done. He trailed down to her neck, sucking on her pulse as Liam lifted her arms up to circle the back of his head.

"Don't move," Liam said.

She whimpered, especially as he unlatched each strap. The dress she wore had removable straps so it didn't have to be worn with a bra. Today she'd opted to wear it with one, but as Liam slid the dress down her body for it to pool at her feet, she had to wonder why she even bothered.

Easton stepped back, and the lust in his eyes was unmistakable.

"You see how perfect she is?" Liam asked.

"She's fucking stunning."

"She's all ours," Liam said.

He flicked the catch of her bra, and her tits spilled

out.

Easton was there, cupping the mounds together, flicking each nipple with his tongue.

"Touch her pussy," Liam said. "Feel how wet she is. I bet she's soaking. I know every single time I've talked about us taking her together, she's been like fire in my arms."

"You've talked about me?" Easton asked. One of his hands rested on her stomach, and she bit her lip to stop herself from begging him to touch her, to do anything. She pressed her thighs together in the hope to gain some friction or anything.

Nothing.

She was at Easton's mercy.

"Yes. Why do you think I made the suggestion? Scarlett wants the two of us together, don't you?"

"Yes." There was no point in denying it.

Liam had showed her only truth made a successful relationship. It's why she always told the truth, even with her son.

Pushing Junior out of her mind, she focused on the two men currently pleasing her right now.

Easton slid his hand between her thighs, touching her clit, and he let out a growl. "Fuck, she's wet."

"Do you want to taste her? She's got the best pussy."

He sank to his knees, and Liam held her hands behind his neck so there was nowhere to go. The panties she wore were slid down her body, and then his lips were on her pussy. "You wax?" Easton asked.

"I shave her regularly. I'm not one to hear her in pain unless it's down to a bit of discomfort from my cock. Only then will I accept her gasps and cries." Liam put his lips at her neck and bit down. There was pain and pleasure combined as Easton licked across her clit. He moved her legs so he had better access to her pussy.

Scarlett couldn't believe this was happening. Easton was licking at her pussy, and her husband stood behind her, cupping her tits.

This was something out of a fantasy, but it was one she wanted to keep on having. Her legs shook from the pleasure.

"Let's move this into my office," Liam said.

Easton stood, wiping the excess arousal from her pussy off his face. More heat flooded her body as he licked his hand. "Tastiest pussy."

Liam picked her up and carried her to his office. She and Liam had been making up for a lot of lost time in his office, and now that Easton was there, it felt complete.

He put her on the sofa and ordered her to her knees. Liam stood in front of her, removing his shirt, followed by his pants. His cock stood out, long, thick, with the vein seeming to pulse at the side. He looked fierce, in control, and as he wrapped her hair around his fist, she knew exactly what he wanted.

Even as Easton moved between her thighs so she straddled his head, she moaned as she sucked the tip of Liam's cock into her mouth. He hit the back of her throat, pulling out, only to dive in again.

The pleasure took her by surprise as she rocked against Easton's tongue. He cupped her ass, rocking her pussy on his mouth. He stroked over her clit, sliding back and forth before moving down to tease her entrance, and back again.

"You can play with her asshole as well. She likes that. I've been getting her ready to take both of us," Liam said.

"You've become really bossy," she said.

"Did you expect anything else?"

"She likes you bossy," Easton said. Three fingers plunged into her pussy but for only a second before he drew them out, going to her anus to stroke over the puckered hole. "She's dripping, and every time you give an instruction, she feels ready to explode."

Liam tightened his hold on her hair, shoving his cock deep until she gagged on the length. He pulled all of the way out of her mouth so she saw the saliva covering his dick.

Wrapping her fingers around the width, she worked up and down before sucking on the tip of him.

Easton pressed a finger to her asshole as he sucked on her clit.

She closed her eyes, trying to stop her arousal from building. She didn't want this to stop. After having Liam talk to her nonstop about how good it would be between all of them, she didn't want him to ever stop.

"She's close, Easton. She's trying to fight it though. She's a greedy one."

"There's nothing to fight."

She cried out as Easton gave her ass a slap. This was different from eleven years ago. They weren't kids anymore fumbling around. This was real. They were man and woman, and not only that, they had Liam now.

Liam pressed the tip of his cock back to her mouth, and as Easton brought her to her orgasm, Liam found his between her lips and she swallowed every single drop of his cum down her throat, wanting more. He let her go, pressing a kiss to the corner of her mouth before he took a seat, watching them.

With the haze of her arousal coming down, she kept her gaze on her husband.

"I want to watch the two of you together," Liam said. "Remember, trust."

"Trust?"

Liam nodded.

Easton sat on the sofa. He still wore his pants, and Scarlett was overcome with shyness. His mouth was covered in her juices, and she could still taste Liam on her tongue.

This was all new to her.

New didn't always mean scary. Reaching out, she tugged open Easton's pants.

"I need a condom," Easton said.

"Scarlett's on the pill."

"Are you clean?" Scarlett asked. "We are. I can go and get our medical documents."

"I trust the both of you. The way Liam's handled everything, I've got no reason to doubt him."

"You don't." Scarlett leaned in close and kissed his lips. She felt unsure, nervous. Should she be kissing him? Liam made no sound of protest, so she cupped Easton's face and finally kissed him with the passion she'd been denying herself.

Even after all these years, her feelings for Easton hadn't changed. They weren't as free as they once were, but she still loved him.

She didn't want him to go, ever.

Was it selfish of her to want two men and for them to want her? Yes, it was. She knew Liam wanted to share Easton, and she was okay with sharing this man with her husband and vice versa.

If only it could work…

It *had* to work.

Easton lifted her up so she straddled his waist. His hands went to her thighs, running up and down them.

"Do you have any idea how long I've been wanting this?" Easton asked. "I spent so many nights with regret. I wanted to find you, but I'd always find some dumbass excuse."

"You've found me now."

"Yes, and you've got the most understanding husband on the planet." Easton reached between them, and the tip of his cock touched her clit.

The grip she had on his shoulders tightened from the single touch of his cock. Biting her lip, she glanced down. This would be the first time in eleven years she'd had sex with Easton. The father of her child.

Looking back up, she stared into his dark brown eyes, mesmerized by the beauty of them.

She felt Liam at her back, and her love for him would never waver. If this worked, she hoped for one day when her love for Easton wouldn't be so broken or shattered.

As she slid down onto Easton's length, they both cried out. In her mind, she traveled back in time to when they crossed this line once before. It hadn't been intentional, and for Scarlett, her first ever time with anyone.

Pushing those bitter memories aside, she focused on the Easton of now, not of then.

Lifting herself up, she began to rock against him, and Easton cupped her hips, working his cock inside her, guiding her pussy over his length.

Liam moved behind her, his lips trailing her neck. "You look incredible taking his cock." She felt his hand between them, his fingers circling Easton's cock as he fucked her. Easton tensed beneath her, but he didn't stop.

This was all new and exciting, and she gasped as Liam's hand moved between her thighs, stroking over her clit.

She needed Liam so badly. He was her anchor.

With him, she knew she'd be safe.

****

Later that night, Liam sat in his office, looking

over some paperwork. Junior was being put to bed and was also having the time of his life knowing Easton would be staying with them for the foreseeable future.

In the next week, Easton would be moving in with them.

For their son, they would keep up appearances and he'd stay in the room he'd been sleeping in. With Junior asleep, Easton would always be coming to bed with him and Scarlett.

Running a finger across his lip, he glanced toward the sofa where he'd watched Easton and Scarlett make love.

They were … scared.

He couldn't think of any other word to describe them. The passion for each other was off the charts. He saw the way they looked at each other, and even as Easton tried to hide his curiosity with him, Liam knew it was going to happen.

What Easton and Scarlett had was broken at the moment. He wouldn't for a second believe he couldn't fix either of them with the right amount of love and care.

Did Scarlett see the shattered man in Easton?

Liam sure did, and it broke his heart to know how sad he was, most of the time. When he didn't think anyone was looking, Easton rarely smiled.

In the past couple of weeks, Liam had made it his mission to find out every single little tiny insignificant and life-changing detail of Easton's life. The only way he could make a success of this relationship with all three of them was to know everything. To Liam, knowledge would always be power.

Easton's past was connected with Scarlett. The death of one girlfriend, happening a mere few months before Junior's conception, spoke volumes.

Not only did Scarlett and Easton share Junior, but

they shared a memory of their last days together. Whatever Easton had said to Scarlett had stopped her from ever finding him out to tell him about their son.

"You okay?" Easton asked, entering his office.

"Where's Junior and Scarlett?"

"He's asleep. She took a swim. Said she needed a few minutes to clear her head." Easton pointed at the chair. "May I?"

"Of course, have a seat."

"I don't think this is going to work out the way you hoped," Easton said.

"Why not?" Liam dropped his pen to the desk, sat back, and waited.

"I know you mean well, and you think you see a future here. It's not possible. It'll never be possible. Not in a million years. I felt Scarlett today, and she's nervous around me." He saw the tears in Easton's eyes, and he looked away, not letting Liam see them.

"Do you love her?" Liam asked.

"Dude, look, it's not going to work."

"Do you love her? I'm going to keep on asking the question. You may as well answer me."

Easton sighed. "You really do like getting what you want."

"I'm a big believer in truth. I don't like people who run from their responsibilities but also their feelings. You don't just hurt yourself if you run, Easton. You hurt Scarlett and Junior this time."

"Did you see how nervous she was with me. How … scared? I don't want her to be that way. Not with me. I will never hurt her." Easton got up and started to pace the office.

Liam watched him. "You did."

"Eleven years ago."

"You've got to understand, Junior will always be

the painful reminder of what you both had and lost," Liam said. "If this is really so hard for you, walk away, but you don't come back."

"You can't keep me from my son."

"I don't believe a coward should raise a gentleman, Easton."

"I'm not a coward."

"Then what would you call a man who is on the brink of having everything he could ever want but because it's not gone so smoothly first time around, you walk away?"

"It's easy for you. She loves you, and she likes your touch. I felt the way she changed when you were there. You can't deny that. You're the one she wants."

Liam stood up. "She wants both of us, you nitwit. Why do you have to push like this?"

"I ... I..."

"You were expecting it to be easy. Believe me, I get it. You think this is easy for me? The love of my life has a lot of pain inside her. I know through her pain she loves you. A part of her will always belong to you!" He pointed at Easton. "My love for her is another reason I'm willing to share her. Not only that, but we can make this work. I know we can."

"What if it doesn't? What if this is going to hurt her even more?"

"What are you so afraid of? Has your father fucked you up that you can't even see the chance of happiness?"

"I don't fucking need this." He didn't want to think about his father in this house. Not with his son or Scarlett, or even Liam.

Liam grabbed his arm, and Easton couldn't help it. He raised his fist as if to hit him, but Liam saw the move and grabbed his fist.

"You don't want to do this."

All of a sudden, Easton was pressed up against the wall and Liam had him completely restrained.

He growled, thrashing, trying to get away. He needed to be free.

"Stop it."

"Fuck you."

"Talk to me, Easton."

"Fuck off."

"You like that word a lot, don't you, Easton? Are you used to pushing people away all the time? Do they even fight to stay in your company?" Easton was so beautifully broken, and Liam was determined to change that. He didn't want any of his family to be like this. He could fix both of them. Scarlett was already changed, but he had no doubt he'd be able to fill the hole in this man's life. Be it friend, confidant or even lover. He'd never force the man but would be more than happy to guide him with everything he needed.

The tension in the room changed, and Easton suddenly stopped trying to fight him. It caught Liam off guard, especially as he was able to feel so close to Easton. The other man was everything he'd ever wanted, and he couldn't believe he'd been right in this city this whole time. The only difference for Liam was he would never hurt Scarlett for his own personal needs.

He'd made that vow once he realized he loved Scarlett more than anything, but now, with Easton in the picture, he was truly starting to know what it meant to love two people with the same kind of passion.

Easton kept on staring at him but not saying a word.

Finally, he let him go. If Liam didn't move back and take a break, he was going to do something about the arousal he was feeling. Kissing Easton wouldn't come like this. Without waiting for a reply from him, he turned on his heel and walked away.

Chapter Twelve

Over eleven years ago

"I hate the rain," Easton said, running into the gazebo for shelter.

Scarlett giggled. "Come on, what did the rain ever do to you?"

"It gets me all wet." Easton laughed as he wrapped his arms around her, pulling her close. "Surely you feel it, don't you?" He pressed his nose against her neck. "How wet you are." Realizing what he'd just said, he pulled away to stare into Scarlett's eyes. Her face was a delightful shade of pink.

"You think I'm wet."

"Yeah, I didn't really think that one through."

"No, no, it's fine. We're both wet."

"I'm hard, believe me," he said. Easton didn't know what possessed him to press the evidence of said arousal against her stomach.

"Easton!" She gasped his name but didn't pull away.

"I want you, Scarlett. Our time together is coming to an end, and I can't stand the thought of going back home without being with you first."

She smiled. "I've never done this before."

"Had a summer fling?"

"No, had sex." She wrapped her arms around his neck. "I'm a virgin." She nibbled her lip, and it was the first time since he'd known her where she looked completely unsure about what she was saying to him. "Does it bother you?"

Carla had been a virgin.

Part of him knew he should back away right now, but the way Scarlett made him feel. The pain was almost non-existent with Scarlett. He completely forgot about everything with Scarlett. All the pain was more a distant memory than actual feelings to him.

"No, it doesn't." Pressing his lips to hers, he vowed to make it good for her. To make sure when Scarlett remembered this moment, she'd do so with a smile. He couldn't keep her for himself; his father would only ruin this woman.

****

Present day

Easton sat in his office after spending the entire weekend with Liam, Scarlett, and Junior. After his confrontation with Liam, he figured he'd get thrown out, but this morning, after Junior was in the car, Scarlett had kissed both him and Liam, and promised them both she'd make an awesome dinner for their return.

He'd also shared Liam and Scarlett's bed, their woman between them.

It wasn't his relationship with Scarlett that was making him nervous. It was the way Liam felt pressed against him. He'd felt Liam's arousal, but the man had simply stepped back from him and walked away.

They hadn't been alone again since, apart from this morning when he got the chance to walk Junior to school.

He'd finally gotten the chance to see his son to school.

"Knock, knock," Axton said.

Pulled out of his thoughts, he looked toward one of his friends.

"You okay?" Axton asked.

"Yeah, why wouldn't I be?"

"I don't know. You've finally been given an almost teenage son. That's got to have some meaning. How are things with your kid and Scarlett?" Axton took a seat, crossing his legs as he did so.

"You're really curious about this or about who my kid is staying with?" he asked.

"I'm not going to lie, I'm curious about Knight and especially about how this all works for you?" Axton shrugged.

Again, he thought about Liam's face and how close he'd been. Easton had wanted to kiss him, and if Liam hadn't moved away, he'd have done it as well.

He'd never kissed a man before. He wondered what it would be like.

Would Liam have nice, firm lips, smooth, sexy?

He was losing his mind right about now. This couldn't be happening. He finally got a chance to be with Scarlett, and now he was fantasizing about her husband as well as her.

"It works for me." Easton shrugged. "Is there any other reason you're here?"

Axton sat back. "I know you're pissed off at me for making you go to rehab."

"I'm not pissed at you for any reason, Axton. I'm actually glad you sent me. I was a mess."

"You're glad?"

"Yes. I fucked up in everything, didn't I? I wasn't good for the company or anything. I had to be taken care of. My father would have killed me and spun some kind of bullshit, but you didn't do that and I'm grateful you didn't. I've been given a second chance. A chance with my son and to know Scar."

"You love her?" Axton asked.

Easton stared at his friend, not wanting to admit the truth.

"We all know you were never in love with Carla. It's not something to be ashamed of."

He averted his gaze. "It is."

"No, it's not," Axton said.

Easton closed his eyes, counted to ten, and focused his attention on his friend. "Yeah, it is. It's not the part about not loving her I'm ashamed of. She's dead because of me."

"You didn't kill her."

"I was determined to pop her cherry. I had this sick bet going on, and I had to complete it. For what reason? I don't know. If I'd simply let it all go, she'd still be alive."

"I wouldn't be with Taylor. Your son wouldn't have been born and you'd never have met Scarlett because you wouldn't have needed a reason to go to camp."

"We can't change what happened though. I did fuck Carla. I knocked her up, and my father killed her, and tried to dump the body. He failed. I went to camp, knocked up another woman, and turned my back on her."

"I didn't want to come in here and reflect on what happened or what could have been. I came as a friend. I've not seen a whole lot of you outside of work. Karson and Romeo said you're not even hanging out with them at the club."

"I've got no reason to or desire. I've got to get this work done."

Axton stopped as if he wanted to say something else.

Easton waited.

"I'll talk to you soon."

He was left alone, and Easton spent the rest of the day catching up on work. At two o'clock he got a call from Liam.

The moment he heard the other man's voice, his heart started to race.

"Are you busy?" Liam asked.

"Erm, I can stop now. I'm one of the bosses, why?" Had Liam felt their connection as well or was it just him? *Get your head in the game.*

"Something's come up at work. I need you to go and pick up Junior if you're able to. Scarlett's busy with the lawyer, as otherwise she'd go and pick him up. Please, Easton, I've already phoned the school. They know you'll be waiting for him."

"What if I'd said no?" Easton asked.

"You'd say no to the opportunity to go and pick up your son? You can pretend to be an asshole all you want who doesn't care, but if it was the case, you wouldn't have come to us, or agreed to the weekends. Are you okay?"

"I wish people would stop asking me that."

"You want people to stop caring about you?"

"It's not about caring."

"It's not? Could have fooled me. When people around you are worried, they ask personal, invasive questions. You should try it from time to time. You might learn something. You're good to pick up Junior?"

"Of course. I can take him out for ice cream, right?"

"You can take him out for whatever he wants. Be warned, he's a very determined kid."

"Will do. Have a good day."

"You too. Thanks, Easton." Liam hung up, and Easton smiled as he put the phone down.

Junior's school let out at three-thirty. He didn't have a whole lot of time to get over there. Quickly closing all of his files and shutting down his computer, he packed everything away and headed out of his office.

Axton, Karson, and Romeo were talking over one of the files he recognized from Paul. He'd opted not to be part of any of the business dealings with Paul for many reasons. One of them was related to Carla. He was aware of the other man's love of Carla, and he'd been the one to fuck her and lose her.

"I've got to take off. I'm going to go and pick up my son from school."

"You need one of us to come with you?" Romeo asked.

"I can handle the drive. Thanks."

He left them alone with their business and climbed onto the elevator. Within minutes he was sitting behind the wheel of his car, his palms sweaty, but he drove out, and took the time to arrive at his son's school.

Music blasted out of the stereo, and as he parked he saw he had over fifteen minutes to spare.

He turned the ignition off and just sat waiting, staring at the school where his son was taught.

His son.

Easton still couldn't get his head around the fact he had a son. He'd missed so much, and he was determined to make this work, one way or another.

Time seemed to slow down so much that by the time the bell rang, his nerves were shot. He'd always had some kind of buffer with Junior. Either Liam or Scar, but now, he didn't have anyone.

This was all on him.

Junior appeared with a couple of friends. He shook hands with them in some kind of special shake, and then headed his way at a run.

"Hey, Dad," Junior said, climbing behind the wheel.

"Hey, yourself." He was going to shoot himself in the head. There was a time he considered himself cool, and right now, he wasn't proving it to anyone.

Junior laughed and climbed in the car.

"You knew I was picking you up?"

"Yep, my other dad sent me a text message."

"Your other dad." Liam, of course. Easton started up the car and waited as several cars were already waiting to pull out.

"I hope it doesn't upset you I call Liam dad as well. I love you both."

"Junior, we're all adults here. Honestly, I don't mind. I think I'd find it a bit disrespectful if you stopped calling Liam dad just because I was here. He's taken care of you and your mom for a long time."

"Yeah, he really helped. I know my mom was terrified when she said there was a man who wanted to marry her. She wanted me to meet him first and get to know him before she made that kind of commitment."

"And you were happy with him, clearly," Easton said, laughing. "You're a smart kid. Smarter than I was at your age."

"What were you like at eleven?" Junior asked.

"Stupid. I never learned a lesson, and I was always getting into trouble and being punished for it." He didn't wish to taint his time with his son with memories of his past. They weren't good memories. "Anyway, enough about me. How about some ice cream?" he asked.

"Sorbet would be good. I don't eat ice cream anymore."

"Oh, right, the vegan thing. I'm good with some sorbet."

Junior nodded and patted his hand against the door, humming to himself.

Easton had run out of things to say. This couldn't be happening to him on the first chance he got with his son.

"How was school?"

"Cool."

"What is your favorite class?"

"Computers, but I love science as well. What was your favorite?"

"I … erm, I didn't have one. I guess I hated them all." He cringed at his response.

Finally pulling out of the spot, he took them toward an ice cream place that served sorbet and ice cream.

Silence once again filled the car.

He glanced over at Junior to see his son looking out of the window.

"Your friends seemed cool."

"Yeah, they love my other dad as well. I think it's why they're hanging out with me. They're a couple of nerds."

"Oh," Easton said. "Well, you know you don't have to hang out with them if they make you uncomfortable."

"I know. It's cool. They're fine with me, but I know they'd like an invite to my house. They won't be getting one."

"Why not?"

"One, they're not really my friends, and two, privacy. My other dad showed me how important and valuable privacy is, and I'm not going to disrespect him for a couple of friends who are only using me."

"You're a strong kid, Junior."

"I know. My mom told me I was her little fighter."

"Your mom's great." His own mother had been a waste of space. So long as she had drink and pills, she didn't care what happened. The oblivion from life was what she sought and she finally had it. "So, how do you like being called 'Junior'?" Easton groaned. "You know what, ignore me."

"What is it?" Junior asked.

"I'm trying here, and I'm falling flat. I honestly don't know what to say to you, and I want to get to know you."

"We're doing good, aren't we?" Junior asked. "It's all new."

"Just so you know, you can ask me anything and I will answer, to a point."

"Okay. Do you love my mom?" Junior asked.

"Wow, you really don't like waiting, do you?"

"I'm curious."

"Can we get back to my question?" he asked. It was by far a safer kind of question.

"I love it. It makes sense. You're Easton, I'm Easton." Junior chuckled. "We won't keep getting confused."

"True."

"Are you going to answer mine?" he asked.

"Yes. It's only fair." It didn't make it any less comfortable for him though. "So, loving your mother. Yes, I love your mother." So true on every single level. No matter how he'd pushed her away when they were younger, he'd done so to protect her. Especially after what happened to Carla. If his father could do that to a woman who he cared about but didn't love, what could he do to a woman he actually loved? "It's complicated."

"You love my mom and so does Liam."

"Your mom's a lucky woman." Now he didn't know if he was saying that because she had Liam's love or not.

His head was so fucked up right now, and he couldn't think straight.

Fortunately, their private conversation came to a close as they arrived at the ice cream and sorbet parlor.

It was busy, but they were able to get a couple of

seats.

Rather than order one scoop of every single flavor, Junior took his time, and ordered only two flavors, and they took a seat in the available booth in the corner.

"You know I wouldn't have minded if you got every single flavor to try."

"Nah, it would have been wasteful, and besides, Mom will be annoyed if I don't eat dinner."

"You're a good kid."

"We'll get to come again, right? You're not going to stop coming around, are you?"

"You want to come here again with me?"

"Only if you want to?" Junior nibbled his lip, looking a tad nervous. "You do want to, right?"

"Yeah, I'd love to take you out for ice cream and sorbet." Easton smiled. He couldn't help it.

In the car, he truly thought he sucked and he probably did with his questions and complete lack of knowing what to say or do, but Junior still wanted to go with him.

Today had been a win for him, and he was going to remember it for a long time to come.

****

Scarlett stood at the stove cooking a vegetable pasta dish. She'd sautéed the onions and had added the garlic when Easton and Junior arrived. Her son rushed to hug her, told her he had no homework, which she already knew, and took off to go shower and get ready for dinner.

As Junior left, Easton entered the kitchen.

"Something smells amazing."

"Just a vegetable pasta. How was your time with him?" she asked.

"It was really good."

She laughed. "Why do you sound so surprised?"

"It's me, remember. I had no idea what to say to him half the time. I've never had a son. I wasn't there for him to grow up. I was ... I don't know. I wasn't anything like him. My father wasn't a good man."

She turned down the stove and pushed it toward the back to stop it cooking. This dish was so fast to cook she had to wait until Liam arrived. Wiping her hands on the cloth on the counter, she tilted her head back to look at him.

"I heard what he'd done. I'm so sorry," she said. "Did he hurt you?"

Easton rubbed the back of his head, looking a touch uncomfortable. "He did, but I don't want to talk about it."

She held her hands up. "That's fine. You're not alone." He had the Four Kings as well, but she wanted to extend her hand of friendship. "I know you had your friends as well. I just wanted you to know I'm here for you, and I care."

Easton moved toward her, taking her hand, kissing her knuckles.

"Be careful, I've got raw garlic."

"It's fine. I'm not a vampire."

She chuckled. "Are you okay?" She hated to see him look so lost.

"Yeah, I'm fine. I will be. I've got you, Junior, and even Liam. Plus, I've got my guys, you know. Axton, Karson, and Romeo. We have a troubled friendship at times, but I know they've got my back for me."

There was something he wasn't saying, and she didn't want to call him on it in case it made him upset.

"And now you've got us as well." She placed her hand on his chest, feeling the rapid beat of his heart. "Our son's a good kid, Easton. You don't have to try with him to get him to talk to you. Honestly, he adores you. Loves you. You're his father."

"I know. You've raised him well. I couldn't have asked for a better mother."

The tension between them grew. She had no idea if Easton felt this connection between the two of them or if it was all her.

Glancing at his lips, she wanted him to kiss her, but it was so wrong. Liam wasn't here. She didn't know the boundaries her husband wanted, but not only that, did Liam want to kiss Easton as well?

She'd seen the attraction for Liam, and she understood it. Easton had been her greatest pleasure and at one time, her biggest mistake. He'd made her afraid to trust for so long, but now, she wanted it all. She wanted to be with him, have this second chance, even if it did mean breaking her heart in the process. She'd do it.

Easton pressed her up against the counter, and she didn't complain. Staring up into his eyes, she waited.

He leaned in close, and as his lips were near to hers, she pulled back.

"We can't."

"Why not?"

"Liam."

"He said we could share you. Junior's not around, and we're alone."

"Not quite alone, but I've got no problem with the two of you kissing," Liam said, drawing both of their attention.

Easton didn't let her go but looked behind him.

She stared at her husband and waited for him to speak. She saw he liked coming home to Easton touching her.

The fire in his eyes a clear indication of just how much he liked coming home to the two of them.

"Where's Junior?"

"In his room getting ready for dinner."

"We know that means he won't come down unless we shout for him," Liam said. "Easton, kiss her."

Easton turned toward her, and she gave him her full attention.

He tilted her head back, and he wasn't in any rush. He ran his thumb across her bottom lip and pressed forward. She sucked on it, watching him gasp as she did.

Suddenly, he slammed his lips down on hers.

His kiss was hard, brutal, and so damn needy. She wrapped her arms around his neck, moaning as he nipped at her lips, and she opened them. He plundered his tongue into her mouth, and she met him, deepening the kiss, very much aware of Liam, who had moved closer.

He didn't touch her though. He touched Easton, putting his hands on his shoulders.

"She loves it when you grip her hair and give it a little tug. She doesn't want pain but to know who she belongs to, and we both know, she belongs to us, and will always do so."

Easton sank his fingers into her hair, gripping the locks and giving them a tug, making her moan as he held her in place, kissing her still.

He broke from the kiss, and those lips trailed a path across her cheek to her neck, sucking on her pulse. She couldn't think as he bit down. Not too hard, but enough to make her ache in all the right places.

"Cup her pussy. I bet she's wet for you right now."

Easton slid a hand between her thighs. Today she'd opted for a dress and it wasn't a revealing one, but feeling Easton's body against hers, she had no doubt it could certainly be mistaken as one.

He cupped her, and she hated her panties for

getting in the way. The only touch she wanted was from his fingers. The need curled deep inside her. He pushed the material out of the way, and he touched her clit.

He slid between her slit, moving down to find just how wet she was.

Liam lifted up her dress, and she glanced down to see Easton's hand on the inside of her panties.

To her, it was so very erotic.

When he sank down to his knees, she looked at Liam. "You don't have to do this."

"I want to," Easton said. "I've spent all day thinking about how good this pussy could taste, and I'm going to have a taste."

"What about Junior?" she asked.

Liam took a step back. "Now I'm on guard. You can have as much fun as you'd like. I've got you both. Remember that."

She gasped as Easton tore off her panties and stuffed them in his pocket. Next, his tongue slid between her thighs. She gripped the counter, hoping to hold herself up as he sucked and licked at her clit.

He spread her thighs open, and she took it in turns to watch Liam and Easton. Both men were incredible, and she didn't know how she'd gotten this lucky with having either man in her life.

Easton bit down on her clit, sliding three fingers inside her. He pulled them out, only to push them back, stroking over her anus. His other hand, he fucked her with, using two fingers to start, stretching her out to three. One of his fingers pushed against the puckered hole of her anus, and she gasped, sinking her teeth into her lip to contain the pleasure.

"Does it feel good?" Liam asked.

"Yes."

"Do you wish it was his cock in your pussy or

your ass?"

"I wish it was both of you," she said. "I don't want to choose between either of you."

Easton bit down on her clit. The sudden pain was almost too much, but he soothed it out with his tongue. She was so close, and she couldn't believe how fast she'd gotten to the edge.

Her orgasm hit hard, fast, and she wasn't able to contain the cry of pleasure she released as she came.

If she didn't have a grip on the counter, she would have fallen, but she also had Easton's hands on her body, doing the most dirty and wonderful things.

He brought her down from the peak and stood.

"That was what I've been wanting all day."

Easton pressed a kiss to her lips, and she smelled her cum on his face.

"I'm going to go and wash up for dinner." Easton left the kitchen. He stopped next to Liam, and she watched the exchange.

Neither of them spoke, but she saw something flicker between them before Easton finally turned and left the room.

"You want him, don't you?" she asked.

She didn't even know where the question had come from. It slipped off her lips with ease, and she watched as Liam, raised brow, smiled.

"Does that surprise you?"

"No. Don't hurt him. He's been through a lot." She didn't know everything Easton had gone through, but she also remembered the man from her past, and he'd have never ended up in rehab.

There were a lot of things in his life plaguing him, and she didn't want it to be her or Liam to be one of the causes of upset in his life.

"I've told you. I've got no desire to hurt him."

Liam moved closer to her.

She pushed down her skirt, and he tutted.

"You don't need to cover yourself for me. You know I love to see every single part of you." Liam grabbed the edge of her dress, pulling it most of the way up her body, exposing her pussy to him.

She gasped as he cupped her in much the same way Easton had.

"You loved having him on your pussy, didn't you?"

One of his fingers slid inside her, and she couldn't look away.

"Do you wish he was here right now?" she asked.

"Touching you." With her free hand, she cupped him through his pants. She felt how hard he was, and she smiled. "Does it turn you on, Liam, to want Easton?"

"You know it does. I'd love to have both of you naked, at my mercy, wanting me to fuck you both." He slammed two fingers inside her, and she cried out, needing more.

She couldn't believe how aroused she was still.

Easton had made her come, and with how Liam was touching her, he clearly wanted to as well.

There's no way she was going to be able to survive these two men, and yet, as he stroked her clit with his thumb, she knew she wouldn't have it any other way.

She'd fallen in love with Liam gradually. With Easton, she still remembered the way he'd made her feel all those years ago. The pain of his rejection was nothing more than a memory as he only served to highlight her own need for him. Easton had done everything he could to protect her, and rather than go and find him, to let him know what they'd created together, she'd left him alone. She didn't like the guilt as she questioned her past actions. She'd acted like a child. At least now, she had the chance to make it up to Easton.

"Let me hear you come, Scarlett. I want to hear every single moan and gasp."

She didn't know it was possible to come so soon after her first orgasm, but Liam's skills brought out a second orgasm that was far stronger than the last.

Liam silenced her cries, working her pussy, prolonging her pleasure until she couldn't stand anymore.

Only then, did he stand back and lick his fingers.

"You can share Easton whenever I'm not around. I want to hear every single little detail. You can't keep anything from me. I want to know how good it felt, what you did, and how you're going to show me later just how much you had fun." Liam kissed her hard. "How did your appointment go?"

"You expect me to be able to think clearly?" she asked, laughing.

Liam smirked. "I love to see you like this. Flushed, ready for sex. I could sink my dick inside you right now, and you'd be so wet, soft, and ready."

"You're both going to be the death of me."

Liam kissed her. "Not the death, the life and love of you. I'm going to go and wash up. Dinner smells amazing."

He left, and she was alone, with no panties, shaking, and with a very wet pussy because of two men.

How had her life gotten to this point?

****

By the weekend, Junior had decided to go and stay at a friend's house. It was the first time he'd done so in months. At first, Junior hadn't wanted to go because of Easton. When Easton convinced him it was fine for him to go and have fun, Junior had looked so happy.

The weekends without Junior were always rare, and Liam didn't have a problem with their son. He loved how close they all were as a family, even before Easton's arrival. This was their first weekend together without Junior's presence, since he'd agreed to share Scarlett.

Their sharing had moved at a much slower pace than Liam would have liked, but they also had to be careful with Junior.

This weekend, such a glorious one, they no longer had to find an excuse for Easton to be in their room. They had the entire house to themselves, and that meant every single room was now available.

Liam glanced out over the garden and saw Scarlett sunbathing outside. She wore a bikini, one he'd bought for her last year.

She had on her sunglasses and was soaking up all the heat waves. She looked calm, happy, and Liam intended to keep them both very busy.

Leaving the bedroom, he kept the windows open, and walked downstairs to find Easton standing in the doorway to the garden, watching.

"You know you can go out there and offer to put some sunblock on her," Liam said.

Easton jumped, clearly lost in his own thoughts. "I didn't hear you arrive."

"Clearly," Liam said, laughing.

"You find this funny."

"No. I find your nervousness endearing."

"How can you do it?" Easton asked.

Liam took a deep breath. He didn't want to waste this weekend with conflict, but maybe he and Easton could finally clear whatever bullshit was going on between them.

"How can I do what exactly?" he asked.

"Share her?" Easton stepped away from the door.

"I don't get it. She's everything, and if I had her, I wouldn't be sharing her."

"You do have her, and I don't see you fighting to keep her."

This time Easton laughed, and it was verging on hysterical. "You think I don't see what you're doing here?" Easton asked. "I do. I know what you're doing."

"What am I doing?"

"I know you're wealthy, and you like to take care of your own. You think I don't know power when I see it? I try to steal her away, you'd tear my company and my friends apart, and not because of money either. There's something about you."

Liam sighed. "You see, this is the problem you have. You're too focused on what it is I'd do, to ask yourself why you're not really fighting for her."

"I've just told you."

He shook his head. "No, like always you've given me a lame ass excuse. Your company. If your company meant so much to you, you wouldn't be risking this kind of conversation to piss me off. I could snap up your company like that, but more importantly, I could end you." He clicked his fingers. "When it comes to love, there is no common sense. We all act so fucking stupid for love. It's why it's so sought after and they make billions off it in movies. Love is what everyone craves, and when they have it, they're so scared to lose it. The reason you're not trying to take Scarlett, is because you don't want to." Easton snorted. "Because even though you wish to deny it and make up some fucked-up reason, you like to share her. You like her being between us." Liam took a step closer. Easton didn't move. "And there is a part of you that's a little curious about me as well."

"You don't have a clue what you're talking about."

"Oh, I do. Believe me, I do." Liam smirked. "You think I don't know desire when I see it? Yearning. Curiosity. For some time now, you've been a little curious about me, what it would feel like to kiss me." Easton looked a little pale, but he wasn't going to back down. "I best you've even wondered what it would be like to have all of the attention and focus on you." Liam didn't touch him, didn't reach out, but he was so close.

The shock on Easton's face let him know he was spot on.

"Did I interrupt something?" Scarlett asked.

"No, I'm just letting Easton know the truth, and he clearly doesn't understand."

"What did you hear?" Easton asked.

He hadn't lashed out or tried to take a step back. Liam considered that a plus.

Clearly, he'd either shocked him into submission, or he'd gotten to the truth of the matter.

Easton wanted him, but he didn't know why or how much.

"I heard enough." Scarlett closed the door behind her. She'd taken off her sunglasses, and she had them closed in her fist. "Is it true? Do you want Liam and me to … be with you?"

"To fuck him, Scarlett. To show him all the attention," Liam said.

"No, this is messed up," Easton said.

Scarlett closed the distance, putting a finger against his lips. "You don't have to deny what you want. We're all adults here. Remember, privacy is key, and we won't share any details."

Easton chest rose and fell as he took deep breaths. He looked close to having a panic attack. Liam waited, but he didn't back away.

"Yes."

The word was whispered, almost in defeat, and then Easton shook his head, and was about to take a step back. The pain, the broken man before him, it broke Liam's heart, and he wasn't going to let him get away.

Grabbing his face, Liam pulled him close and slammed his lips down on his.

This wasn't how he'd imagined their first kiss going, but it was enough to start.

At first, Easton was tense in his arms, not moving, shocked. Liam didn't stop. He kissed him hard and deep, and after a few seconds, Easton shyly responded.

His touch was unsure, nervous, and so sexy.

Moving him back, Liam pressed him against the wall, aware of Scarlett right beside them, waiting.

Breaking from the kiss, he stared at Easton, who had his eyes closed.

His lips looked a little swollen.

Finally, he opened his eyes, and the heat shining back at him replaced whatever fear he must be feeling.

"Isn't it your turn to kiss me?" he asked, turning to look at Scarlett.

Chapter Thirteen

Easton had never kissed a man before.

He'd never craved a man's touch.

He'd never wanted another man near him.

Liam was so different in everything.

Not only did he want him, but he didn't want the kiss to stop. His lips, they tingled, and something felt so incredibly right and good.

One glance at Scar, and he wanted her.

"Kiss me," he said.

She stepped toward him, only a few steps. Liam gave them enough room for her to fit between them. His love of this woman, it hadn't diminished in the years they'd been apart. It had only gotten stronger, and now, he didn't have to hide it.

She ran her hands up his chest to wrap around his neck. When her lips touched his, he sank his fingers into her hair, holding her head, as he kissed her.

Liam stroked his fingers through his hair, trailing down his back. The touch was intimate, sexy, and it helped to reassure Easton.

Breaking from the kiss, he looked at both of them, unsure.

"I don't know what I want anymore," he said. "I've never been with a man. I'm so sorry, Scar."

"Why are you sorry?" she asked. "You think I don't want to see this? You and Liam together." She ran her hands up and down his chest, smiling. "I think it's going to be so sexy watching the two of you, and I'll get to join in as well. This isn't about just us, Easton. This is about you as well. You're not here out of some obligation, are you?"

"No, of course not."

"Then why can't we do this?" she asked, smiling. "Have a weekend where today is all about you, and tomorrow, is all about him." She reached out, putting a hand on Liam's chest.

Between them, she was the buffer, the one to bind them together.

"I'm game. Especially if I get my own day."

Scar chuckled. "You're already thinking of all the dirty things you can make us do."

"At least until Junior comes home."

"Until Junior," she said, turning back to Easton. "What do you think?"

"One day of being in charge. Of having the two of you devoted to me?"

"Yes. So long as it doesn't involve hurting ourselves or each other," Liam said.

"I wouldn't do that," Easton said. "I have no wish to cause pain to anyone."

"Yeah, well, it needs to be warned about. You can't go around trusting everyone, believe me," Liam said.

Easton stared at the other man, wondering what exactly that meant. He would find out, someway.

He wanted to know all of Liam's secrets. Not to bring the man down, just to be there for him. Did Liam have anyone who took care of him? Who watched out for him? Easton had a feeling for a long time, Liam spent most of his life taking care of others, and even though he admired that, he wanted to be the one to take care of him, to offer some comfort back.

"Do you want to do this?" she asked.

"We won't force you, Liam said.

"Yes, I want to do this." He stroked Scar's cheek and turned to look at Liam. "I don't know what this is. I don't get it. I've never been attracted to any other men in my life. I've always been with women." He looked toward Scar. "I don't want to hurt you."

"You're not going to. We couldn't expect our time apart to be celibate. Not with the way we ended things." She kissed him.

"We can all learn together," Liam said. "I won't push you, Easton. Whatever you want to do, it's all on you. Not me. You're in charge, until tomorrow, or the stroke of midnight." Liam winked at him, and he laughed.

"Then we're at your mercy," Easton said.

"What would you like?" Scar asked.

"I'd like Liam to kiss me again." He touched his lips. "I need to know something."

Scar stepped to the side, and Liam stood in front of him.

His heart pounded, and his cock was so painfully hard. He'd never been in this position before.

"Liam's a good kisser," Scar said. "No one would ever be able to resist him."

He couldn't look away, and as Liam pressed his body against him, Easton felt the evidence of Liam's arousal.

"You feel what you do to me? What you and Scarlett do to me?" Liam asked.

"Yes."

"I want this, and more than that, I want *you* to want this," he said.

"I do," Easton said.

Scar took his hand; she was so close.

When Liam kissed him, Scar was there, grounding him.

Easton was terrified, aroused, curious, desperate, hungry, wanting more. So much more.

Liam slid his tongue across his lips, and Easton

moaned, opening his mouth for him to plunder inside. When he did, Easton let go of Scar's hand and cupped Liam's face, deepening the kiss. Wanting more from him.

There was a hunger inside him that had awakened, and now he needed these two more than anything.

"We've got you, Easton," Scar said. "You don't ever have to be alone again."

He didn't know how long he would have these two, but he would hold them for as long as possible.

"Let's take this to the bedroom," he said.

"I thought you'd never ask." Liam took the lead, picking Scar up on his way past. Easton followed behind them. His excitement grew with every single passing step. He wanted this more than anything.

His dick was so hard, and he wanted Liam as much as he did Scar. Again, where the fuck was this need coming from? No man had ever appealed to him in his life, and yet, here he was, craving Liam's hands on his body.

They entered their room, and Liam dropped Scar on the bed. She gave a quick bounce, a laugh, and her gaze moved to his. "You want to join me?" she asked.

"No, I want Liam to undress me and you to get naked so I can watch."

Scar knelt on the bed. The bikini didn't exactly hide anything, but he wanted her open, exposed, and ready to take his cock when he was ready.

"Are you going to order me?" Liam asked. His brow raised, hands on his hips. He looked formidable, but Easton saw the clear outline of his dick pressed against his pants. Liam wasn't a small man, and from the times he'd seen Liam with Scar, the man was packing some serious length.

Now, he didn't want to just look at Liam. Easton wanted to touch.

"Undress me, Mr. Knight."

"I like you all commanding," Liam said, approaching him.

Easton expected him to be rough, but again, he was surprised. Liam didn't need to be rushed to do something he wanted.

Slowly, he ran his hands up his chest, and one by one, opened up the buttons on his shirt.

He stared into Liam's blue eyes, hypnotized by the sharpness of them as he pushed the shirt off his body.

Liam stroked his fingers down across his chest, and Scar moaned.

Staring across the room, he saw she was still in her bikini, but she was biting her lip, rubbing herself between her thighs.

"You like what you see?" Easton asked.

"Why wouldn't I? You both are so handsome."

"Just handsome?" Liam asked.

"You're both so much more than that," she said.

"Didn't he tell you to get naked?"

"I'm the one doing the ordering. Get naked, Scar. Let's see your body. It belongs to both of us." It felt so good saying those words.

She *did* belong to both of them.

The bikini bra was the first to go, those glorious fat tits of hers spilling out. They were more than a handful, and by the end of the night, he wanted them swinging in front of his face as he fucked her hard.

Liam took his attention away for a split second to sink to his knees. Seeing the powerful man kneeling before him had Easton's stomach twisting. It didn't feel right to see him like this, and yet, as he loosened his belt, it was exactly what he needed without even realizing it.

As Scar pushed her bikini bottoms down, Liam released Easton's aching dick. It was so hard it was at the point of pain.

He watched Liam wrap his fingers around the length, working up and down. The tip was already leaking copious amounts of pre-cum.

"Fuck."

"Do you like that?" Liam asked.

"Yes."

"I can make it feel even better."

Easton didn't know how he could do that, but he wasn't about to argue with the man.

Liam's lips went over the tip of his cock, and Easton cried out.

Looking over at Scar, she sat on the edge of the bed, watching.

"Spread your legs. Play with your pussy as you watch your husband suck my dick."

The pleasure was so intense.

Liam wasn't playing around. The man knew what he was doing, and Easton felt close to coming. He'd been with his share of women, and not since he was a young virgin boy had he come so quickly.

He closed his eyes and tried to think of anything, even Carla, to try to keep his orgasm from spilling out of the tip.

Nothing worked.

Liam took him to the back of his throat, and as the man gagged, he reached behind him, stroking over his anus, and it was all just too much for Easton.

Against his own wishes, he came and did so hard, spilling his cum deep into Liam's throat.

The man before him wasn't disgusted. He swallowed his cum down, moaning as he did. Easton didn't think he'd ever be sane again as he collapsed against the wall.

"Now, I think it's only fair I go and pleasure our woman," Liam said, licking his lips clean of the creamy cum.

Easton nodded. He'd wanted to be the one to make Scar come but for now, he would settle with watching her with Liam.

Finding the will to move, he walked over to Scar, and as Liam licked and sucked at her pussy, Easton cupped her face, turning her toward him, pressing his lips to hers, capturing every moan and scream Liam evoked.

These were all his.

Scar belonged to him, just as he was hers. He wasn't sure yet what this all meant with Liam, but he was willing to give this a shot.

As Scar came, he broke away from the kiss to watch. She shook in his arms until Liam finally let her go. He sat back with her cum on his chin.

Silence fell between them.

Scar pushed some hair off her face and smiled down at Liam. "You look happy with yourself."

"Two people in less than thirty minutes, I'd say that was a job well done," he said.

She burst out laughing. "I see you have a problem yourself." She turned to Easton. "Do you think we should take care of his need? You're the one in charge, Easton. You get to help him or we can leave him. What will it be?"

****

Easton demanded Liam get naked, and the moment he did, Scarlett's arousal heightened. Since Easton had come into her and Liam's life, and her relationship with her husband had grown, she had fantasized about these two men. Especially knowing Liam wanted to be in this kind of relationship. When he'd warned her of his intentions years ago, she had truly believed he would never find it, but now, with Easton, and even herself, she knew it was possible.

She stood beside Easton as Liam was ordered to lie down, and Easton wrapped an arm around her waist.

She noticed he shook just a little bit, and she tried to offer him comfort with her body. Resting her head against his, she waited for his instruction. This was Easton's show, not hers, and certainly not Liam's.

Waiting, standing beside him, her heart racing, she wanted to show both of her men how she felt and how good it could be with them. Junior would always be loved and taken care by all three of them, but they'd be able to find happiness with each other.

"I think you should go and suck his cock," Easton said.

She tilted her head back. "Whatever you demand."

Crawling onto the bed, Liam smiled at her, and she wrapped her fingers around his length.

Liam let out a moan.

"Do you think we'll be able to make him come as fast as he did us?" she asked.

"We will have to see." Easton watched them both.

She'd already started to notice how Easton would look at Liam. There was an attraction there, and she was surer than ever before that Easton wanted Liam.

The tip of Liam's cock leaked pre-cum, and she swiped her tongue across the tip, listening to him moan as she took him to the back of her throat. She gagged a little on the length before pulling up.

Easton moved up behind her and placed her into a position. His fingers traced over her spine, going to her ass cheeks and spreading them.

He teased her pussy, sliding two fingers inside her. She was still sensitive from her orgasm, so any touch to her clit seemed heightened to her.

As he strummed her clit, she closed her eyes and let go of Liam's cock, to use only her mouth, and to suck him in deeply, bobbing her head as he had taught her to do.

Easton pressed the tip of his cock to her entrance and with a grip on her hips, he slammed all the way to the hilt, making her jerk and release Liam's cock.

"Is he deep inside your pussy?"

"Yes."

"Does it feel good?"

"Yes."

"Suck his cock, Scar," Easton said. "I want to fuck you and see him come."

She had no choice but to hold onto Liam's cock and start to work him with her mouth, swallowing him down as Easton pounded her pussy.

He wasn't gentle, but she didn't need sweet tenderness. She just needed Easton. All of him, every single part of him, eradicating the past, making it only the two of them. She was totally drawn to these two men, and as Liam wrapped his fingers around her hair and began to take over, forcing his way into her throat, she relished his brand of control.

Liam would never hurt her.

Easton would never hurt her.

She'd finally found her freedom with these men, and she didn't want to let it go.

"Do you have any idea what you do to me?" Easton said. "I love this fucking pussy. I'm going to want to fuck her ass soon as well."

"She's never had a cock in her ass before."

Easton's fingers slid over the puckered hole of

her anus, and she gasped as he pressed forward just a little before pulling back.

He slickened up her asshole with his saliva and began to work his finger inside her. At first, it burned, almost as if it was too tight to accept him. He wasn't one to give up. Easton pressed his finger in deeper and began to pump the digit inside her ass as he fucked her at the same time.

Liam didn't let her stop in her ministrations with his cock, and she sucked him in deep.

"I'm so close," Liam said.

She glanced up his body as Easton added a second finger, spreading her ass. As she looked at Liam, he came hard, filling her mouth with his cum, and she swallowed every single drop, not letting a tiny bit leave her lips.

At the same time, Easton found his climax, filling her pussy as he did so.

When it was all over, she collapsed against Liam's legs, wrapping her arms around him, but she should have known better than for her men to be done with her.

Easton was still deep inside her, and he moved her off Liam, withdrawing his dick from her. She went to roll over, but Easton stopped her.

"I think the only way to get her ready to take a cock is to prepare this really pretty ass. Tell me you've got something," Easton said.

"I do. I've been preparing for this moment for a long time."

Liam got up and moved toward the closet. She watched him go to his side of the closet, pulling down a box. It was quite large, and as he opened it, she saw the abundance of anal plugs, dildos, and there were some chains as well.

"Are you into BDSM?" she asked.

Liam chuckled, holding up the chains. "Nah, I'm not into that. But I do like to play a whole lot." He winked at her. "I think she'd look rather sexy all tied up and at our mercy. What do you think?"

Easton laughed. "We'll be playing with them, but I was thinking of tying you up. What do you say?"

"So long as I can have my way with you. Moving on for the time being." Liam picked up a rather large-looking plug, but compared to the others, it was in fact small.

"You got any lube?" Easton asked.

"I'm a man who always comes prepared." In his other hand was a tube of lubrication.

"Good."

Liam opened up the anal plug. All of the sex toys he had were brand-new, and as he threw the trash into the bin, he opened up the lubrication.

"Here, hold this." Liam got Easton to hold the plug as he covered lubrication all over the toy.

Easton still held the plug as Liam got her ass nice and prepared to take it.

She couldn't believe her men were preparing her ass for one, or both of them.

Gritting her teeth, she felt the tip of the dildo, but Easton wasn't in a rush.

Liam moved beside her head, his face so close to hers. "I want to look into your eyes as he fills you. I've got a couple more dildos, and then when we take your ass, you're going to be ready for it."

She clenched her hand into a fist as Easton began to push it inside her. It was a little too tight, but at the same time, not enough. She wanted pleasure.

"Get her to her knees," Liam said.

"Why?"

"I'm going to lick her pussy."

Easton helped her to her knees, and she aware of the fact he'd come inside her. The excitement in Liam's eyes wasn't hard to miss.

Liam moved between her thighs, and his tongue licked across her slit, sliding across her clit, then down to fuck inside her.

She cried out, hungry, desperate, in need, and full as Easton worked the plug into her ass.

Liam's hands grabbed her hips and held her in place as he licked and sucked at her pussy. He was relentless, even as the plug filled her ass.

He didn't stop until she came, and as she did, she pressed her pussy against his face, needing all the pleasure.

She had a plug in her ass.

Two men, around her naked, and she collapsed to the bed, even as Liam came out from between her thighs, licking his chin.

"You want a taste?" Liam asked, looking at Easton.

She turned in time to watch her men kiss. It wasn't gentle.

It was two men clashing to get a taste and devouring each other.

Their cocks were hard, and both of them looked so sexy the way they were.

This weekend was going to be one of the best of her life. She just knew it.

****

Within one night, Scarlett's plug was changed a second time to the next size up. While Liam had Easton desperate and hungry for sex and attention, he didn't want to miss an opportunity with him.

Fucking Scarlett's ass would be a dream, and

sharing her with Easton was exactly what he wanted. He'd just need to make sure all next week, she rested, and he prepared her asshole again.

He rested on his elbow, staring down at his two people. Scarlett slept between them, and Easton snuggled up against her.

They both looked perfect together. He couldn't believe Easton had given her up for fear of what his father would do. At the same time, he couldn't judge Easton for his actions ten years ago. He was nothing more than a boy himself, and stepping up to his murderous father had to be hard and dangerous.

Liam had never met Easton's father, but tales of Nial's reputation had spread far and wide. Whenever it came to doing business with the Four Kings, he'd shied away from it.

"How long have you been awake?" Easton asked.

"A while."

"What time is it?"

"A little after five."

"Are you kidding me?" Easton groaned, quietly so as not to wake up their sleeping beauty. "Why are you awake so early?"

"Light sleeper and besides, this is my day." Liam winked. "I think I need to let Scarlett rest a little. You want some coffee?"

"Sure, I can have coffee. How do we not wake her?"

"She won't wake yet. After last night, we've got a couple of hours." Liam slid out of the bed, grabbed a pair of sweatpants, and left the room.

Scarlett would join them when she was awake, and he really needed a cup of coffee. He'd also get started on making her breakfast. He'd seen her press tofu the day before, and she was probably going to have the tofu scramble she'd begun to love.

Easton joined him in the kitchen, and he wasn't naked, which was a shame.

Liam filled the coffee machine and got two cups ready.

"I figured you'd be the kind of guy who had a live-in cook and staff."

"Why?"

"I don't know. I used to have a bunch of cleaning crews and a personal relationship with the local takeout place near my apartment. I guess you'd be the same."

"I was, many years ago when I made my fortune."

"You didn't inherit your fortune, did you?"

"No. I earned my fortune after I got out of the military."

"So why don't you have a whole host of people working for you?"

"I do. I know how to protect my family. I've also got people at Junior's school as well to make sure he's always safe. I won't have anything happen to my family. When I want to take Scarlett and Junior away, I arrange for the home, villa, cabin, or apartment to be cleaned before our arrival, and then I'll take care of everything else."

"Again, you don't keep anyone around."

"Privacy. I've been burned one too many times by people claiming to have my best interests at heart. The truth is, the only people who have my best interests are myself, Scarlett, Junior, and I'm hoping you. Lies are told in magazines. Stories made more exaggerated by their need to sell more papers. It's a ridiculous makeup as far as I'm concerned and not one I wish to help further. It's why we as a family clean. It's why Scarlett does most of the cooking." He poured out a cup of coffee, handing it to Easton. "Or you get the rare occasion like today where I cook for Scarlett."

He grabbed the tofu out of the fridge along with some peppers and tomatoes.

"What the fuck are you making?"

"Tofu scramble. Scarlett likes to experiment with it, and well, I don't mind it either. Junior loves it, and it was one of the first recipes he came into the kitchen to cook."

"I missed so much," Easton said.

"I wasn't there for the early stuff. Scarlett has pictures though. She tried to take as many pictures as possible to document it all."

"She does?"

"Yeah. I'm pretty sure she wouldn't mind sharing them with you. At least let you look at them. You're spending more time here."

"Yeah. I'd like that. Can I ask you something?"

"Sure."

"How would you feel if I started to clean this place?"

"You don't like it? Is it too messy?"

"No, no. It's just, after I got out of rehab for my drinking addiction, I, erm, I started to clean. It became something to help me heal. I will totally understand if you wouldn't want that."

"Did you used to clean your apartment all the time?" Liam asked.

"Yeah, it's the most spotless place in my life, and well, now that I've moved here, I've been cleaning my bedroom with a washcloth. I like to do something with my hands."

Liam chuckled. "You can clean. I'll show you where all the cleaning stuff is. Scarlett would probably appreciate the help. She loves to clean and to keep on top of stuff like this."

"Yeah." Easton let out a chuckle.

"There's something else?"

"Yes."

"You don't want to talk about it?"

"I don't want you to think I'm a crazy person."

"Too late. I already think you're crazy."

"Ha, ha. Okay. What do you think to people who see … ghosts of their past? You know they're made up, but you have full conversations with them. Even hang out with them."

This time Liam frowned. "You're seeing ghosts?"

"I don't mean ghosts. I know she's not there, and I've not seen her in a little while."

Liam paused in crumbling the tofu. "You're going to need to help me out."

He listened as Easton told him about seeing Carla. One of the girls from his past. Liam was aware of the story. It had been in the news not too long ago after his father's arrest.

"I'm not crazy. I promise you. I'm not."

"I didn't say you were, but I think we need to take you to the hospital."

"I know she's not there."

Liam washed his hands. "Easton, no one should be seeing or talking to beings that are dead."

"He's right," Scarlett said, surprising the two of them. "We need to go and get you looked at. We can't have you hurt."

"I'm not hurt. I'm telling you."

"Please, Easton, for us," Scarlett said, moving toward him. "You shouldn't be seeing Carla."

"She's not here. She's … not here."

Liam saw the panic in her eyes, not to mention his own concerns. "The fact she has been with you, I'm worried. I'm not going to take no for an answer. We're having you checked out today."

He grabbed his cell phone and started to call the hospital he'd donated and they promised him no matter his demands or needs, they'd take care of him.

"What about your day?" Easton asked. "I didn't tell you this for us all to run to the hospital."

"I'm glad you did tell me. I'm not going to take my day knowing there could be something wrong." It could be Easton's way of dealing and creating an imaginary friend of some kind. But it could also be more sinister, and he wasn't going to lose Easton to his own selfish needs when it came to him.

Stepping out of the kitchen, he arranged an appointment with the head doctor, and once he got back into the kitchen, he saw how pale Easton was.

"I'm fine."

"We've already got an appointment. Get dressed. I will take you to him, even if I have to knock you out and take you myself."

"Junior's coming home today."

"And Junior will have other nights away with his friends. Do you really think I give a fuck about my day when your health is by far more important to me?"

"Please, Easton, stop fighting this."

"I know you're not used to having people take care of you like this, but I'm not someone who can walk away or pretend I didn't hear something. I'm here for you. We're both here for you, and we're not going to let you go. Not like this. Not ever. Do you understand?"

Easton nodded.

"Go and get dressed."

Liam went to follow him, and Scarlett held his hand. "Is he going to be okay?"

"He will be. I won't let anything happen to him."

He kissed Scarlett on the lips and followed Easton upstairs.

There was no way he was going to let the other man run, and he had a feeling Easton would run the first chance he got.

Not on his watch.

On his watch, Easton was going to stick around a whole long time.

Easton didn't talk to him as they got dressed, or on the way to the hospital.

Liam and Scarlett sat with him as he explained everything to the doctor.

"I know she's not real. I know she doesn't exist."

"I think it's best we do some tests, just to make sure you're okay, Easton."

"This is crazy and a waste of time."

"Not to us, it's not," Liam said.

He and Scarlett couldn't wait with Easton, and so had no choice but to sit in the waiting room.

Liam wasn't exactly a patient man. Not with something like this.

"What if there's something wrong with him?" she asked.

Tears were in her eyes, and Liam knelt before her, not caring that people watched them.

"If he is, we'll be here to help him fight it." He gripped her thighs, offering her as much comfort as possible.

"Do you like him?" she asked.

She whispered the words, and he nodded.

"I do too."

"I know you do. It's one of the reasons why I know this with all of us will work. I can see us being happy for a really long time."

"Do you think we should call his friends?"

"The rest of the Four Kings?" Liam asked.

"It might help him, in case there is something more serious."

He had no desire to bring the Four Kings to Easton's side, but he also didn't want to be accused of trying to hurt the competition in any way.

"I'll make the call," he said.

"I can make it if you want."

"No, I can." He kissed her head, and left the room, putting the call through to Axton.

He didn't have anything against the Four Kings, but none of them had noticed Easton talking to himself, and because of that, Liam wasn't happy to be working with them in any way.

Chapter Fourteen

Over eleven years ago

She'd had sex.

Scarlett had been with a guy.

Glancing over at Easton, she saw the blanket they had used to try to warm them from the cold was pushed down to his waist.

He looked so handsome, especially in sleep.

All she wanted to do was to take care of him. She'd noticed the sadness in his gaze from the first moment he arrived, and it had made her want to ward off all the pain and fear he might be feeling.

Reaching out, she pushed some hair off his forehead.

He didn't wake, but he did move a little, getting comfortable.

This wasn't supposed to happen between them. She'd come to camp to help out. The final hold of a childhood she would no longer have when she got home. Her family already had a fiancé lined up for her.

A life she didn't want. A man she hated. She had no control, and she'd been told many times a woman like her didn't have a chance at her own life. She had to learn to do as she was told and to deal with the consequences of it.

She hated it, every single day.

"I think I'm falling in love with you," she said.

Easton wasn't like any of the men in her life. They didn't try to make her smile or to figure out what was bothering her. Easton did all of those things. He gave her a voice, a reason, an opinion, and he even cared about it as well.

In the twenty-first century, her parents believed

her place was to look pretty. They had told her there would be a makeover, and the woman she was now would no longer be acceptable in their house.

Her long hair would go. Her clothes would be changed. She would have no choice but to look like the proper wife of the man they had picked.

Tears filled her eyes as she thought about what she was going to have to do. Unless she admitted the truth to Easton and took a chance with him.

She didn't want to spoil their summer. The time they had together was so short, and even though he'd made love to her, taken her cherry that had been meant for someone else, she couldn't let him go.

Soon, she'd tell him what she felt, but until then, she was going to enjoy him.

****

Present day

Easton hated waiting for anything. Tests pissed him off. Gossiping nurses irritated him. Bossy doctors made him want to throat-punch them.

When he pulled off the pulse ox monitor on his finger, the machine beeped, and he ignored it.

He'd been forced to wear one of the hospital gowns, and again, he wasn't fucking impressed with that either.

There was a lot of stuff he was angry about.

He shouldn't have told Liam, and even though the doctor had said he should have, Easton didn't want to believe them. Climbing off the bed, he was going to find Liam and give that son of a bitch a piece of his mind.

Their weekend had been ruined because of his fucking mouth.

As he was walking out of the room, the nurse rushed toward him, but he ignored her. He wanted to throw her across the room so she would back the fuck off. Instead, she followed him out to the waiting room, where he spotted Liam and Scarlett, but also Axton, Taylor, Karson, and Romeo. There were a couple of other people, who he figured were waiting for their own loved ones.

Liam spotted him first and got to his feet, drawing the others' attention.

He didn't know why the fuck his friends were there. He didn't need them in the hospital.

"What are you doing here?" he asked.

"I called them, just in case."

"Do you think I'm going to die?" Easton wasn't impressed.

"Sir, I need you to go back to your room," the nurse said.

"I'm here because I fucking want to be. Back off, now!" Easton yelled the words, becoming the center of attention.

"I'm thinking we should take this to your room," Liam said.

He was tempted to scream at all of them, but if it wasn't for the no cell phone rule, he'd have been filmed screaming at the nurse.

Turning on his heel, he entered his room but refused to sit down.

"You can't have this many people in his bedroom," the nurse said.

"You either let them in or I swear I will have your job so fucking fast you wish you kept your mouth shut," Easton said.

His anger had hit an all-time high. He was livid and looking for anyone to take it out on. The nurse was merely an easy target for him, and one he really fucking needed.

"Easton?" Scarlett said.

"I don't care right now what the fuck you think of me." The door had been shut, and they now had privacy. "Why are you here?" He turned toward Axton, Karson, and Romeo.

"We're your friends."

"So. I'm fine."

"Liam said there could be something wrong with you. We were worried," Axton said.

"You didn't tell them?"

"It wasn't my place. I just figured they were your friends."

This time, Easton laughed. "Oh, yes, we're friends, aren't we? The Four fucking Kings. The empire. All of it. We're supposed to be the best fucking friends, but you know what, I don't want you here."

"You don't mean that," Taylor said.

His nostrils flared. "You know why I'm here?" he asked.

"You might be sick."

"Since I got to rehab and even getting out of it, I've been having conversations with Carla. You know, the dead girlfriend from years ago. The one I knocked up, before I knocked up her." He pointed toward Scar. "The girl who I pretended to care about."

"Easton, you loved her."

"No! I fucking didn't. I didn't love her. She was nothing more than a bet that I used to amuse myself, and it backfired. I cared about her. I won't deny that, but I didn't fucking love her. God!" He let out a scream. Behind all of them, Carla was smiling at him.

He ran a hand down his face.

This wasn't going to happen. He couldn't believe this was happening to him.

"I fell in love with you," he said, turning to Scar. "I thought you were poor. I thought you couldn't handle my family. I didn't want to lose you, Scar. I never did. I had no idea we'd made a baby. A really precious baby. A sweet, beautiful son. I wish I had known him back then. There are so many mistakes."

The door to the room opened, and Easton growled for them to get out.

"I need to prep Mr. Long for surgery, now."

Nurses, security staff suddenly rushed into the hospital room, and all Easton saw was Scar. Liam was in control. He would take care of him. Easton had no doubt. There was a look of panic on her face, and the world began to slow down a little.

He had a tumor.

They needed to operate.

Carla wasn't a figment of his operation.

He was in fact, very sick.

****

Liam sat in the waiting room. He'd put a call to the parents Junior was staying with and asked to keep him one more night, and they were more than happy to keep him. Scar held him. They were sitting in the family room.

Axton, Taylor, Karson, and Romeo were also in the room. They hadn't spoken since they had been led to this room nearly thirty minutes ago.

The doctor he'd called was the best neurosurgeon in the country, but even still, he'd warned him of potential complications, and they were prepping for surgery in such a short time.

Liam had already done the math. Easton had been seeing Carla for over eight months, maybe even longer.

Eight months of a tumor growing inside his head.

Eight months of … being alone.

He'd had no idea Easton was suffering, and he couldn't stand to know, he'd been the one to fuck up.

"What if he doesn't make it?" Scarlett said. "I've never seen him look so angry and so afraid." She sniffled. "Oh, my God, I kept his son away from him, and he … he might die. I never got to apologize for not sharing Junior with him. What am I going to do? I'm such a horrible person."

"He'll make it," Liam said. "And when he does, you can apologize to him. You can make it right with him. Easton is ours, and we'll take care of him. We'll love him, and we're going to make sure he gets through this."

"How do you know?"

"I just do. Easton's a fighter. He won't let this get in the way."

"This is about more than being a fighter. This isn't an illness he can kill with antibiotics," Romeo said. "They're operating on his brain."

"I know that. You think he needs us in here, arguing?"

"I don't know what the fuck he needs," Romeo said.

"He needs us all to be strong, and if none of you can provide that and just want to blame each other, you see the door. Walk yourselves right out of it," Liam said.

All three men got to their feet. The violence was clear, and Liam was more than happy to go toe to toe with all of them.

"Liam," Scarlett said.

He stepped up to them, refusing to back down, refusing to let them push the blame of this shit on anyone.

"You want to start with me, let's do this. I got no problem with all three of you. You think you can use your numbers against me, fucking try it with me, boys. You're nothing more than a bunch of kids playing at being men."

"You don't know what we've been through."

"I've got a fucking idea, and you know what, still don't give a fuck," Liam said. "Your friend has been seeing a dead woman." Taylor sobbed. "Shut the fuck up. I don't care which one of these people you're marrying. Your friend died ten years ago, and none of them were responsible for it. If you were any kind of woman, you'd get over your shit and stop making others guilty for moving on with their lives."

"Don't talk to my wife like that," Axton said.

"It looks to me someone's got to put a little perspective on life. Your woman is living in the past. You want to move on, you got to let her know you're not going to keep being sorry for being happy. People die, and we have no choice but to move on. It's the fact of life, and if you want to stay in the past, you're going to end up fucking lost." He glared at Axton and turned his attention to Taylor. "You're going to kill that man in there. I get you're sad about what happened, but Easton is a living, breathing person and he has a right to be happy."

"I don't need to sit here and take this," Taylor said. "I've offered him support. I don't want to see him suffer."

"But you do it every single day you bring up the past. You think I don't see how broken he is by the time he comes home?" Liam asked.

"Liam?" Scarlett said, grabbing his hand.

"These people are supposed to be his friends, and they're not helping him. They're crushing him. He could die on that operating table today. What do you think about that?" he asked. He looked at Axton, then Romeo, before going to Karson.

All of Easton's friends look scared.

"I'm going home," Taylor said, stepping toward the door. Liam watched her. He knew about this woman's revenge plot. From the moment he found out about Easton, he'd made it his business to know every single little detail of the people in front of him right now. "Are you coming, Axton?" she asked.

"You're going to sit down and wait to hear about my friend," Axton said.

"Excuse me?"

Axton stood up and turned to face Taylor. The woman looked shocked to see Axton standing up for himself.

"You heard me. One of my best friends could die tonight, and you think I'm going to go home and wait. You're wrong. If you love me, if your promises meant anything, you'll sit down, take what has been said, and deal with it."

"And if I leave?"

"Then you get the fuck out and you leave Carla. It's as simple as that. I love you, Taylor, I will die for you. I've put up with all kinds of bullshit, but I'm not walking out of this room."

Liam took a seat as Scarlett wrapped herself around him. He felt her shaking, and he had to keep it together.

This weekend, he'd been so close to getting what he wanted. He'd seen the attraction in Easton's eyes, and knew it was only time he needed to finally have the family he always craved.

Taylor, much to Liam's shock, sat beside Axton. She was tense and looked like she wanted to be anywhere but at the hospital.

He didn't blame her.

"It's good Easton has you looking out for him," Axton said. "He's been so secretive about everything.

How is he getting on with his child? His son."

"We've not gotten a chance to meet him yet," Karson said.

"He's part of Easton, and we'd love to meet him," Romeo said.

Scarlett sniffled. "When all of this is over and if Easton makes it through."

"He will," Liam said.

"We don't know that."

"I'm not going to sit in this room and think for a second he's not going to make it through. He's a strong man, and I know he's going to make it. He has to survive."

He didn't see any other way for this.

Easton had to survive.

Scarlett held him a little tighter. "When Easton pulls through, we'll have lunch or dinner. Or something. We'll make it work."

These men were Easton's family, and Liam was more than willing to accept them, but they would only be allowed to come around if they had Easton's best interests at heart.

He took care of his family, and he used any means at his disposal to do it.

****

Why was the time going by so fucking slowly?

Scarlett stared at the clock and couldn't be sure if it wasn't broken or something. It was like time was finally mocking her. Making her wait for the scariest outcome of her life. What if Easton didn't make it? What would she tell her son? How would she be able to handle that kind of pain?

"I need to go and get myself a drink and some fresh air," she said.

Liam got to his feet. "I'll come with you."

"No. I'll grab you a coffee. You don't need to come with me." She patted Liam's hands, trying to give him comfort. It felt impossible to do.

She knew he always went out of his way to comfort her, and no matter what she tried, she would be failing him.

"Black, no sugar," he said.

"Okay."

Without a look toward the others in the room, she made her way out of the tension-filled space and went straight to the vending machine near the elevators. She didn't want to drink coffee, and without seeing some of the labels on the cans of soda, she opted for bottled water.

Bending down, she twisted off the cap and pressed the button for the elevator. Stepping inside, she closed her eyes, resting her head back against the wall.

"Hold the elevator," Taylor said.

Opening her eyes, Scarlett watched as Taylor stepped onto the elevator.

"You're leaving?"

"No. I just needed some air. Axton should be here for his best friend, and I'm here for him." Taylor stood in the corner of the elevator. "I'm sorry you had to see that."

"I don't care," she said.

"You've known Easton a long time?"

"No," Scarlett said.

"You have a son."

"We do."

Taylor smiled. "Forgive me, but how do you have a son and not know each other?"

Scarlett stared at Taylor and Liam's words kept playing in her mind. She didn't owe this woman an explanation.

"I know enough about Easton to know he's hurt by something that happened in the past," she said. "Why are you so determined to live in it?"

"Carla was my best friend. She was pregnant when she died, with Easton's child."

"Did he kill her?" Scarlett asked. "I saw the papers about the incident. The exposé on his dad. Easton had nothing to blame."

"He should never have been near her. If he'd just left her alone, she would be alive now."

Scarlett stared at the woman and shook her head. "You don't know that."

"The only reason Nial Long killed her was because of Easton."

"So you're going to blame him all of his life?"

Taylor gritted her teeth and looked away. "You don't understand."

"No, *you* don't understand. I get you're upset about your friend dying and I'm truly sorry for what happened. I really am, but holding it against Easton is just fucking wrong." Scarlett couldn't believe she was having this conversation. "He didn't kill her. He didn't put his hands on her, so why should *he* be the one to suffer all the time for it? You don't think he's suffered enough? He's not been plagued by guilt. He's in that hospital bed because he was seeing his dead girlfriend and didn't tell anyone about it."

"Good! He deserves it."

Scarlett reacted. She didn't even know what was happening. One minute she was standing in her corner holding the bottle of water. The next moment, she had her hands wrapped around Taylor's throat, pressing her up against the corner of the elevator.

"You want to keep on blaming him, go ahead, but I can tell you now, you toxic little bitch, I will make sure you, your husband, and your fucking kid struggle for the rest of your natural born lives. Do you hear me? You can keep thinking this is all Easton's fault, but your friend, she didn't have to fuck him, did she? They both made a choice, and you are just as much to blame as everyone else. If you had been a good enough friend, she'd have come to you when she started sleeping with him, telling you all of her secrets. Instead, she chose to keep it a secret from you. What does that tell you, huh? It tells me you weren't as good a friend as you think you were. And if you had that big of a beef with what happened, you wouldn't be fucking one of the Four Kings. I bet they knew what had happened and who did it. You've got to make a choice in this world, darling, and it's not chasing after Easton. Otherwise, I, no one else, *I*, will end you." She let go of Taylor, grabbed her bottle of water, and left the elevator.

Without looking back, she took the stairs back up to the waiting room.

Liam was waiting. Romeo and Karson were still there.

"Are you okay?" he asked.

She spoke quietly to him so he was the only to hear what happened.

"Is it wrong to think of how hot you are right now?"

"I didn't mean to get so angry."

"She threatened our man. We can't have that, and all you can do is whatever it takes to save and protect our family. I'll have your back always. I'm not having anyone throwing Easton's past back at him."

Scarlett held onto Liam as Axton and Taylor returned. The couple were holding each other, and it looked like Taylor had been crying.

Good. She had no desire to end Taylor's

suffering. She didn't even want to think about how long Easton had been suffering at her hands.

This was the first time since being married to Liam she'd been violent. The emotions of the day were starting to finally get to her. Pushing some hair off her face, she let out a breath.

Just as she closed her eyes, she heard the door to the waiting room open. The doctor was there to finally tell them all what had happened. She couldn't lose Easton. They had a fucked-up past, but that didn't mean she wanted to see him dead. Not ever. They were given a second chance at this. She wanted to apologize and to make up for all the lost time they had missed.

A second chance to be together and she didn't want to fall apart. Liam held her hand, but it was all too much.

Would Easton live or die? He *had* to live. She had so much to make up for.

Chapter Fifteen

Over eleven years ago
This was it.
He had to go home.
Had to go back and face reality, which really fucking sucked. His friends would be waiting for him.
Easton glanced down at the time, waiting for Scarlett to arrive. The last couple of weeks with her had been the best time of his life. He hadn't loved Carla, and it made her death even worse. She'd been a fling, a bit of fun. He cared about her, but after knowing Scarlett, he didn't love her.
He loved Scarlett. His Scar. His world.
They had come together and it had been the most magical time of his life, and now, he was going to have to walk away even if it killed him.
As he ran his fingers through his hair, rain fell down around the gazebo.
Part of him hoped she wouldn't turn up. She'd stay gone as just a summer camp fling, but there was no stopping Scarlett when she started.
She ran toward the gazebo, all in white. It made this so much harder.
He couldn't run with her.
His father would find him, and when he did, Scarlett would die. He'd underestimated Nial before, and he wasn't going to do it again.
"Hey," she said, wrapping her arms around him. "I'm so sorry. A couple of the kids didn't want to leave, and I had to see them off. You know how it is." She kissed his lips. She'd already admitted she loved him the other day. He'd told her the same thing. He loved her and wanted to be with her for the rest of their lives.

Now, he had to break her heart, shatter it, destroy every single trace of love he had for her.

"What's wrong?" Scarlett asked, letting him go.

He'd not held her back, not given her any indication he wanted to even hold her.

He stood, hand in his pocket, waiting for the right moment.

Even as he smirked at her, he knew he was screaming inside, begging for her to not listen to him. to know he never wanted to hurt her.

"I'm heading home tomorrow," he said.

"Easton?"

"Look, I hate to do this, but it was a summer fling, you know. Not really anything for us to think that was great and wonderful. It was sex. Granted, really great, and fucking amazing sex, but that was all it was."

"You told me you loved me."

"Yeah, about that, I kind of lied. I'm sorry. You were this persistent bitch in fucking heat all along, and you know, a guy can only handle so much."

"You're lying. Why are you lying? Why are you being this way?"

He sighed. "You're really going to make me spell it out for you, aren't you, babe? It was just sex. I wanted a nice wet cunt, and the only way of getting it, was by telling you what you needed to hear. Come on, Scarlett. You really think I would be happy with a lifetime with you? With being with a woman so fucking poor it was sickening. I can't stand the thought of having to wake up every single day, staring at you. I mean, no offense, you're not the prettiest girl in the world now, are you? I can do way better. By the time I get home, I will have a whore on my face and another sucking my cock. If I wanted, I'd probably even get one licking my asshole if I so desired. You are nothing. You will never be nothing to me. I lied. I don't love you. I never could, but I have to say, it was really nice popping that cherry. It'll be a good old story I tell to the Four Kings when I get home. Give them something to beat one out. The next guy you fuck, tell him he's welcome. I broke you in."

Tears had filled her eyes and started to fall down her cheeks. Easton's heart was breaking inside and he wanted to take it all back, but he had to shatter her. "You want another round for the road? I mean, it's a little boring all the moaning and gasping, but I can give you a pity fuck."

Scarlett didn't say anything.
She spun on her heel and left.
It was over.
Done.
Finished.
His heart shattered in a way he'd never known it could.

He had broken the only good thing in his life, and it made him no better than his father.

****

Present day

"You know I can take care of myself," Easton said as Scar brought him a cup of coffee, his morning tofu scramble, and his laptop.

He'd gotten out of the hospital four months ago, and even the doctors had said he was fit and ready for work. His surgery had been a success. When he first woke up, he'd panicked as he'd not been able to speak, but the doctor had said they had to give it a couple of days. Liam and Scar were by his side every single step of the way.

Axton, Karson, and Romeo were there as well. They were his lifeline, and he'd seen the worry his friends had.

Liam had allowed them to stop by for dinner during his recovery. Junior had talked to them constantly, and his friends adored his kid.

"I know you can take care of yourself, but while I'm willing to do all of this, you should allow me. I want to take care of you."

He wrapped his arm around her, hearing her cry out as he made her straddle his lap. "Like this? I think you should take care of another problem I have." His hard cock pressed against her core.

"Wait, there's something I really need to say to you, and I don't want you to get me all excited, and I need to tell you."

The last thing Easton wanted to do was to stop, but from the desperate look in Scar's eyes, he knew he had to.

"What is it?"

"I'm sorry."

"You're sorry? For what?"

"For keeping our son away from you. From not realizing sooner that there was a reason you broke it off with me. I was so hurt and blind by my own feelings, I didn't even think as to why you'd want to break up with me. We were so close during camp, and I thought you had faked it, but I know now you were only trying to protect me. I was wrong keeping our son a secret and not giving you the chance to be a father with him."

"Scar, I don't need to hear this."

"You do."

"I don't know if I'd have been a good father then."

"I don't care. You're still his dad, and I was still in the wrong. Can you ever forgive me?"

"Yes, you're forgiven." Now, he wanted to get back to what he truly wanted. He could draw out Scar's apology, make her suffer, but he didn't want to. They had already lost enough, and he wasn't willing to lose any more time with her.

So far, they hadn't shared her again yet. Liam had said he expected a day of his own soon, but that hadn't happened. Liam had been busy working, and with Junior at home, having that kind of fun seemed in the distant future.

He wanted his woman and his man back.

Yes, he'd started to see Liam as his.

"You really think you're ready for me?"

"Come on, Scar, you know I am."

"And I can't wait to see it," Liam said, leaning against the door.

Liam was in a suit, the jacket open as he had a hand on his hip, resting against the door. Easton's cock hardened more, if that was even possible.

"I thought you were at work," Easton said.

"I was, and now I'm home. Junior's going to his friend's tonight, and I spoke to your doctor. You're all well and can handle anything. So, I was thinking I can have my day. What do you guys think?"

"I thought the guys were coming over?" Scar said.

"I canceled them. The way I see it, I got a day to myself, and I intend to take it."

"You didn't have to worry about me," Easton said.

"You had a tumor, stupid man. Of course I had to worry about you. Taking care of you, Scarlett, and Junior is my life. I will do it because I know I'm the only one good enough at the task. Now, Scarlett, get your clothes off. It's such a waste to hide that body of yours."

She stood up, and Easton wanted her back to straddling his waist.

"Easton, come here," Liam said.

Getting to his feet, he walked toward Liam. Anticipation filled the room as Liam grabbed him, slammed him against the wall, and kissed him, hard.

It was the kind of kiss that left Easton breathless, and he was so fucking happy. Arousal flooded his body, and he heard Scar moan.

"She likes it, you know. She likes the two of us fucking, making out. It gets her all hot and horny, doesn't it?" Liam asked.

"Yes." She was already naked, and her fingers slid between her thighs, stroking her clit.

Easton dropped to his knees in front of Liam. "I've been thinking about doing something, and I want to do it now."

"I'm not going to stop you," Liam said.

He'd been wanting to do this for some time, especially after watching Liam fuck Scar. They hadn't stopped sharing a bed, and he'd wake up to see Liam watching him.

He loved this couple. No doubt about it.

Liam had found a way into his heart, his thoughts, his mind, and now, he was totally consumed by this man. His level of care was addictive, and he couldn't give it up, not even if he wanted to.

"Do you have any idea what you both do to me?" Liam asked.

Easton pulled out the long length of his cock, feeling how firm and stiff it was in his hands. "I've got a rough idea." The tip was already soaked in pre-cum, and he licked that right off, moaning as he did. He'd licked Scar's pussy when she had some of Liam's cum inside her, and he'd known he'd wanted to do this.

This wasn't about being with just any man. This was about being with Liam.

The man was impossible to deny, and above all else, he didn't want to.

Taking the head of his dick into his mouth, he swallowed him down, moaning as he sank the dick to the hilt, almost gagging on it.

"Oh, fuck!" Liam growled, and he gripped the back of Easton's head.

Staring up his body, he looked into Liam's blue eyes as the man fucked his mouth, shoving his length to the back of his throat, repeatedly.

It felt so good, so incredible, and he didn't want it to stop.

Just as suddenly as he sucked Liam's cock, he was pulled off him.

"No, I don't want to come in that pretty mouth of yours. I want us to come inside Scarlett, together."

Easton turned his gaze toward the woman in question. She was sitting on the sofa, fingers between her thighs, and he saw how wet she was from where he knelt.

"Are you ready to take two of us?" Liam asked.

They had talked about the both of them being inside her, often. Easton had been thinking about the moment they'd both be joined.

"Yes."

"Should we take this upstairs to the bedroom?" Easton asked.

"No. I think we're more than okay to do this here." Liam moved to the sofa and picked Scar up.

She let out a little scream and a giggle as she was settled between Liam's spread thighs.

Of the three of them, Scar was the only one completely naked, and Easton liked it.

"Easton, if you check my briefcase, you'll see some lube. Grab it."

"Why do you have lube in your briefcase?" he

asked.

"You never know when the situation would call for it, and I'm thinking it calls for it right now."

Grabbing the briefcase, Easton flicked the locks open, and sure enough, a nice fresh tube waited.

He picked it up, closed the case, and turned in time to watch as Liam took Scarlett's pussy. He slid her down his length, and he wondered what it would feel like to have Liam inside him. He'd never been with a man before and for the most part, he didn't think he'd ever want to, but with Liam, it was different. It was always so different.

"Does that feel good?" Liam asked.

Scar cried out as Liam held her hips and began to slam his length up within her as he pulled her down.

It looked amazing, and Easton wanted to be part of it.

Stepping toward them, he opened the tube of lube and released himself from his sweatpants.

Wrapping his fingers around the length of his dick, he spread copious amounts of lube. His hands shook a little from the excitement, but he got control of himself. He wasn't going to spoil this moment.

Reaching between them, he stroked Scar's clit, hearing her gasp and go a little wild on Liam's cock. Kissing her neck, he used the tube to smear a good amount of lube on her anus and his free hand, after dropping the tube onto the floor.

Pressing the clear gel into her anus, he heard her cries and loved them. This was what he wanted, and he was desperate to be inside her.

Liam stopped his thrusts just as Easton got her close to the peak, but not allowing her to go over it.

"You're so beautiful," Liam said. "It's time. You tell us if you want him to stop."

"I won't."

"It's up to you. You're the one in charge."

"I know."

"Please, I want to feel you."

Easton ran his dick across her puckered hole. Liam had both of her ass cheeks in her hand and had spread her open, making it a lot easier for him to slide in. She was so tight, and at first that ring of muscles kept him out, but after stroking her clit, she started to open to him, and he pushed the first couple of inches inside her, before going as deep as he possibly could go.

They both paused for just a moment, allowing them to get accustomed to what was happening.

Easton held her hip, with his other hand between her thighs. He felt Liam's cock, the pulse of it, and, staring over Scar's shoulder, this felt so right.

"I want to keep you both," he said.

"You will always keep us," Liam said.

Easton would hold them both to that promise.

Liam was the first to move, sliding out until only the tip of him was inside her, and as he plunged back Easton pulled out. They set up a pace. It was slow at first, giving Scar a chance to get used to the feel of both of them inside her.

He'd never felt more connected to anyone than he did these two in this very moment. He didn't want to let either of them go.

As the pleasure mounted, there was no denying the need rushing through them. The instant hit of need and there was no waiting. He and Liam fucked Scar, drawing her to not one, but two orgasms before they found their own within her body.

****

Scarlett sat at the table, watching her men as they played cards. Her body was on fire, and it had been a couple of days since Liam finally got his chance to be with the two of them.

Easton was well.

He was back to fitness and should probably go to work at some point, but she found it impossible to let him go.

She wanted to take care of both of her men. Liam and Easton, they belonged to her just as she belonged to them.

Junior had decided to have another sleepover, and with the holidays coming up soon, he wouldn't be leaving the house all that much. He always had so much to say about his time with his friends. She missed him all the time, but like tonight, she was really pleased.

"You know," she said, entering the room. She ran the tips of her fingers up the length of the table as she walked toward her men. "I've been thinking about something."

"What's that?" Liam asked.

She smiled.

If anyone would know what she was about to ask, it would be Liam. The man knew her better than she knew herself.

"Well, you guys have enjoyed your fun, but what about me?"

"I know what's happening here," Liam said.

"And me," Easton said. He sat back, this hint of a smile on his face as he watched her.

This man, he reminded her of the boy she had known during camp. The one who wasn't trying to break her heart and shatter her, but the man who had cared about her, even as he was afraid.

"She's horny," Liam said. "Her nipples are nice and hard, and this house is warm."

"And she's wearing a pair of shorts, so easy to

see, and if you look closely, you'll see she's not wearing any panties, and her arousal is very clear."

Her cheeks heated under their assessment.

"You know, I could go and help myself," she said. "I know where your secret drawer is."

"It's not so secret, and you don't have to go anywhere. You just have to tell me what you want, and you know I'll give it to you," Liam said.

"Yes, but what I want will require Easton as well, if he's willing."

"I'm willing."

She held her hands up. "I wouldn't be so quick to jump in and offer your services. I may ask for something you're not willing to give."

"There's nothing you can ask that I wouldn't be willing to give." Easton stood up, and she saw the outline of his cock pressing against the front of his pants. "And whatever you want, I will do it for you."

"I want you to fuck Liam while I watch and then, later on, while you're fucking me, I want him to have you." She nibbled her lip. She hadn't wanted to speak the words aloud, but now they were out, there was no reason for her men not to know the truth. She wasn't going to hide from them. From either of them. This could make or break what they had.

The men were happy playing with each other, but she had a bigger stake in this game.

She wanted both Easton and Liam.

The dream Liam had told her about when they first got married, was so close, she could taste it. But she had to give these men a nudge in the right direction. Otherwise, it would all be lost, and she couldn't have that.

Easton looked at Liam, and she saw the men exchanging glances.

They didn't speak.

"Do you two have your own special language I don't know about?" She forced a laugh, hoping it didn't sound nervous.

"It's called guy talk," Easton said. "I'm curious if Liam's attraction to me extends to wanting to fuck me and have me inside him. I'm game for anything. I've been wondering when these games would move along."

She tried to hold her wince. "Easton, this is not a game."

"I know it's not a game. I want to fuck Liam. I have no idea why I want to, but when I look at him, I want to kiss him, fuck him, make him mine. I want to do everything to him to keep him close."

"I've got no problem with that," Liam said.

He got up, and she watched her men as they kissed. She loved watching this as they both lost themselves in each other.

"Bedroom," Scarlett said.

She rushed out of the room and went straight to the bedroom. She'd already set the scene. There were rose petals on the floor and on the bed. It had taken her some time to pick the petals off the flowers, and she'd gotten a thorn or two for her trouble, which was no real trouble at all.

Removing her clothes, she lay on the bed, waiting for her men.

She didn't have to wait long as they entered the room. Liam was first and Easton following up the rear.

"Do you want to do the honors of getting us naked?" Liam asked.

"Nah, I'm more than happy to watch the two of you." This wasn't just about her. She wanted to watch her men lose themselves in each other and to know she'd been the one to help bring them together. It was what she wanted more than anything.

Easton was the first to react, grabbing Liam's shirt and pulling it over his head. Getting naked was more like a wrestle with each other, but it didn't detract from Scarlett's overall need for both men.

They were sexy, and each one had their own set of ink as well.

By the time they were naked, Liam took the lead, pressing Easton to the bed. She watched him wrap his fingers around the length and working his cock. Pre-cum was already leaking out of Easton, and Liam went to his knees, wrapping his lips around the length. Easton groaned, sinking his fingers into Liam's hair, holding him in place as he fucked his mouth.

It looked so good, and she moved her own fingers between her thighs and began to stroke her clit.

The pleasure hit her, and she slowed down her movements as Easton pulled Liam's mouth off his dick, in much the same way Liam had.

"Are you ready for me?" Easton asked.

"Yes." Liam moved to the bed, and he grabbed her, pulling her down so her pussy was at the right level with his mouth. "I'm going to have you come all over my face as he fucks my ass."

"You are so dirty."

"And you love me for it."

"Yes, I do."

She stared over his shoulder at Easton, who already had a condom on and was spreading lube all over his shaft. Easton had felt amazing in her ass, and Liam had also taken her ass. She loved these men so damn much.

The past could suck it.

She knew the truth.

Easton, even when they were teenagers, had tried

to protect her. She had forgiven him. It hadn't been easy, but seeing Taylor, witnessing that woman's spiteful grief, she knew she didn't want to turn out that way. The only way to get over what happened was to accept, and move on. She didn't want to spend her life hating someone who really didn't deserve it.

She loved Easton just as she loved Liam. They were her men, the loves of her life, and she would do whatever was necessary to keep them both.

Liam stopped licking her pussy as Easton started to slide inside him.

"How does he feel?" Scarlett asked.

"Amazing. I don't want him to stop."

"You heard the man."

Easton gripped Liam's hips and worked his cock inside him.

Only when Easton was deep enough did Liam go back to licking her pussy.

She wanted to watch, but with the pleasure on both of their faces, and her own orgasm so close, she found it hard to focus on all senses.

Easton leaned over, biting onto Liam's neck as he fucked his ass, working his length in and out of him.

"He's going to come soon," Easton said. "His cock is so big, and he's going to make a mess of the bedding."

"I don't care."

Easton had become her cleaning helper. They spent many hours a day cleaning. That time would come to a close when he had to go back to work, but it had reminded her just how much she loved spending time with him.

Liam would help in his own way when he was home, bringing them coffee. In the time it had taken Easton to recover from his surgery, they had become a family. A united unit. A collective.

Together.

As one.

This was what she had wanted for so long.

And she hadn't even realized she craved it.

She came hard on Liam's face, and he wasn't willing to give her just one but he brought her to a second orgasm, quickly, and she screamed his name.

Easton grunted next, and she watched the pleasure rush over his face as he did so.

Liam was the last to come, and as he did, he collapsed to the bed.

"I like when you're in charge," Liam said.

She chuckled. "You do, do you?"

"Yes, that was incredible."

He kissed her stomach, and for the first time, it made her wonder where all of this was going with them.

The past pushed to one side, was there any chance of a future for all of them?

****

Liam finished up the call he'd just made and sat back.

It was done.

Finished.

Glancing across his office at Easton, he smiled. Scarlett was out with Junior to pick something up for Easton's birthday. He had a small celebration in mind, and even though Easton was at home, he'd kept him confined to his office so they could throw a special party for him.

It wasn't every day a guy turned thirty, and Easton had tried to keep it from him.

"You look happy."

"I am." Liam grabbed his stress ball, tossing it into the air and catching it. "I love it when all my little plans come together in a nice neat tidy bow without me even having to lift a finger. Especially now."

"And a plan has come together that you didn't instigate."

"Yes, in a way. Scarlett's family will no longer be an issue. Their company has gone completely bust. Every single small holding, company, haven, you name it, it is gone. They are also being investigated for tax fraud. *That* little detail is not on me. I don't break those kinds of laws. I was surprised actually they were able to keep their finances that close to their chests."

"Wait, hold on a minute. You have completely destroyed her family, but it will all come down to their link to tax fraud?"

"Bingo. I didn't even need to make the final call to cut them down. It would appear when I started the process for them hemorrhaging money, they made mistakes, and in doing so exposed their underhand dealings. Not to mention lawsuits filed against them. Turn on the news. You'll see."

Easton got to his feet, and Liam always paid careful attention to the other man. The doctor had warned him of potential dangers like loss of balance and memory for him to watch out for. It could show signs of either another tumor, or possible clot, or something else. Liam was going to take care of his family.

The next person on his list to deal with, now that Scarlett's family was taken care of, was Easton's father, Nial Long.

Easton turned the television on to breaking news about Scarlett's family. Liam smirked as he watched it all unfold once again. This was going to be such a fun day.

"You're not worried in case Scar sees this and wants you to stop it."

"No can do, and when I asked Scarlett about going after her family, she was more than happy for me to do so. Believe me, she is not worried about this." They had tossed her out of their life, and it was up to him to put her back together.

Glancing down the length of Easton's body, a need stirred within him, which he tried to hide.

Easton whistled. "I'm so glad I'm not them, and I won't ever be on your bad side."

"You can try it being on my bad side, I don't mind." Liam winked.

"I know that look."

"What look?"

"It's the look you're giving me that says you want to fuck me," Easton said.

"Am I? What do you think to that?"

"It doesn't matter what I think. Is it true? Do you want to fuck me?" Easton folded his arms, waiting.

Liam smirked. "You know, you look sexier when you give me the smoldering look."

"You think this is a smoldering look?"

"Yeah, it's the one that is telling me to fuck you without saying the words aloud." Liam glanced down his body. "And I want to fuck you so badly, Easton."

He'd been holding back with this man, giving him the chance to get comfortable with their situation. There's no way he wanted to rush this, not if he wanted it to last.

"Then come and get me."

Liam stood up, and without a second invitation, he grabbed Easton, slamming him against the wall and kissing him hard. Running his hands down his body, Liam took his fill of this man.

"That feels so fucking good," Easton said.

"It's going to get better." Popping the button on

his jeans, he slid down the zipper, and pushed his hand inside, cupping his dick. Running his hand up and down the length, he watched as Easton threw his head back, moaning as he did so. "I love your cock, Easton. I love how it feels inside me, and I love watching you with Scarlett. Taking her pussy."

"She's got the best pussy."

"And she belongs to us." He kissed Easton again and this time, moved him so he was near the sofa.

Breaking from the kiss, he turned Easton so he was bent over the sofa.

Pushing his jeans to the floor, he spread Easton's ass cheeks, admiring his asshole that was going to belong to him.

"Stay there." He barked out the instruction, not wanting his man to move. He had lubrication hidden all over the house for an occasion like this. Returning to Easton, he unscrewed the cap on the lube, and squirted a generous amount over his anus before going to his cock. He got himself nice and slick and ready. "I'm going to take it nice and easy." He put the tip right at the puckered hole, and slowly began to push inside.

Easton groaned, but Liam hadn't gone too far.

"Play with yourself," Liam said.

As Liam sank inside his tight little ass, Easton followed instruction and worked his cock. Full to the hilt, Liam gripped Easton's hips, and basked for a few seconds without moving, without doing anything.

This man, he'd been waiting for him for a lifetime.

Pulling out slowly, Liam took his sweet time. At first, he made love to Easton's ass, letting him become accustomed to the feel of his cock.

Only when he couldn't stand to wait anymore, did he speed up his thrusts, powering into his ass at a pace that had them both growling.

Liam waited for Easton to come first before he found his own release. Seconds passed, and they both filled the air with their panting.

"I had no idea it would be like that. It felt incredible."

"You can't have any other man," Liam said. "No one else will ever make you feel that way." He was being entirely selfish, and he didn't care.

"There will never be anyone else but you, Liam. Don't worry. I know you've staked your claim." Easton glanced over his shoulder, smirking. "We better get cleaned up before Junior and Scar walk in and well, you know."

"Scarlett would be aroused. Junior would need therapy."

"Yep."

Liam leaned down and kissed Easton. "Thank you."

"You don't have to thank me. I love being here with you." Easton gripped the back of Liam's head, holding him in place. "I'll stay for as long as you'll have me."

"How about forever?" Liam asked.

He knew without asking Scarlett that his wife wanted to keep Easton. They both did. They loved him, and he was going to make sure to take care of both of them.

Chapter Sixteen

One week later

Easton couldn't believe he'd decided to visit his father. The letter had been stuffed in his jacket, and he'd forgotten about it until yesterday when he'd grabbed said jacket to leave the house.

He lived with Liam and Scar full-time now, and he'd put his apartment on the market. At the end of a busy day, he had no desire to go to a cold, empty apartment. His life, the people he loved and cared about, were in one large house.

A house he was finding felt more and more like home than his childhood one.

Sitting in a room, waiting to hear from his father, Easton knew it was a mistake even before seeing the man who'd raised him.

One look at Nial Long, and Easton was shocked. He no longer looked like a scary monster of a man who could ruin his life.

Nial Long looked old. Old and full of cruelty.

He was pushed down into the metal chair, and Easton picked up the phone.

Nial glared at him as he picked up the other side.

"What the fuck brings you here?" Nial asked.

"Hello, Dad," he said. "If I recall I got your letter demanding my presence."

"I sent that months ago."

"Been having some personal problems."

"What the fuck is that supposed to mean?" Nial asked.

Easton looked at his father. For so long he'd been afraid of this man, had spent so many hours in the day scared of what it actually meant to be his son. Worry, fear, anger, all of it had combined throughout his childhood, and it hadn't dissipated until the past year.

"I had a tumor," he said. Staring at his father, Easton felt all of the worry ebb away. This man meant nothing to him. He wasn't even worth the time to take talking to him right now.

"A tumor?"

"Yes. In my head." Easton stayed perfectly still as he watched the man he called father. He didn't even know why he was here.

"You okay?" Nial asked.

"Yes."

"Then let's move on, you fucking pussy. I want out of this damn cell, and you're going to help me do it. I've been talking to some of the other guys, and there was no proof. I can…" Easton listened as Nial listed all the reasons for a jury to overrule the conviction of him being in prison.

Easton didn't interrupt. He listened.

No one looked at them.

They were all interested in their own lives. His father was a murderer, crook, asshole, and rotten from the inside out. There was no redeemable quality in him.

"Well, what do you think?"

"I have a son," he said.

"What?" Nial asked.

"I have an eleven-year-old son. He'll be twelve soon, and the past year I've gotten to know him." Easton smiled. "You know, after you killed Carla, I honestly thought I would never father children. It turns out, I did at camp. The place I was sent to. I met a girl there. The most amazing, beautiful woman, and we fell in love, but I pushed her away. Now I have her back, and I'm not going to let her go. I've got a son who loves me, and I now know I'll never be a bad father to him. I know what a bad father does to your soul. How it shatters a part of yourself and you can never get it back. I will never be the kind of man you are. I don't want to be. I'm not going to help you, Nial. You deserve to be here, and I'm not going to be the person who helps you get away with what you did." Easton put the phone back on the cradle as Nial began to spew anger and hatred toward him.

He was done.

It was finished.

Getting to his feet, he went to the door, and the guards let him out. He didn't stop walking until he got to his car. Climbing inside, he sat for several minutes just watching the prison.

That place housed his father, and it was the best place for him to be.

Easton expected his hands to shake, but they didn't. He was ready for this. His father would no longer touch him or hurt him. He wouldn't carry the guilt around with him for a moment longer.

Turning over the ignition, he drove home. Not to the city, but to his, Liam, and Scar's home, where his son was waiting for him.

He guided the car through traffic, taking his time so he wasn't in any kind of serious accident.

When he arrived home, he saw Liam's car parked in the driveway.

It had been on the tip of his tongue to tell his father that not only was he in a relationship with Scar, but also a man. A very powerful man who could crush him like the bug he was.

Shaking off those thoughts, he climbed out of the car, and as he made his way up the steps, Liam was already there, waiting for him.

"You okay?" Liam asked.

Staring up at the large, imposing man, Easton felt

a flood of heat and shame rush through his body. "I went to see my dad today."

"You did?"

"Yes."

"How do you feel?"

"Like shit because I didn't tell you or anyone else I was going."

Liam stepped down toward him, cupping his cheek. To anyone else, they were just two friends sharing a moment. To Easton, it meant so much more.

"What is it?" Liam asked.

"My father killed my ex-girlfriend who I had knocked up. He's in prison for a whole lot of other shit, but he killed a woman I cared about."

"What did he want?" Liam asked.

"He wanted me to help get him out by discrediting Paul. He's the guy who testified and saw him dump the body in the lake back home. Carla's buried there."

"She's the girl you imagined," Liam said.

It wasn't a question.

"You've got to stop feeling this guilt, Easton. You didn't kill her."

"But I did. I know everyone is pissed off at Taylor for being angry at me, but she's right. I did kill her because I didn't leave her alone."

"No. You didn't push her. You were willing to leave everything you'd ever known to be with her. I know you, Easton. You told me the entire truth, and I believe you. You're not capable of murder. You're too good to ever do that."

"But I was relieved. When she died, I felt like I'd dodged a bullet."

"So? You were eighteen. Your father had spent your entire life hurting you. You weren't ready, but if

Carla was still alive today, you wouldn't have been at camp. You wouldn't have had Junior, and you wouldn't be here now with me. You know why?"

"Why?"

"You'd be with Carla and your children. You are a good guy. You would have done the right thing, regardless of your own happiness. That has to mean something. No matter what your father says or does, *you* are a good man. An honorable one, and you should never doubt who you are because when I look at you, I know you're a great man. One who shouldn't have to justify his life for others. Only you should matter. Only you should care." Liam pressed his head to Easton's.

The closeness helped to take the pain away. Liam spoke so much sense to him, but he loved it when he was like this, and held him.

The pain slowly filtered away until there was nothing left.

"Now, Scarlett's got dinner on the table. You're home, and Junior's excited to show you his science experiment."

"Can I confess something?" Easton asked.

"Yes, of course. You can tell me anything, and I will protect you."

Easton had no doubt the man before him would do whatever it took to protect and love him. Liam was the man who protected those he loved, and Easton vowed to do the same for him. To always look out for him, no matter what.

"I hate science and I think my son is a nerd, but I love him so much for it."

Liam burst out laughing. "Yeah, your son is a nerd, that is right." Liam brushed his lips against his. "Let's go in and party. It'll be fun."

Holding Liam's hand, Easton walked into the

house, and sure enough, his nerdy little son had conducted a science experiment and Easton wouldn't have him any other way.

****

Scarlett closed the cardboard moving box with the last of Easton's things from the bedroom. They had put off packing up his apartment for a long time, and she didn't really know why, but now they had started, there was no stopping it. Putting her hand on the lid of the box, she sighed.

She never thought there would be a time she was so happy she thought she would burst.

This day, it was magical.

Knowing Easton was willing to move in with them meant everything to her. There was no guarantee he'd stick around though.

He slept in her bed every single night, and made love with her and Liam. She had watched her two men together as well, but there was no other commitment.

"That box ready?" Romeo asked, entering the bedroom.

Axton, Romeo, and Karson had offered to help them move Easton into their home.

There hadn't been any conversation about what it meant for Easton or his relationships with other women.

"Yeah. It's all done."

"I cannot believe he's doing this, you know," Romeo said, reaching for the box. "I always imagined Easton would stay a bachelor forever."

"He can still do what he wants. His life is still his own."

"I'm not stupid," Romeo said. "You should stop treating me like I am. I see the way you and Liam look at Easton. The love between you all."

"You're mistaken," Scarlett said.

"I'm not. Some may not see it, but I'm glad he's been able to find not just one person who loves him, but two. All of his life, Easton has been seeking love. He doesn't know he's been doing it. I think it's why he was so easily smitten with Carla. She took his shit and still smiled at him afterward." Romeo looked so sad. "I thought I was going to lose him after what happened to Carla. We sent him to camp because he just wasn't dealing like the rest of us were. Why would he? We'd not been with the victim. We'd not gotten to know her and put a baby inside her."

"What's your point?"

"When Easton came back, we all knew something had happened, but we figured it was closure on Carla. It wasn't. He'd met you, and once again, he had to give something up he loved. Carla was ripped from him, and the chance of any kind of happiness. With you, he pushed you away. I don't know the exact nature of your relationship. What I'm saying is, take care of our guy, love him. He deserves to be loved and to have everything his heart desires. Please."

Tears filled her eyes, and she had to look away and wipe her face to stop them from falling.

"I don't know what you're talking about, but I can promise you, Liam and I, we only want the best for him. Easton deserves a chance to have a clean slate, and unfortunately, one of you isn't exactly giving it to him." She looked past Romeo into the other room. Taylor had her daughter on her hip.

She didn't look threatening and there was a smile on her lips, but Scarlett wasn't convinced. The woman had made her feelings known within the hospital, and whenever she was around, Scarlett would keep an eye on her so she didn't hurt Easton.

"Yes. It would seem the pain is still there for her.

We all know that. Axton, he can deal with her."

"Really?" Scarlett asked. "Because if she thinks she can hurt his future, she will have to deal with me. She's a brand-new mother, but I've been one for eleven years now. I know how to protect my family, and Easton, he's my family."

"He's all of our family," Romeo said. "We're a fucked-up bunch. I'll give you that." Romeo hauled the box out of the bedroom.

Scarlett sat down on the edge of the bed. The mattress was bare, and Easton had told them there wasn't any furniture he wanted to take.

It wasn't lost on her the lack of possessions he had. For a rich man, he had a few items of clothing and jewelry, nothing of any real value to him that he wanted to take. He'd not set down roots. The only true enjoyment she saw he had was in cleaning. His cleaning closet was packed with clothes, polish, buckets, bags, and everything a cleaner would need.

Easton had it in abundance.

Seeing his supplies had made her smile.

Now, she felt gutted.

In the past eleven, nearly twelve years, he'd not found anyone else to share his life with or who had shown him how to live properly.

"You okay?" Liam asked, entering the room.

"Yeah, I'm fine," she said, standing up.

She stepped toward him, wrapping her arms around him. "This doesn't look like someone who is okay."

"I'm fine, or I will be when we get him back home. I just can't help but feel like he's missed so much, and I know I'm the one to blame for that."

"Guilt, life, it has a way of knocking you down and making you fight every single last breath you take."

Liam kissed her head.

"Life fucking sucks," she said. She closed her eyes while resting her head against his chest.

"We'll take care of him. We'll help him find roots, settle down, and we will make sure he's happy. It's what we do."

Scarlett opened her eyes, and tilted her head back. "Have you found it?"

Liam smirked. "Yes. I have."

"Do you even know what I'm talking about?"

"I know what you're talking about, and yes, I found it. I'm going to keep it as well. What about you? Will you be happy if I keep it?"

"You're speaking in riddles."

"Riddles you know."

Scarlett smiled. "Yes, I'd be happy if you kept it and you never let it go. I don't know how I got so lucky to be with a man like you, but I'm so glad I did. I'm so glad I went to that interview and met you."

Liam stroked his fingers down her back. "My only regret is I didn't fall for you sooner. We could have had more time together."

"We will. With Easton and with Junior. I can't believe that stuck, you know."

"What?"

"Junior. One day you mentioned it, and we all just started following."

"It's because, my dear sweet, sexy wife, I know what's best, and everyone around me knows that I know best."

"I know what you did to my parents and their company," Scarlett said.

She'd not spoken to Liam about it. She had seen the news.

"I didn't know of their tax fraud and evasion," he

said. "I simply helped them to grow desperate. Are you pissed at me?"

Scarlett ran her hands up and down his arms, thinking about her father. The words he'd spewed her way.

"You think we're going to allow you to raise a bastard child? You're nothing more than a common whore. A slut who spread her legs for the first man that would offer you a smile. You are not my daughter, and your spawn will never know the life you had. Get out of my house because I have you locked away for trespassing, you fucking whore."

Her mother had said near enough the same thing.

Her family, the ones who were supposed to love and protect her, had cast her out in her time of need.

"No. I'm not. Does that make me a bad person?"

"No. It doesn't. You're a good person." Liam kissed her. "And together, we'll protect Easton. We'll make sure he knows love and happiness again. I promise you."

"You guys ready?" Easton asked, coming to the room.

"Are you sure you're ready for this?" Liam asked. "I want you to not regret this."

"I won't regret it. This is what I want, and I know it's to spend the rest of my life doing what I want to do. It's not being alone here."

It was good enough for her for now.

"Come on, let's go home." She grabbed Easton's hand and Liam's, walking with them, side by side toward the elevator.

****

Liam rarely took a vacation. He wasn't the kind of guy who needed to be away from his home. However, after Easton moved in with them, and Junior's term ended, it was only fair to take his family to a remote island.

He called ahead to make sure supplies were ready and he had the house completely cleaned, and as they arrived, it did truly feel like home.

Easton grabbed Junior and took him to the beach, while Scarlett did all the unpacking. For Liam, he simply watched his family.

It wasn't complete just yet, but he intended to make those changes while he was on the island.

Sipping a bottle of water, he watched as Junior and Easton built sandcastles together.

Scarlett, finished, came out and made up a smoothie for them all.

"They look so happy together," she said. "I never thought my life could get any more exciting and happy."

"And now?"

"And now, I'm happy. I'm excited, and I look forward to the future. I'm not wanting to rush into anything, but I'm happy." Scarlett pressed the blender on, and it whizzed to life. Once it was finished making some fruity goodness, she poured it into four glasses. "Are you going to tell him?"

"Not yet. I don't want him to be upset."

"The man spent his entire childhood being hurt by the man. I think you should tell him."

"Tell me what?" Easton asked, walking in. "Our little boy wants a drink, and I see you've already beaten me to it."

"I always know what my men want," Scarlett said.

"So, what do you have to tell me?" Easton took his glass, taking a sip.

"It's about your father," Liam said.

He'd learned the news that very morning, and

well, he didn't want to cancel the trip and have Easton dealing with all the bullshit.

"What about him?" Easton asked.

"Have you heard from him recently?" Liam asked.

"No. I told you when I last went to see him, he wanted me to find a way of getting him out of jail. I told him no, and he got pissed. The end."

"He's died," Liam said.

He watched Easton. The other man's eyes went wide.

"He died?"

Scarlett took the smoothie from him. "Are you okay?"

"Yeah, yeah, I'm fine. Do Axton and the others know?"

"No."

"I think I should tell them. They have a right to know," Easton said.

Liam moved toward and helped Easton into a chair.

This wasn't exactly how he imagined Easton reacting. He'd expected more tears, anger, pain.

Easton just sat, and his mouth was slightly open in shock.

"Are you okay?"

"I'm relieved," he said. "I'm fucking relieved my dad is dead. Is that wrong? What happened?"

"He picked a fight with another inmate who had a shiv. He stabbed him in the jugular, and he bled out within seconds," Liam said.

"Wow, you know, I'm not surprised."

"I'm so sorry, Easton," Scarlett said.

"I'm not. I'm fucking glad. He was a monster. He was the reason for so much pain and suffering. With him dead, I know he'll never hurt our son, or any children we may have."

"Any children?" Scarlett asked.

Easton turned to Scarlett.

"I love you," he said. "I should have said it all those years ago, but I was too much of a fucking coward to stand up for what I wanted, and that is all on me. There's no getting away from the mistakes I made. My fear stopped me telling you the truth. It held me back, and I didn't get to marry you, or watch my son come into this world. I missed his first steps, and I don't blame you for not seeking me out. I wasn't a good man, but I want to be. I want to be the best for you, for Junior." Easton turned to look at him. "And for you, Liam. I love both of you. I don't know how the fuck it happened, but it did. Call me crazy, but I love the both of you. I've been thinking about this for a long time, and I want us to make it work. I know I can never marry you, but in here." He put a hand over his heart. "I am married. I will make the vows to love, honor, cherish, obey, and to be whatever you need me to be. I've never felt or been more in love than I have with you guys."

Okay, now Liam was taken aback. He'd expected to have to nudge them both into this step.

"I love you too. So much," Scarlett said. "I know it's crazy for us all, but I want us to make this work. I know we can, with Junior, with each other." She turned toward him. "What do you think?"

Liam smiled. "You think I'm going to turn down what I've been wanting for a long time? I didn't see it being like this, but this is perfect."

"Liam, I've got one thing to ask you, and then I'll never bring this up."

"Go on."

"Did you have anything to do with my father's

death?" Easton asked.

Liam smiled. "No. I didn't. I'm not lying. I told you before. I don't make it a habit of breaking the law, and if I do, it's not something that will get me thrown away. Believe me, I know how to cover my tracks. I didn't arrange to have your father killed. I was planning to make his life uncomfortable and looking into his past deeds to get him put in a more secure and locked-down prison, but his death means I don't have to look into that. Shame. I really wanted to see the look on his face when he was locked in a cell for a longer time with the key thrown away."

Easton grabbed his hand. "I don't need that. I only need the two of you."

"Will you be telling your friends?" Liam asked. "If so, they will have to sign non-disclosure agreements. I don't negotiate in any other terms. I'm protecting all of us, and I know they're your best friends, but I need to know you're safe as well. One day, I will tell you everything as to why it has to be this way. For now, can you accept that it is for your own protection, and not because I'm being a selfish asshole? Friendships come and go, and I don't want you hurt in any way."

"I'm not telling them. I don't want them to know everything about me. I like this. I like that no one can meddle with this, that no one can take it away from me. When I eventually tell them, we'll have everything in place. I don't want them to try and talk any sense into me or think they have a right to tell me what to do. I don't want them to have that kind of power. For once, I do want something that is just all mine, and I don't have to go to my friends to do it."

Chapter Seventeen

One month later

The vacation with Scar, Liam, and Junior had been exactly what Easton needed. He'd been trying to find the perfect words to say how sorry he was to Scar for what he'd done in the past. The lies he told her.

The truth was, he'd fallen in love with her against all the odds, and he'd not wanted to lose her.

In having to follow his father, he had no choice but to let go of the only woman he'd ever truly loved.

Now, it was time to move on again. King's Ridge cemetery was to his left where Carla was buried. It had been some time since he'd been here. The last time, he'd ended up talking to Taylor, and he'd not come back since.

Picking up a single white rose, he climbed out of the car and made his way to where she was buried.

Staring at her name, Easton didn't feel the pain or the guilt.

"Hey, Carla, it's me. It's the fucked-up boyfriend. I don't know if you can hear me, but I wanted to say sorry for so many things. You shouldn't be here. You shouldn't be dead. In fact, you should be arguing with Taylor right now, or maybe even doing your hair, or any of the list of things you wanted to do. I thought, for a short time, I loved you. In a way, I did, but it wasn't the love you wanted or needed. This was the kind of love of two friends finding something more, and I'm sorry. I'm sorry I wasn't enough. I will always regret what I did to you. What I did to all of us. If I could take it back, I would."

"You can't take it back.".

Easton turned to see Taylor with an entire

bouquet of flowers.

"Hello, Taylor," he said. For the first time, he didn't flinch at her words or the glare she was firing at him.

"You shouldn't be here. You have no right."

"I have every right. You can hate me all you want to, Taylor. It's not going to change the fact I'm happy."

"She's dead because of you."

"Maybe, but I didn't hurt her. I never hurt her. You seem to be under this impression that you and Carla were tight. You had the whole best friend thing."

"And? What is your point?"

"If you were such good friends, why didn't she tell you we were together?"

"You told her not to."

Easton laughed. "I know best friends, and when they want to, they tell each other all of their secrets. Carla and I were together a lot longer than you think. I enjoyed being in her company, but what she loved was the secrecy. She liked having a life that didn't revolve around her friend."

"She can't even defend herself."

"And I can't defend myself to a fucking woman who refuses to listen. I didn't kill Carla. I never wanted to. I was more than willing to do the right thing."

"But you've found your happiness, haven't you? You've got a son and a whole new family, and you get to live your life while she doesn't." Tears fell from Taylor's eyes. "She will never get to hold my little girl, or know what it means to fall in love, or have any of those things, and I can't handle it." Taylor dropped the bouquet of flowers, and he realized, Taylor wasn't angry with him. She was angry with herself, and with it, she was guilty. That's what she felt, guilt.

Sinking to his knees, he wrapped his arms around

her. "She wouldn't want this."

"She would have wanted to live." Taylor sobbed. "I can't do this anymore. I can't keep coming here."

"Axton doesn't know you're here?" Easton pulled away to stare at her.

"No, he doesn't. I'm fucking that up just as I do everything else. He's talking about a break if I don't get my shit together. I can't help it. I feel so guilty all the time. When I look at my little girl and Axton, I'm so happy, and in the back of my mind, I know she'll never have that."

"We've got to let her go. I know Carla, and she wouldn't want us to be hurting for her. Think about it. Carla would want us both to live and to have a life that meant her death didn't hold us back."

Taylor nodded. "Yes, she would." She laughed. "I can see her now, angry with me."

"Pointing that finger that she loved doing whenever she got angry."

Taylor nodded. "She always pointed her finger and glared at me. Always told me to live my life how I wanted. I've spent so much time angry and hating myself for not knowing the truth. I heard about your dad."

"Don't for a second tell me you're sorry he's dead."

"I'm not. He was a monster, and he deserved what he got. I'm sorry you're related to him. I'm sorry for all the pain I've caused you. I'm really glad you didn't die," she said. "Your head."

"Yeah, I'm glad too. I get to be with my son."

Taylor nodded. "I can't promise you this isn't going to be easy. I've had my anger for so long it seems a part of me."

Easton took her hand, and they laid their flowers on her grave. "This is going to be the last time I come here. I need to make a clean break, and I think you should as well. Carla doesn't want this. We both know that. You should talk to Axton. I hate to hear of you two fighting, and I know it's killing him as well. I've seen the way he is at the office, and he's worried about you."

"I know. I fucked up. I'll make it right."

They left the cemetery together. He saw her car parked a little behind his.

"You didn't ram my car?"

"No. I didn't want Axton to know I'm here. I'm going to tell him though. I owe him that." Taylor was still crying.

"I'm not going to let you drive home like this, Taylor." He held her hand.

"I've got to. My car."

"I'll have it towed back or I'll drive Axton back, but regardless of if you can stand me or not, I'm not going to let you kill yourself."

He pulled her toward his car, opening the passenger side and helping her in.

"I don't want to be too much trouble."

"You won't be. Believe me, I'd like the company."

"I'm not very good company."

"Then we can both be miserable together, but I'm not going to abandon you. We've allowed this distance to build between us when it doesn't need to be there." He started up the car, and turned the car around, leaving King's Ridge behind and going straight home.

For the first couple of minutes, Taylor was silent.

"Thank you," she said, finally speaking up.

He glanced over to her.

"What?" he asked.

"For not abandoning me, and for not throwing everything in my face. You're a good man, Easton, and

I've been the worst bitch in the world."

Easton laughed. "Apology accepted. We can move on. I know it's what we all want. I don't expect this to be easy, but we'll make it work."

Just like he, Liam, and Scar were making it work, and he also had another plan as well. Today had been about closing off the past and moving onto the future.

For him, his future was with two people he loved more than anything else and his son.

He dropped Taylor off at the office and went straight back to his home.

Parking the car, he stared up at the house.

This was his home.

Climbing out of his car, he made his way inside and found Liam, Scar, and Junior in the sitting room. They were playing a board game, and he leaned against the doorframe, and watched them.

This was his family.

"I need to go pee," Junior said. "Dad! You're back." His son hugged him tightly, and Easton felt at home. This was his life.

"I am, and I'm staying. Can I play as well?"

"Yes, yes. I'll be back. Got to pee."

"Language," Scar said.

"Let Dad play." Junior rushed off, and Easton looked at Liam and Scar.

"You okay?" Liam asked.

"I want to stay," Easton said. "I don't want to be anywhere else but with the two of you. I love both of you, and I want to have this life with you all."

Scar stood up, and Liam looked shocked. He stood as well.

Easton stayed perfectly still, not moving, watching them.

"You love me?" Liam asked.

"Yes. I know I don't want this with anyone else. I'm willing to give it a shot, if you'll have me. I fucked up all those years ago, Scar. I won't fuck up again. I promise you." Tears filled his eyes, and he stepped away from the doorframe.

He stepped in front of both of them, reaching out, grabbing both of their hands. "I will never do anything to hurt what we've got. I love you both and I want to share you and to be shared. Please say you'll have me." He'd never begged for anything in his life, not since his father showed him begging wasn't going to get him anything. Sinking to his knees, he pressed his head between them.

Easton felt their hands on him, running fingers through his hair.

"You belong to us," Liam said. "I'm not giving you up, Easton. We're your family now, and if I could, I'd bind you to us in marriage."

"I would gladly marry you."

"Then how about we start a family?" Scar said. "I want to have another baby, and this time, we can all be together. I know Junior wants a brother or sister."

"You want our children?" Easton asked, looking up at her. He couldn't believe this was happening.

This was more than he could have ever hoped for.

Scar sank down to her knees as did Liam.

"We finally found each other. It wasn't right before, but now it's perfect," she said. "This is our life, and I will love you and Liam for the rest of my life."

She kissed his lips before Liam did.

Cupping both of their faces, Easton knew he'd finally come home. His broken world was no longer shattered. He was finally whole, and he wasn't ever going to fuck it up again.

Epilogue

Five years later

Liam sat in the yard, watching as his wife, his husband, and his children all ran around. Easton and Scarlett were laughing so hard, and he couldn't help but smile as he watched them.

They were crazy as they shot each other with water guns.

"You're too cool to join in?" Liam asked, looking toward Junior.

"I need to finish up this paper." Junior looked toward the group.

He was sixteen years old, going on seventeen, but Liam recognized the yearning in the young man's face.

"Go, your paper can wait. I know you'll get it done. You need to have fun as well."

Junior closed his folder, lidded his pen, and rushed off to join in the water fight.

Axton, Karson, and Romeo would be joining them all soon.

It was a family picnic in his home, but it was also a celebration.

He, Easton, and Scarlett had taken their vows on this very day. Easton's friends knew of the momentous day as Easton wanted them present.

Liam had made them all sign non-disclosure agreements before they were allowed near them. He'd been fighting for his happiness all of his adult life, and he wasn't going to allow three young boys to spoil it for him.

When he met Scarlett, he had no idea she would have such an impact on his life. Slowly, month by month, year by year, he'd fallen for her, and she had brought him

Easton. He had no doubt if it wasn't for Scarlett, Easton wouldn't be in his life.

Liam didn't care.

This was his family.

Scarlett broke out from the fight and rushed toward his side. She threw herself into his arms, and he wrapped her up in his arms.

In the past five years she'd given birth to two more children, and after seeing the test in the trash today, he knew she was going to give them a third. The family he had always wanted. It didn't matter to him who had fathered them. They were equally his and Easton's.

"Hello, beautiful," he said.

"Hey, you." She kissed his lips, and he groaned.

"You've got to take it easy." He put his hand on her stomach so she knew he was aware of her condition.

"What?" Easton asked, startling them as he approached.

Scarlett went bright red. She took Easton's hand and placed it over her stomach. "I was waiting for the right moment to tell you, I'm pregnant. I took the test this morning. We're going to have another baby."

"Another baby?" Easton pulled her in close, and Liam wrapped his arms around both of them.

Their family knew they were all together. For Junior, he'd been happy to have two dads.

Against all the odds, it had gone smoothly for him. Liam was always prepared for any potential backlash. To the outside world, they were the best of friends, making the most of their situation.

Behind closed doors, the truth was there for the three of them.

"Yes. Are you happy?"

"Happy? I'm fucking ecstatic. I want us all to have a big family. There are a lot of bedrooms for us to fill, and I want us to fill every single one of them."

The broken man had been healed, and Liam watched this man thrive. All he'd needed was patience, love, and stability.

Surrounded by his family, Liam knew he'd made the right choice in not destroying the Four Kings. He could have done so easily.

After all, they all had skeletons in their closet, and one day soon, someone was going to fall. Liam would catch Easton; he would protect him.

The love he had for Easton and Scarlett wasn't fleeting. This was the kind that lasted a lifetime, and he intended to make every single moment with them count.

The End

SAM CRESCENT

EVERNIGHT PUBLISHING ®

www.evernightpublishing.com

www.ingramcontent.com/pod-product-compliance
Lightning Source LLC
Chambersburg PA
CBHW030118180626
46812CB00002B/472